Cover artwork by Sue Massey

# A RIP IN TIME

**THOMAS J. STONE ©2021**

Cover artwork by Sue Massey

# A RIP IN TIME

## THOMAS J. STONE ©2021

# PART ONE

**1888, Whitechapel, London.**

The tall man walked through the dense London fog carrying his large black medical bag. This last one was the most spectacular yet. He'd outdone all his previous efforts. This one felt different though. Special. She was the last of the six he needed before he could sleep again. He seemed to need more sleep than he ever did, the number of days of wakefulness diminishing every time. Years ago he would wake a full six months before he took what he needed. Now it was just a scant few weeks, He dreaded the time when he'd only have a few days freedom before he had to strike again and then hide. He didn't understand why he was getting less time now. Would there ever be a time where he just wouldn't wake again? Maybe that would be a relief. He sometimes wished it would just end and he'd be at peace for the rest of eternity and not a monster roaming the countryside, taking innocent lives to survive.

Every twenty-two years he'd awaken and need to kill six more to take the essence to keep him alive, although maybe alive was the wrong word. He was immortal. In a few more days he'd make his way to the caves where he would hibernate for another generation, wondering what life and society would be like when he returned to a different era. What changes would he see in 1910?

The newspapers were full of his exploits, the names of Martha Tabram, Polly Nichols, Annie Chapman, Elizabeth Stride, and Catherine Eddowes would go down in history thanks to the reporting by the sensationalist press. All the work of the man they had dubbed 'Jack the Ripper'. He liked his new name. He didn't know the identity of this last victim yet but she will be the one most remembered, he'd made sure of that. He'd had plenty of time with this one unlike the others, he'd killed her inside her own home. It was messy but the fear generated as he cut and cut was exquisite. He took it all, all she had. He would rest very well this time while he regenerated.

More people roaming the streets of the city meant he'd had to rush the other five and he was nearly caught after the first of the pair the papers were calling the 'double event', he was so close to being discovered. But what could they do if he was caught and convicted? Hang him and bury him? He'd pretend to be dead and dig himself out again after a few days. He'd done it before years earlier. He couldn't die. He had no heartbeat. That was his power... or his curse. He could never die.

Two days later he'd read the name of Mary Jane Kelly. Brutally mutilated in her own home and now the whole city was in a panic wondering who was next and what dark depths this evil killer would stoop to. He knew there would be no more this time. Six were needed to ensure that he could stay alive, or his version of it. The blood and gore and the mutilations were secondary, just for show. It was their fear he fed off. Their 'essence'. No children this time, that was a shame as they generated more fear as they died, but these six would do. It was hard to find children in the dead of night in a large city, even in Victorian London. Much easier to steal them from their beds in the country. Next time he'd find another village. The Home Counties were still mostly rural, but would they be as quiet and undisturbed in another twenty-two years? No matter. He'd find his six victims anyway.

The inept police had several suspects but no evidence, all suspected on hearsay or gossip. It was good for him that their efforts were aimed in the wrong direction. Someone even suggested royalty. He laughed at that. He'd known royalty who were far worse monsters than him. Some of them were depraved, but that part of their lives was kept well hidden. He wondered if the truth would ever come out about them and their fetishes. Princes with a lust for young girls and even murder, unknown to the public.

It was finally time. He left his meagre lodgings in Wentworth Street, also leaving all his possessions. He wouldn't need them again. He hailed a Hansom cab to take him to his normal resting place. It was a long journey, even longer in years gone by but the new roads coming out of London made it slightly easier and less time-consuming. At one time he would have had to walk but with these better roads and forms of transport he could venture further afield from his place of hibernation. It was slightly more than fifty-five miles to the caves. He could have walked. He didn't tire like everyone else but why not travel in style? A carriage would be less conspicuous too.

The cab was black, as they usually were, with large windows on either side of the enclosed seating area. The driver, a squat, swarthy man in his late fifties with long white hair under a top hat was perched at the back on a wide bench seat. The reins reached across the cab towards the front and the two large bay mares, which would take him to his destination, snorted and stamped their hooves on the cobbles, waiting impatiently to get underway. The man gave the driver a square piece of cream paper with an address on it.

"That's a fair trek, guv," said the driver with a sly smile. "It'll cost you."

"Take me there, I have the money!" said the man menacingly.

"With pleasure, guv." The driver already spending the money in his head. A new hat and the rest on gin, maybe a doxy or two.

It took just over five hours for the cab to reach the village of West Wycombe. The horses trotted for around ten miles on the journey, and then rested while they walked for one or two more miles, then repeated the process. It was now approaching dusk but the man in the cab could still see the huge hexagonal mausoleum perched on the top of the nearby hill. He knew it well. The cab made its way through the high street to the end then made two sharp right turns and climbed the hill. A couple of hundred yards up the slope was his real destination but the man didn't want the cab driver to know that. Instead, the cab carried on up the ever steeper hill that twisted its way to the top and level ground.

He paid the driver, who nodded at the man and then turned the cab around and the mares trotted slowly down the hill again. The tall man waited until the cab was out of sight, breathing the cool evening air at the summit for the last time before another period of peaceful hibernation. He then walked slowly towards the mausoleum. He'd known Francis Dashwood's family well and some of those he had known were now residents of the impressive dark grey building in front of him. He stared inside the structure, at the well-kept lawn within, at the urns mounted high in the alcoves within the flint walls. The monument in the centre was dedicated to Dashwood's wife Sarah. The man had stayed at the Dashwood estate with Sir Francis on occasion in 1756 and found the wife to be quite pleasant, although not Dashwood's type considering his strange appetites. He wondered if Dashwood had even consummated the marriage, there had certainly been no legitimate heirs. He could see the vast estate from where he stood. He said a silent prayer for Sarah, dead for more than a century. Even though he was a monstrosity it did not mean he didn't believe in his God. He moved onward to the churchyard, walked amongst the graves for a while, recognising the odd name as he passed by the stone markers. Then he reached the church with its great golden globe on top. Originally a medieval church, it was remodelled and restored by Dashwood in the 1750s. He'd seen the improvements to the chancel and nave when he'd returned in 1778. Sarah had been dead by then. It certainly was an unusual and impressive sight.

It was almost full dark when he made his way down the wheel-rutted track again. It didn't take him long to reach the cave, the entrance housed in a mock-Gothic church front. He silently walked into the cave, moving slowly downhill through the dark passages. After almost twenty minutes he'd found his destination, a hidden passage with a small alcove off to his right. He entered the small hidden area and stood with his back to a strange beige-grey patch on the wall and melted into it, feeling the warmth it gave off. He was ready for his sleep, already dreaming of his exploits in another twenty-two years. Outside the cave, the moon shone down on the entrance, and bats flitted in the half-light. In London, everyone was prepared for the worst that night but it didn't come. It took several months before people started to feel more relaxed and safer again. As the man faded away for another generation he started to remember, as he always did, when the time to hibernate came round again.


## 62 A.D. Britannia

His name was Consus and he was born in a village outside Rome called Gionco in the year 27 A.D. He had been recently promoted to a centurion in the Roman Army and was serving in Britain in Verulamium, called St. Albans in later years after the martyr who died there around two hundred years later. Consus was there when Alban was brutally executed. He was not a soldier then, he had already died and became what he was now, an immortal who returned every twenty-two years and then returned to his hibernation again.

Consus wasn't a bad man when he was alive. He missed his family badly and needed money to desert from the army and return home, gather his wife and two small children, and move somewhere, anywhere, another region or even another country. Away from the constant wars and colonisation the rulers of Rome decreed. He had been approached by a wealthy Briton, a merchant who had heard of his disillusionment with the Roman regime. The merchant was called Vericus, a name given to him as he was now a Roman citizen, derived from his Celtic name, Veritagus. Vericus had told him that Queen Boudica was trying to drive the Romans out of Britain and was about to attack Verulamium and he wanted information, for a price. Consus jumped at the chance. Either the Romans would be forced out of the country and he'd be stationed nearer home or he'd have the money he needed to get back to his family and take them all to safety. All he had to do was give Vericus the troop strength and any weakness in the Roman defences in the town. Verulamium was strategically important for Boudica and taking it would give her a stronghold in the south and a base to push on to Londinium and then drive the Romans back into the sea. Taking back the country invaded over a hundred years before by Julius Caesar.

Boudica was successful in sacking Verulamium and the escaping Roman forces retreated to Londinium. Vericus was captured and tortured and gave the names of his fellow conspirators in the plot to oust the Romans from Britain. Consus was named amongst them. At first, Consus denied everything but when his quarters were searched a purse of gold coins was found hidden in an earthenware jug. After being tortured himself he was brought before General Festus Augustus, known as a fair man but treason was unacceptable, as it is with all men who demand loyalty.

Festus has been in Cyprus several years earlier and had picked up quite a few artifacts on his travels including the spear that was reputedly used to kill Lazarus, the man who was allegedly returned from the dead by the Christ. Little is known in modern times about Lazarus after he was resurrected but he roamed several towns in Judea over the subsequent years and finally fled to Cyprus after rumours of a plot to murder him. He was found in Kition on Cyprus and put to death with a bronze spear that pierced his heart and then they decapitated him. Festus acquired the spearhead as payment for a debt owed to him by Titius Marcellus who was the governor of Cyprus at the time. The spear was the most prized possession of Festus and he carried it at all times. Few knew of the rumour that the spear had killed the resurrected Lazarus and must have had a special power to be able to do so.

Festus, still reeling and angry from the defeat to Boudica at Verulamium, decided to make an example of the traitor Consus. Instead of the usual punishments of beheading or crucifixion, the manner of Consus's death would be more personal. Festus felt betrayed by the centurion. He would execute Consus himself. Consus was roughly pushed to his knees in front of General Festus, already bleeding about the head from the fierce beating given to him by the guards for several days in his cell until he was summoned by Festus. Consus looked up into the eyes of Festus, knowing he had just a few more seconds to live, a defiant look on his face. He had no regrets, he did what he had to for the sake of his beautiful family and would see them all again one day. He would soon be met by Mercury and taken over the River Styx and his family would join him when their time finally came. He calmly closed his eyes and waited for the fatal blow. Festus raised the spear over his head and plunged it down into the upper chest of Consus, down into his rapidly beating heart. Consus ignored the searing pain and pictured his family as they were on the last day he'd seen them three years previously on his final day of leave before the legion was deployed to Britannia. There were tears as he left and then a single tear trickled down his right cheek as he died in a faraway country.

The lifeless body of Consus was dragged unceremoniously from the building by two sturdy soldiers and thrown onto an awaiting cart. He was transported several miles outside of Londinium and dumped in the swampy ground surrounded by tall ash trees. Festus didn't want the remains of a traitor anywhere near him or the remainder of his forces. There was no burial for him. He would be left for the crows, the scavengers, and the other vermin to feed off. His family at home would never know his whereabouts but they would certainly learn of his treachery. Word had already been sent to Rome to be conveyed to the family of Consus. The name of the traitor would not be forgotten and will serve as a reminder as to the loyalty expected of every Roman citizen, either at home or throughout the Roman Empire.

That very night Consus opened his eyes slowly. He was confused. He was dead, surely? He had felt the spear pierce his drumming heart. How could he be staring up at the stars far above him? His hand moved cautiously up to the wound in his chest. He pushed his forefinger into the deep gash and felt no pain. He *was* breathing though, hearing the rattle as air and a little blood escaped his damaged lung. He then heard a rustling in the undergrowth near him and a large brown rat poked its head out of the thick tall grass and eyed him suspiciously. *A free meal for you gone, I'd wager,* Consus thought. He just couldn't understand what had happened to him. He was certainly dead, yet alive too. He had to think. What was his next move? Was he free to return to the village of his family? First, he needed to get away from the immediate area. As far away from Londinium as he could for now. A strange craving was gnawing at him though, something he didn't understand. An urge to kill, but why? He didn't even want revenge on the guards who beat him or even Festus who took his life from him. He knew he deserved his execution for his treason. He knew what the punishment would be if he was discovered.

The next day Consus moved west, deeper into the countryside. To the north was Verulamium, now in ruins after the attack by Queen Boudica and the Britons. It wasn't safe there either, even though he'd helped them he was still a Roman and it was possible only Vericus knew of his involvement and could guarantee his safety. But he knew Vericus was dead. He stole some clothes from an unattended wicker hut so that he would blend in until he found a safer place to stay. West, that was best for him, wait a few months and see if Boudica could force the invaders back to Rome. Maybe then he could travel back to his family in the confusion. He decided on Cornwall. He knew there wasn't a great military presence by the main Roman army, just the odd outpost of auxiliary infantrymen recruited from countries like Germania, happy to be away from the more populated, and dangerous, areas. There to keep the peace and not much else. He wouldn't have any problems avoiding them. It was well known all they cared about was drinking and gambling at their remote outposts. They were never considered real soldiers.

Over the next two weeks the craving to kill increased and also the sense of straying from where he should be. His newfound instinct told him he was moving in the wrong direction. He was in two minds but eventually decided to move north again, maybe he would find answers there. He realised that he had not eaten in the last two weeks, not even considered it. Something so basic for survival never even crossed his mind. If he didn't eat he couldn't possibly be alive, he didn't drink either, nothing had passed his lips since the scraps thrown to him in his cell in Londinium. The gnawing in his stomach was a different kind of hunger, one he needed to satisfy soon.

On the rutted, grass-covered road he was using to walk northward he saw a young girl who had been gathering firewood, coming towards him from the other direction. He assumed she lived nearby because the pile of sticks in her arms was almost too large and heavy to carry, so her dwelling can't have been too far away. As he walked towards her the craving was unbearable. Just a few more steps to go. She shyly looked up at him as he neared then she saw the strange look in his eyes. He had the hungry look of a grey wolf. She dropped her sticks and tried to run but he had grabbed her by her long hair and pulled her into his chest and his other arm encircled her neck, tightly choking her, she was unable to scream for help. Then something strange happened. A thin red mist started to emanate from her. *What is she doing to me?* he thought. Maybe she was a fairy and had some sort of defence against attackers, could she be a demon? She looked ordinary enough, no obvious look of a supernatural entity. He wanted to release her but also knew if he did she would raise the alarm and he would be hunted like a wild boar across the countryside. He had to finish her. He tried to hold his breath, not wanting to breathe in the mysterious vapour but knew eventually he needed air and hoped she would die before he had to gulp in the much-needed oxygen. He had no need for food or drink but he still needed air because dark speckles were starting to invade his vision. Even though he knew he was dead/alive he wondered if he could die again. He was eventually forced to gulp in the red mist together with the oxygen. He immediately felt invigorated, alive again, no… more than alive. He felt stronger and healthier than he had ever felt before his death. Even better than in his youth. He wrapped his arm tighter around the girl's neck and more of the faint crimson cloud escaped her. He sucked it in greedily. He felt like one of the Gods he worshipped, maybe even stronger than them. He was here, now, and not some mysterious entity from the past. The struggles of the girl began to fade and she went limp, a last puff of the mist was released which he quickly sniffed up his nose, like the scent from a beautiful flower. She wasn't a fairy after all, it was her fear escaping and he knew that was what he needed to sustain him in the future. One of the most powerful natural forces that anyone could possess, fear, was what he needed to survive, to continue 'living'. To thrive. It was in everyone, even the Emperor of Rome himself! Fear was the thing that protected people from dangerous situations like walking too close to a cliff edge or straying too far while swimming in the ocean. Self-preservation. The fear of death was strong as a bull. And now it had a colour to recognise it and the power to preserve what now existed as his life. He was dead, alive, and not a God! He believed he could no longer die like an ordinary man. The spear! The one that took the life of Lazarus, the extended life given to him by Jesus had somehow been transferred to him. Would he ever die? Could he ever die? He felt guilt in killing the child, but he could see what he did was necessary to carry on his existence. He wondered how many more he'd need to kill to survive in his resurrected state. Dozens, hundreds… even thousands? Could he cope with that sort of guilt? Ending innocent lives so that he could exist. Avoiding the finality of bodily death. But wasn't his body already dead? He felt no pain from the wound in his chest so would his body eventually decay? What would happen to his mind and spirit if it did?

The girl lay limply at his feet, he needed to get away but hiding her would give him a bigger head start. He gently picked her up, showing respect for the corpse who had shown him the way of his future, and carried her into the thick copse to the right of the road. He lay her down on some dried leaves and calmly walked back onto the road and carried on to the north. On the way, four more children had died over the next few days and their fear gulped down into his lungs. He felt immense, immortal, but also knew that he had almost his fill of the mist. One more would be enough for the time being and then he'd move to a different area. He wondered how long he could last without the vapour. He felt shame for murdering children but he knew he never wanted the exhilaration he felt to end permanently. There was no other feeling like it. He'd also learnt that by killing the victims more slowly he could extract more of the life-enhancing mist. He felt more guilty about killing these children now than he did about his treacherous acts against his people but he needed to survive. They were necessary. And with sadness, he realised he could never go home to his village. He couldn't risk his children to his strange new appetite. He decided he needed to stay in Britain and feed off these heathens. They worshipped different gods and they meant little to him. He regarded them the same as a boar or an ox or fowl, just food. There for the taking. There to satisfy his need.

While walking through a village close to a range of hills he heard two men talking about good work a few miles away at Hambledon, near the caves. A road was being built and would provide work, and good money, for anyone willing enough and would last several months. No slaves were being used. Consus wasn't interested in any work, he didn't need money for food, or shelter either as he could sleep in the open in all weathers anyway. He didn't feel the heat or the cold and the rain didn't bother him much, it was cleansing. The word that piqued his curiosity was caves. He was sure a group of men were on his trail for the killings, he'd heard talk in the villages he'd passed through, and he needed somewhere secure to hide if need be.

Consus found the caves easily, perched halfway up a steep hill. He entered the large chalk opening and saw how dark it was further on as the light from the entrance faded. Then the path became clearer. His eyes could cut through the gloom, maybe his new power gave him other advantages like seeing in the dark. He'd not noticed it while walking at night as his way was lit by the moon and stars but in this enclosed space his vision returned. There was a bluish tinge but his eyes had adjusted enough to see fairly clearly. He moved slowly along the slight descent of the long corridor until he came to an opening to a small chamber where narrower paths branched off from it. In time he would explore them all to find a suitable hiding place or refuge. Men would need blazing torches to search the caves and he would be able to see the glow from far off and easily move around the caves to conceal himself. He knew they were coming, the gossip in the villages told him so. They would be here within days, he estimated. There was no need for him to procure provisions as he didn't need to eat or drink so no cache of stores to reveal his hiding place. No need for blankets either. It would be easy to hide here as long as he avoided the men. He slept sat against the chalk wall of the chamber. Later he would explore.

It took two full days to explore all the various paths leading off from the main chamber. Some doubled back to join with other paths and some had even narrower passages branching off them. One led to a smaller chamber but it was a dead end. Just a diameter of around twelve feet but very difficult to find, especially for the men who would come with their flickering torches, causing shadows to bounce off the narrow passage walls. One part of the wall did look different though. Instead of the usual chalk, the surface looked flat and a greyish light brown. It intrigued him. He was reminded of villas under construction and the surface of floors and walls readied for a mosaic to be laid, very smooth. He touched the surface, expecting dampness but the area was slightly warm and dry and gave him a tingling feeling on his fingertips. There was a strange cloying smell in the enclosed space too which he couldn't quite recognise - sort of muddy and mossy but not quite. It was almost overpowering but that was another advantage of this hiding place. The men would probably avoid the stench without investigating too closely. This place was almost perfect and after a while, he probably wouldn't even notice the stifling odour filling the alcove and passage.

He knew he would need to feed soon, the strange hunger had returned. He made his way slowly through the tunnels and out of the main entrance. As he suspected it was night time, even though he'd been in the caves for two days his inner sense of time was still acute. He walked down the hill into the valley where the road was being built, abandoned now as it was night time, no sentries or watchmen around. He could see how the road was constructed as he walked along it as sections of this new road were in varying degrees of manufacture. Parts of it were just the lowest level consisting of a couple of layers of flat stone blocks set in a mortar that was drying into a solid mass. The next layer was of rubble and small stones which were also set in the lime mortar they used. As he walked he could see the third and fourth stages, a layer of sand and gravel mixed with lime cement and then one of the smooth stones embedded in the cement. He knew Romans had built their roads in the same way for decades and the design would never change all over the Empire. They were designed to last centuries, maybe a thousand years, probably longer than the empire would.

He roamed silently through the night, the countryside around him was deserted. Eventually, he found a small round stone cottage with a conical thatched roof, no more than a bleak hovel set in a field. He quietly crept around it, looking into the windows. A man and his wife were fast asleep in separate cots, presumably exhausted by a long day's work in the fields. In another room were a small child and a baby of no more than six months. He crept into the room through the small wooden door set into the side of the building, well away from the main entrance. The baby snuffled in its sleep. The infant child was too young to understand death so would have very little fear. No use to him. The older one was around six and was a boy. He crept silently over towards the sleeping child and looked down on him. He remembered his own two boys at that age and felt sad that he would never see them ever again, maybe not even in the afterlife. He covered the child's mouth and nose with one large hand and pressed down on the boy's chest with the other, expelling the air from the lungs, his strong arm and weight pinning the boy to the thin bedding. The child's eyes snapped open immediately and looked into the eyes of Consus, panic already setting in. The red mist rose slowly and Consus bent slightly to draw it into his lungs. It took over two minutes for the boy to suffocate silently which maximised the amount of vapour Consus could inhale. He straightened and turned and was shocked to see the sleepy farmer trying to comprehend what he was seeing. His child was murdered in his bed. Consus grabbed the man around the throat with his left hand and brought his closed fist down on top of the man's head which seemed to stun him more than his sleepy drowsiness. Consus spun the man around and wrapped his arm around his neck, expecting more of the red mist to appear but none came. Wasn't he afraid of dying? It seemed impossible. The man barely struggled as he was starved of oxygen, seeming to accept his fate. The man sagged to the straw-covered floor. Consus was concerned about the lack of mist from the man… why? What was different about this man?

Consus was about to exit the building when the wife screamed, he needed to finish her too, no witnesses. He moved towards her. Then he heard the noise of a rabble. The group of men hunting him must have been camped nearby and heard the scream. He ran. There were shouts when he was spotted and the men chased after him. They were less than forty yards away. He flinched when a spear rushed past him, inches from his shoulder. He ran over the soft ground, he knew he could probably outrun them eventually as he never seemed to tire but the chance of a spear hitting him while he was so close was still possible. They could bring him down and capture him. Then what? Executed again? He almost laughed to himself as he ran. They could not kill him again, he was almost sure of that. He was pulling out a strong lead on the group as they began to tire but the land was flat, and he was still visible to them as the light of dawn approached slowly. He could see the hill that housed the caves far into the distance, the only raised land in the area. He knew they would see him enter, so he had two choices: either keep running and draw them away from his planned hiding place or let them follow him into the cave system and test his hiding place. Would it matter if he was caught in the caves? They would try to kill him again, and then he could possibly feign death and come back again. They would think their job was done and revenge was taken and would go back to their villages, satisfied that he was dead.

He decided to try out his hiding place. He was half a mile ahead of the group when he scaled the steep hill and entered the cave. As he entered the mouth he turned and looked at the chasing mob. Several were pointing to the opening with their torches and probably assumed they had him trapped. Maybe he was? The next few hours would tell as they searched the dark chalk labyrinth. They only had three torches between them so Consus knew there would be a maximum of three groups they would split into after they reached the large chamber. They didn't have the advantage he had, being able to see in the dark. As he approached the junction of the tunnels his eyes were adjusting to the blackness by the second and he took the second passage on his left - the one which would lead to his possible haven. He heard the echoes of the mob as they entered the cave system, he knew he had time to reach his private hiding place. The walls of the passage were getting narrower and he knew that anyone following would have to do so in a single file which would make them more nervous about an attack by him. None of them would be comfortable leading the chase. The sound of the horde diminished and he knew they hadn't entered the branch that led to him yet. Probably organising themselves in the main chamber, deciding if to split up. They would need to leave one or two near the entrance, of course, worried that Consus would double back through the passages and escape. They couldn't afford that now they were so close to capturing him after the last three weeks of their manhunt.

Consus had reached his haven, guided by the smell of the place, he didn't even need to see the small entrance. He squeezed into it sideways and stood with his back against the strange, smooth wall. He felt a slight tingling, a tiny buzzing that he sometimes felt when there was a great thunderstorm approaching. The smell of the place changed too. The awful moss and mud odour had gone and replaced by a slight burning aroma, almost like incense. He could feel himself being drawn into the wall. He tried to pull himself free but it was impossible, he was held in it's grip. Was this the end for him? Trapped inside the wall of the cave for eternity? He began to struggle in his desperation to be free of the chalk and rock. He'd rather face the angry gang chasing him than be walled up in there forever. He was getting drawn in inch by inch, the sounds of the pursuing pack fading as his ears were covered in liquid stone, just his face and chest now showing. He was slipping further and further into the rock. He felt sad that he may never see the light of day again, the sun over a cornfield, or the face of another living soul ever again. He'd never feel anything again. He missed his family. He was absorbed by the rock which then began to solidify over him. For him, there was just silence.

After several hours the men found the small chamber, sickened by the damp mossy smell they didn't spend too much time there. It was obvious this was a dead end and they were satisfied he couldn't be hiding there. One of them wondered about the smooth brownish-grey surface of one of the walls and ran his hand over it for a few seconds before being driven out by the stench. The killer wasn't there. He left with the other two of his companions and decided to regroup with the others in the large chamber near the entrance to the outside world. Maybe one of the other gangs had captured the murderer.

## 84 A.D. Britannia.

Consus woke coughing. He found himself on the floor of the small inner cave. The area stank even more than he remembered. Where had he been? He vaguely recalled being sucked into the wall. Was that a bad dream? How long had he been asleep for and why had he not been captured by the gang? He ached in his bones and felt so empty. He picked himself up from the dark, damp floor and stretched, trying to think. He needed to get out into the fresh air. Even if it meant capture.

Consus groped his way through the widening tunnels until he got to the main chamber. It seemed he couldn't see as well in the dark as he did before. He staggered up the small slope which eventually led to the entrance and discovered it was close to dawn. He could see the faint glow of the rising sun on the horizon. There was no sign of anyone else around. The men working on the new road would be arriving soon and he needed to scout around before they arrived. Consus walked down the hill to the valley and what he saw amazed him. There would be no workmen arriving that morning. The road had been finished and had been in use for a while. How long was he in that cave? It must have been months at least for them to finish the road. Being swallowed up by that wall can't have been a dream. But how was that even possible? What manner of trickery was he a victim to? Was he the only one it had ever happened too and why was he released from his prison? Question after question rushed through his mind and no answers were forthcoming.

Consus stood in the centre of the long straight road and looked into the distance. Far away he could see a small settlement. He couldn't recall that being there before, but he was confused. He slowly walked towards the new collection of houses. He was wary of the fact that people could still be looking for him. He needed to be very careful who he talked to. The Roman trudged along the road as the sun rose higher to his right. The birds were singing, flitting and fluttering from tree to tree at the side of the road. Still no sign of anyone else. The gnawing was in his stomach again as it had been weeks after his death at the hands of General Festus. He would need to feed soon, he felt. He started to remember the last time he had gorged on the red mist. The boy in the cottage and then the father. But there was no mist coming from the father. Why not? Was he totally without fear or was it something else? Could he only take from six victims until he was full? What if things had changed and he could never take in the recuperating crimson vapour again? Was he now doomed to roam the land with this hunger inside him until he went mad? There was only one way to find out. He needed another victim… and soon.

As he approached the settlement he could hear voices and the grunting of pigs. Two men were in a small pen and one of them straddled a large pig, using the force of his legs to stop the beast from moving. The other man walked calmly towards it from the side brandishing a long knife. He bent slightly and sliced the pig across the throat. There was a brief squeal from the animal and then a gurgling sound and the pig sagged between the other man's legs and was silent. They carried the pig's carcass between them through a small gate in the pen and then into a nearby hut, presumably to be butchered into cuts of meat and then salted to preserve it. He suddenly remembered the taste of pork roasted on a spit and missed it slightly. His body didn't need that kind of nutrition anymore but he missed the taste of the succulent meat.

He moved on. Consus passed several other huts, all circular with thatched conical roofs as was the normal style in the area. Two people were talking about the upcoming census. He knew there had been one in Britain a couple of years before he died, in 60 A.D. and they were taken every twelve years. Was this another one in such a short space of time or was it still the same interval? Was this 72 A.D and could he have been trapped in that wall for ten years? It was impossible to believe. It would explain the road being finished and the new settlement though. At least there was one advantage to it being true, he was no longer hunted by that mob and was free to roam the country and choose his next victim without the fear of a horde pursuing him for a time. He was desperate to know if he could still induce his kills to emit the crimson cloud of panic and terror as they died. He needed it so badly, he felt incomplete. Consus approached the men with a friendly smile.

"I heard you talking about the census, I've been away for a while and wasn't aware of it. The last one I knew of was in the year sixty, is it still held every twelve years?"

"You have been away for a while, you missed the one in the year seventy-two then?" laughed the stout man standing in front of him. His friend wondered where the stranger had been. An escaped slave maybe?

"I seem to have lost my memory of certain things. I was injured… somewhere, my head," he lied, "I know my name and that I am in Britain but little else."

"Well friend," the shorter man said, "You may have missed the last one on your travels, but it's certainly unwise to avoid this coming census. Those Romans are harsh on anyone who doesn't pay their taxes, where have you been for the past twenty-four years since the one you remember? You must have been a child then, were you in slavery?"

"I'm not sure," Consus lied again. "Are you telling me this is the year eighty-four?" he asked incredulously.

The man nodded and looked at him strangely.

Twenty-two years inside the wall in that cave. It didn't seem possible. He thanked the men and wandered in a daze for miles, impossible thoughts flying around in his head, unbelievable things! Was he mortal again? Had he been reborn into his old body? Could he now die? The urge to feed was still within him. He could feel the cramping of his stomach as he walked. There were so many unanswered questions about who he was, what he was. He realised he'd been ripped from his own time into another.

Consus waited until dark before he risked taking someone. He hid in the trees next to the long, straight road, far from any village, biding his time even though the craving was almost unbearable. Long after night came, a lone woman appeared on the road about half a mile away. She must have been a domestic servant who had finished for the day and was returning to her family. Consus wondered what had become of his wife and two sons over the last twenty-two years. Had the boys joined the Roman Army? Were they killing in the far-flung places of the empire? Maybe even stationed in Britain? He would never know but he hoped they were doing something more worthwhile and safer. That they had trained for a trade like a carpenter, maybe they were fishermen? The anticipation was almost too much to bear as he waited for the woman to approach the thicket he was hiding in.

Eventually, she had walked past the copse and he slowly emerged from the trees and followed her, gradually gaining as she wearily traipsed along the road, exhausted from the work of the day, oblivious to his stealthy presence. She gasped, shocked from her mundane thoughts, as he flung his strong arm around her neck, his forearm biting harshly into her fragile windpipe. She tried to pull the arm away but with his strength combining with her tiredness it was impossible. She flailed with her arms trying to beat at his head and kicked backwards hoping he would loosen his grip but the vital oxygen she needed was not replaced in her burning lungs. Consus was relieved and grateful that the red mist was emanating from the young woman. He gulped greedily, eager to replenish his body and his soul… if he still had one. He released his grip slightly, letting the woman draw in one last breath, trying to prolong her fear. His right hand was clamped over her mouth, stifling any scream. He bent slightly and whispered in her ear that he was not going to spare her and the mist virtually gushed out of her. Consus smiled, knowing that he could squeeze even more terror out of his victims this way. She died slowly in his arms, and as he furtively looked around him for any witnesses, dragged the body into the copse and left her hidden there. He walked into the night, satisfied. He was back! The gnawing pain in his stomach had ceased and the elation and relief he felt that he could still extract the life-giving vapour from his victims after the twenty-two years he had spent in hibernation soothed his mind. It still bothered him that the seventh and last victim of all those years ago failed to give him what he needed. He was still at a loss as to why. Maybe he'd find out when the time came for the seventh this time around. The man may just have been fearless or maybe too shocked by the death of his son to realise what was happening. He would take a seventh again, maybe more.

Over the next few weeks, Consus was careful when and where he struck next. Another woman walking home, a teenage boy working in the fields, a girl of about six or seven he found sitting in a patch of daisies and happily talking to herself, and another boy who was foraging in the woods. He made sure he hid every body, hoping that their remains would take weeks or months to be discovered, the cause of death presumed natural. After every kill, he always returned to the cave he thought of as his home now. Sleeping for days on end. He was wary that he could be taken by the wall again but his intuition said that if it was going to happen again it was not time yet. The sixth victim was another young girl. She was maybe eighteen and walked dreamily through the woods on a dirt path worn bare by the local woodcutters. He stepped in front of her from a thick clump of bushes and stared at her. She stared back, no fear showing on her face but he noticed her hands were trembling slightly. She stepped towards him. He was confused. Hadn't she heard of the other missing people?

"What is your name?" asked Consus.

"I am called Aurelia," she answered.

"Where do you live?"

"I live in the villa outside of the settlement, my father is the governor in this region, Festus Augustus, you may have heard of him?" she said proudly.

"Oh yes, I have certainly heard of him," grinned Consus. "We met many years ago when he was a mere general."

"What do you want?" asked the girl warily, "My father will punish you if you do anything to me."

"He already killed me once," he smiled. Consus grabbed the girl roughly by the arm.

Aurelia pulled a long knife from a sheath on a brown leather belt hidden behind her small back. She plunged it between his ribs. There was no pain, very little blood escaped either. She looked on in shock as the man refused to die, seemingly unaffected by the blade sticking in the left side of his torso. Aware that he still gripped her and he was applying even more force, she could feel the bones in her wrist grind together. Pain radiated up her entire arm as her shoulder twisted in its socket. Consus looked down and pulled the knife from his side. He had strangled or suffocated all his previous victims but he thought using her own knife on her would be interesting and fitting too. She deserved it after she had attacked him.

He pushed her to the soft ground and straddled her then easily moved her hands together so that he could hold both wrists in one large hand. She screamed. He didn't care. By the time anyone could come he would be finished with her. He ran the blade down her left cheek, she screamed even more and tried to kick him off her but he was almost double her weight and muscular too. The red mist started to flow from her. He smiled as he breathed it in, thin trails of the vapour drawn into his nose. He cut the other cheek and the girl started to whimper. She was now terrified, her previous defiance gone, and the mist flowed even thicker and faster. He continued to cut and slash, blood flung into the air with every stroke. She was still alive and resigned to her fate when he drew the blade across her slender throat, more blood gushed as it pooled around her upper body.

Consus smiled as he got up and looked down on her bloody corpse. He had thought previously that he didn't care about revenge, but once the opportunity presented itself he had enjoyed it immensely. More satisfaction than even killing Festus himself. This would hurt the old Roman even more than his own death. He wished he could witness the pain Festus would feel at the loss of his daughter. Not just the loss but at the way that loss was inflicted. Consus decided not to hide the body. The sooner she was found the better. That way the quicker Festus would have his heartbreaking pain. A figurative spear through his own heart.

Consus looked down at the wound in his side, the small flow of blood had already stopped and very little had stained his clothing. There was a slight tingling, deep inside the puncture. He moved slowly along the path, intending to return to his cave. He needed to rest for a while. Suddenly he was faced with an old Roman soldier who had heard the screams of the girl. He may have been her bodyguard. He looked vaguely familiar to Consus.

"This can't be, I saw you die!" said the man.

Then Consus remembered. The man was one of the guards who had beaten him while in the cell, waiting to be brought before Festus.

"The Gods saw fit to spare me apparently," replied Consus, grinning at the man.

"It's not possible! You must be a relation of his," the old soldier said.

"No, the precious spear of your general, his most treasured possession, gave me back my life after a few hours. Were you one of those who discarded my body in the marshes? Left for the scavengers to feed upon?"

"N-no, no, that wasn't me," the older man replied, fear now creeping into his voice as he realised he was faced with some sort of supernatural being, a dead man brought back to life. He pulled his short sword from the scabbard at his side and moved towards Consus, knowing he had to strike quickly.

"You know I can't let you live to tell Festus what you have discovered," said Consus coldly.

"I must!" replied the soldier.

The man lunged at the immortal, slashing at the air as Consus stepped back then spun to his left, ending up behind the ageing soldier. Consus swung his arm around the throat of the man and flexed the muscles of his forearm, tightening his grip. He still held the knife he had used so effectively on Aurelia in his other hand. He pushed the blade deep into the bicep of the soldier, forcing him to release the sword and scream in pain. The sword dropped between his feet and lay there, impotent.

"Would you like to know what I will do with you?" said Consus, knowing that telling the soldier his fate would increase the fear in him. Knowing that the man would expect a soldier's death, and not to be mutilated.

The man shook his head, fear and panic overtaking him. He knew he was finished. The dead man was incredibly strong.

"I will cut your eyes out, then your tongue, and finally your ears. You will be deaf, dumb, and blind in the afterlife. He started to cut. There was no red mist. Consus immediately knew then that he could only take six victims for their vapour and had to return to the wall in the cave. He wondered how long he'd be shut up inside the stone for this time, but was sure he'd return again. He knew it would be pointless to mutilate the soldier further, there would be no mist from him even though he looked terrified. Consus slashed the man's throat open, so deeply he could feel the knife grating on the soldier's spine. The man dropped to the ground and Consus walked calmly away in the direction of the caves, the bodies would be found soon and he wanted to be away from the area. Only six at a time, he thought. He felt disappointed, but at least he knew there was a limit to his killing before he could rest again.

He got to the caves just before dusk and wearily descended to the main chamber and took the narrow tunnel that would lead to his particular grotto, his safe haven. He was nervous though, doubt creeping into his mind. What if it didn't work the same way again? Maybe he could only be taken and returned once? He knew he had no choice though, if he couldn't extract any more of the mist then he'd be doomed to wander the land with that craving, eventually going mad with bloodlust. No choice at all. If he couldn't get back it was best to end things here.

He entered the small cave and smelt the ozone which had replaced the damp, mossy odour again. He knew he would be taken again and prayed that he would return once more. With a mixture of trepidation and anticipation, he walked slowly towards the smooth, brownish area of the cave and turned and rested his back to the wall. Again, the stone seemed to melt and he slowly sank into it, his last thought was that he'd miss the look on the face of Festus when he found out about his daughter's gruesome end. Consus smiled as he sank further into the soft, living rock. Revenge was undoubtedly sweet.

**106 A.D. Britannia.**

Consus woke on the floor of the cave. Took stock of his situation once more. He considered everything he knew about his new life. He had died by the point of the Lazarus Spear, somehow it had given him eternal life but it was limited to short stretches of a few weeks at a time before he had to return to the wall of the cave. He needed to kill to obtain the red mist of fear from his victims. That mist quelled the hunger and the gnawing pain in his stomach for a while and it seemed he could only take the mist from six victims each time - none was forthcoming from a seventh kill, twice that had happened. The strange, smooth brown/grey surface set into the white of the ordinary chalk that melted and took him in, hid him for however many years. How many this time? It was twenty-two last time the wall spat him out. Was it different this time? He had to find out. He was curious. Maybe it was a shorter span this time, or was it even longer?

He felt full of energy and well-rested like he'd had a very good night's sleep. He walked the short incline from the main chamber to the cave entrance. It was bright sunlight, maybe around noon judging from the position of the sun and it seemed like late summer to him. Not much had changed. The road was still there, as expected, at the bottom of the valley. It led far into the distance, so long and straight. The hill leading to the cave had a definite track now. It ran from the valley past the cave and carried on to the top of the hill. He decided to go up for a better view of the countryside around him.

The view from the top was spectacular, from the flat plateau he could see for miles. Lush green fields full of vegetables and others with the golden-brown of wheat. It looked peaceful. He wondered if the Romans still occupied the land, it looked so tranquil. At the top of the hill in the long grass, he saw a movement so he went to investigate. He found a hare caught by a rear leg in a primitive snare. He wondered if animals could produce the red mist as well as people. He gently picked the animal up and untangled the snare and proceeded to choke the rabbit. Nothing. No mist coming from it. He supposed that animals had no real concept of death and what it would mean if they were dead. Maybe they didn't have souls? Maybe only humans had a fear of dying, wondering if there was an afterlife or if it was all a lie and there would be nothing, just blackness. An end to everything they had ever known. He dropped the hare before it died and it limped away. Consus walked back down the hill.

He moved down to the valley and walked along the road to the village he remembered. It was a lot larger now, a lot more people were there. He spotted an old man sitting next to the village well. The man must have been in his late sixties or early seventies, a good age. Consus needed to question him without raising too much suspicion.

"Greetings sir, I have been travelling far and wide over the years, and I find I have lost my way. Can you tell me where I am?"

"You are in the village of Hambledon, young man, an old settlement from before the time of the Romans," replied the old man, a long bit of straw hanging from the side of his wrinkled mouth.

"I had a friend who used to live nearby, he worked for a general called Festus Augustus, I heard the general was made governor in this area. I'm wondering what became of him," said Consus.

"I remember the governor, a long time ago, he went mad after his daughter was murdered nearby, what was the name of your friend?"

"Marcus Cornelius," lied Consus.

"No, I don't recall the name but all the governor's men were replaced by the new man, Gaius Vida. That must have been over twenty years ago now, your friend is long gone from these parts." He sucked on the straw and then spat on the ground.

Over twenty years? Could it be twenty-two again?

"You look like a man who has lived through a lot in your time, can I ask how old you are sir?" asked Consus.

"I'm seventy-two years of age and not much use for anything apart from collecting sticks in the woods for the fires and telling stories to children."

"So you were born in…," Consus prompted.

"The year thirty-four, I may be old and feeble but my mind is still quick and sharp," grinned the old man with a toothless smile.

*It's 106, so it was another twenty-two years.*

Consus thanked the man for his help and wished him many more years of good health and stories to tell.


The years rolled by for Consus. Twenty-two years in hibernation and then six kills for the red mist and then repeating the cycle. So many victims and who knew how many more as he roamed through history, becoming more and more depraved. He tried to vary the methods he used. Strangulation and suffocation were used a lot but also the long blade he had taken from the daughter of Festus, and drowning his victims too. The mutilations also got worse. He never used to enjoy inflicting such wounds but he thought they were now necessary to extract the maximum amount of the mist. Sometimes he wished he could have been able to get the mist from animals but he knew it was impossible after the experiment with the hare. He felt sorry for the families of the children he took but they had the most fear, riper for culling. And he needed their fear to survive.

Centuries passed. The Romans eventually left Britain just before their entire Empire collapsed. He didn't consider himself a Roman anymore, he had no country. He was just a man who was presumably one of a kind although he had wondered over the years if the Lazarus Spear had done the same to anyone else, given eternal life, but at a price. He wondered where it was now. Was it lost and buried? Did it belong to another rich man in a collection of artifacts? Did anyone even know what it was and what power it wielded, it's history long forgotten?

Consus marvelled at the new inventions appearing every time he returned. Clocks to tell you what time it was instead of relying on the sun. Printing, mass farming using machines that tilled the soil and planted seeds and even harvested too, machines to spin yarn and weave cloth, vaccines to combat some diseases, better sanitation to prevent them, the telegraph. People could send messages hundreds of miles down a wire, steam being used to run machines like trains. He has taken his first train ride in 1822 and thought he would die of fright or even lack of oxygen if he wasn't immortal. And of course, the weapons of war improved, killing more people at a time and faster than ever before. There were always wars, it seemed. It was now 1888 and he'd finished his work for another generation. The newspapers had made him famous as 'Jack'.

And so it continued….

# PART TWO

**1976, Kingsford, Hertfordshire.**

Frank Kelly had turned fourteen a few weeks previously. A typical teenager, heavily into music and football, rode home from school on his ten-speed racing bike. It was the last day of the summer term and the first real day of summer for him. Freedom at last. Freedom from the rigid timetable of subjects he hated. *Who needs religious education anyway?* he thought. They didn't even cover Satanism. It's discrimination, he cried inwardly with a smile. He wasn't a real Satanist, he just loved horror films and fiction. He'd love to be a writer or a director one day or even a cool actor like Peter Cushing or Christopher Lee. He'd concentrate on the subjects that would get him there. Stuff bloody R.E.

His first stop was not home. As usual, it was to the playing fields where all his mates hung out, playing football or chatting up the local girls on the swings at the bottom of the field. His best friend Martin Frost was already there. They'd been mates since nursery school in the Hertfordshire village.

Kingsford wasn't a big place but at least there were three schools there and no one had to go out of the village for education unless you were a pretentious posh prat and went to the grammar school in the next town. The nursery school was next to the old church and if you were brave your mum would walk you down the short cut through the graveyard, or if you weren't, along the path to the Rose and Crown and cross the main road there and then down the hill to where a hundred screaming kids congregated in the sun, rain or snow.

Junior school was a bit more serious (if you were six). Proper lessons in proper subjects like History and Sums and proudly segregated into 'Houses' which brought the first taste of real rivalry and competitiveness later in the year for sports day and the football tournament. Frank was in Tudor - bitter rivals of York, Lancaster, and Stuart. His favourite teacher was Mr. Rolt. Frank was bright enough to go from the end of the 2nd year to the 4th year for two years. One of six or seven kids who were promoted to even out the classes a bit. Two years with Mr. Rolt were brilliant. He not only taught them the usual stuff but things about nature, balsa wood and polystyrene modelling, and even taught them cricket. He used to give away personal possessions if anyone did particularly well and Frank had got a plaster goose egg which he treasured until he dropped it one day and it shattered. It upset him and he would never tell Mr. Rolt what had happened to it. It was at junior school when he'd joined the Boy's Brigade. It was either that or the Scouts but he didn't like the sound of all that 'dib dib' rubbish so joined the BB like most of his friends. That was probably where he'd learnt a bit of discipline and self-respect. He also had to go to church, he hated that part. He made friends for life, and life back then meant about a hundred years.

Now, Frank was in senior school, he'd just finished his second year there. And it was *really* serious. It was the time for him to choose his 'options' - subjects which would supposedly help him on his path to some sort of a career. Not allowed to drop bloody R.E. though! He thought that if people wanted to follow a religion they should do it in their own free time and not have it all drummed into them at school. Who cared about Christianity, let alone Islam, Shinto or Buddhism? They could have another period of football instead if he had his way, but no one listens to a kid!

"Martin! How did you get here before me? I've got the fastest bike in the village!"

"Bunked off this afternoon, mate, couldn't be bothered. It was so hot. I didn't fancy doing double Maths and double History. I just nipped over the fields and had a nap at the old barn. They say it could get even hotter this summer. It's already hot enough for me."

'They' could always be relied upon as they seemed to be experts on everything… even though no one really knew who 'they' were. Maybe they had a lot of reference books or maybe that Almanac that predicted things that Frank's mum bought every year.

The rest of the lads turned up one by one or in pairs, H, Little Gary, the Twins, and a few others, and then they started to have a kick about in the cloying heat with the old football which was kept behind a garage next to the field. It started five-a-side until more arrived and joined in. Maybe about ten on each team by the end of the game which finished 21-16 to Frank's team although no one was entirely sure of the correct score. No one cared. It was summer!

Frank eventually went home for his tea, fish fingers and baked beans, a staple in his household, along with beans on toast and shepherds pie… and beans. Sometimes he was allowed to go down to the chippy near the canal for cod and chips, maybe plaice sometimes, if he was lucky. The TV was on in front of him as he ate. A cool new series had just started, The Bionic Woman, a spin-off from The Six Million Dollar Man which he loved. She was a tidy-looking bird, that Jaime Sommers. He wondered if Steve Austin would be in it every week, he was really cool. He didn't think so or they would call it The Bionic Couple or Steve and Jaime maybe. Frank thought that in another ten years everyone would have bionic arms and legs and eyes. That would be great if it didn't cost too much. He wondered if he should start saving. Maybe he could be a professional footballer? He thought he was good enough and having bionic legs would make him even better. After the programme finished he ran out on his real legs and down to the playing fields again. It was time for another game of football until just before nine when they would all go back in to watch The Sweeney. Then bed and reading at ten. He was reading Murder On The Orient Express. It baffled him and he'd changed his mind a few times as to who the killer was. Poirot wasn't far off revealing the culprit judging by the number of pages he had left to read. He still had no idea. It could even be Poirot himself, he chuckled. You never could tell with Agatha Christie. He loved the Miss Marple films with Margaret Rutherford. She was mental, but sharp. He'd love a grandmother like her, he could even help her with those investigations.

Life was very simple. Get up at six, do his paper round, go to school most of the year, hang about with your mates and play football and that was pretty much it before bedtime at 10 p.m. Nothing much out of the ordinary happened. Not until a couple of weeks later. Life in Kingsford would change drastically - and unfortunately not for the better.


*****


The first death he saw in the newspaper while eating Findus Crispy Pancakes, which were like a sauce in between two bits of cardboard, with Smash and… tinned beans. The pancakes always burnt the roof of his mouth, but he didn't notice on this occasion. A young eight-year-old girl, Jackie Marshall, had gone missing. She'd been found by an un-named farm worker a few days later in a field on the outskirts of the village. She had been mercilessly sliced from her throat down to her groin and her entrails were missing, presumably taken by an animal as she lay there semi-naked in the wheat field. A fox or a badger maybe. He heard later that there was a look of abject terror carved on her face. She was a pretty girl, or she used to be, looking at her grainy picture in the paper. Frank lost his appetite but carried on eating, knowing he'd get shouted at for wasting food again, because *food costs money*.

He went up to his small bedroom to listen to the songs he'd recorded from the chart countdown on the radio the previous Sunday evening. He popped the tape in his cassette recorder and set the volume to maximum. He needed to take his mind off what he'd just read. *Strange Magic* from ELO was followed by Slik and *Requiem*. They looked cool wearing American baseball shirts when he saw them on Top Of The Pops the last Thursday. His mum shouted up the stairs to turn the volume down, he did very slightly. He turned it up again when Queen's You're My Best Friend came on and he wished he could increase the volume even more than the maximum when the opening riff to Thin Lizzy and *The Boys Are Back In Town* blasted away at him. Their black singer was *really* cool. Frank was a member of the Britannia Music Club. After the initial offer of four cassettes for a pound each he usually bought a new one with his paper round money every month. He now had a collection of Thin Lizzy, Black Sabbath, Queen, and Slade, the latest being from a Canadian band called Rush who sounded a little weird but rocked.

There was a banging from downstairs as his mum thumped the living room ceiling with a broom. He didn't know why she had one. She never used it apart from that one purpose.

A farmer, John Baldwin, had been arrested. He was still in custody but denied everything, of course. The police had no more leads, no evidence to lead them to a different suspect, so they thought Baldwin was their man. They just had to prove it… by any means. He was grilled by detectives for days.

Baldwin was still in custody when the second murder happened. The police had to release him, assuming the same person was responsible for both deaths. A mile from the spot where young Jackie was left, they found another body, this time a twelve-year-old boy, Paul Maddox. Frank had sort of known him, although anyone who was in a lower year at school was usually anonymous to people of his age. The boy was a promising footballer and played for Watford's youth team, which made him into a minor celebrity at the school. He too had been sliced open, but nothing was missing. His blackened face was the worst part. He'd been strangled with his own Watford scarf first, the air choked out of him. Frank wondered what that was like and tried to hold his breath and managed just over three minutes which he counted off on the Timex he'd been given for Christmas.

People in the village looked at their neighbours in a slightly different way now, although it was thought that the killer was from outside the community, everyone was suspicious of everyone else. They hoped the police would get the man soon, or at the very least, he would move on to somewhere else to continue his killing - anywhere but Kingsford.


*****


Alan Taylor lived happily on his narrowboat, the Lucky Lucy, moored on the Grand Union Canal which passed through the bottom half of the village. He was reading a horror paperback, a new James Herbert called The Fog, and smoked his pipe while his old collie lay sleeping at his feet. He was almost fifty and worked as a labourer on a local farm. When he was ready, or bored, he would move on down the canal to another area for a few months and find work there. He never had any problem getting a temporary job, especially in the summer in rural areas and he could turn his hand to almost anything. He'd worked on farms, in shops and warehouses on his travels, and liked the life he led. No ties to anything apart from his barge and his dog.

His reading was disturbed by a muffled banging on the outside of the barge, way down on the hull near the waterline. Thinking it was a small branch swept down on the current he tried to ignore it. It would probably move on with the prevailing flow of water, maybe even a rush of water if someone was coming through the nearby canal lock. It was getting annoying though. He couldn't concentrate on his book and this was *his* time, the time he used to relax after a hard day's work. He got up, told his old dog to stay where he was, and hauled himself up onto the deck through the small opening to the outside world and shuffled along the narrow walkway at the side of the barge. He got to the bow of the canal boat and looked down and then, in shock, almost fell in. A body. The headless corpse of a child was repeatedly banging on the hull. There was a bright red smudge on the light blue paint as the bloody stump of the neck floated just above the water and repeatedly hit the boat. He threw up into the water, missing the corpse by inches. The remains of sausage and potato floating near to the body, then his vomit was drifting away, slowly down the canal. He got his thoughts together and tried to remember where the nearest public call box was. He had to call the police. He clambered over the front of his barge on wobbly legs and threw himself onto the towpath. He landed on his knees and the light gravel cut through his jeans and into his bony joints. Despite the pain, he sprinted along the towpath until he came to the bridge over the canal. He clambered up the embankment and then over the bridge and ran to the phone box which was outside the corner shop where all the kids congregated. He had to pull two girls out of the red kiosk and told them it was an emergency and dialled 999.

It took nearly twenty minutes before Taylor could hear the sirens in the distance. A white Ford Cortina with a red stripe along the side flew around the bend next to the pub and screeched to a halt near the phone box, scattering the kids who hastily put their cigarettes out and threw their half-full bottles of Double Diamond over a garden wall as the light was beginning to fade.

Taylor led the officers to the canal towpath and showed them the body stuck to his barge. One, a large barrel-chested man, was immediately on his radio and uttered the words 'not a hoax' and looked a little green. An hour later a uniformed inspector arrived and interviewed Taylor about what he saw, and also what he'd heard. Did he notice anyone out of the ordinary? Anyone acting suspiciously? How long had he been berthed there? Where did he work? It was almost dark as the police roped off the section of path where Taylor's boat was berthed.

Taylor answered all the questions and the inspector looked satisfied for now. One of the officers unhitched the barge and reversed it twenty yards up the canal, nearer the lock. It would make it easier for the police frogman to help with the retrieval of the body and to search that part of the canal for any evidence, any weapon… and the poor victim's head.

Taylor wasn't allowed back on his narrowboat so the police took him to a local bed and breakfast for the night and dropped his dog off at the kennels about half a mile away. Taylor wasn't happy being separated from his dog for the night but knew he wouldn't be allowed in the B&B with the old boy in tow.

The body in the water was identified as Colin Wilson, the son of the local greengrocer in the high street. Colin was nine and known to be a good lad, often delivering parcels of fruit and veg to some of the elderly in the village. His blue Raleigh bike was still missing. And so was his head, the search by the frogman was fruitless. The local inspector was informed a more experienced detective would arrive in the morning to take over. The gruesome story was all over the papers the next morning. Someone had tipped the media off to another horrendous killing in the village. The inspector was put in charge of the hunt for the leak. He assumed it was one of his own men.

*****

Detective Chief Inspector Paddy Mallen, along with his team, Sergeant Ray Carter and Detective Constable Danny Daly were called in now that the case had received nationwide publicity. He was one of the top men at the Met. after a stellar career in Belfast. He was sixty-two, not far from retirement after over forty years on the force, and considered the best when it came to serial killers. Britain hadn't had too many in the past but they were becoming a lot more common in modern times, maybe influenced by America, and American TV in particular. He was involved in the capture of Graham Young, the notorious poisoner in 1971 and also Patrick Mackay, who had allegedly killed eleven people between 1974 and 1975 in London and Kent but was convicted in only five cases. Mallen was by far the best-qualified man for the job. He was considered a 'living legend' by his peers. Maybe not by the media though, who rarely got anything directly from the man's mouth.

Mallen started right at the beginning again. He, and his team, interviewed Billy Nott, who had found the first victim in a field he was working in. He wasn't a suspect because he was visiting family over a hundred miles away when the girl went missing and had only arrived back the day of discovery. Mallen had that confirmed by Plod from that area who had visited Nott's family and had taken a statement. Nott worked for the farmer John Baldwin who owned the land where the body was found. Baldwin was re-interviewed. Originally the prime suspect, but released because he was in custody at the time of the second murder. Mallen considered a partnership between Baldwin and Nott, one giving the other an alibi for each murder. It was still a possibility, Nott's family could also be giving him a fake alibi, it wouldn't be that unusual. The third victim, the greengrocer's son; where was the boy's head? Mallen thought decapitation unusual for a serial killer. The methods of all three murders were different, a knife, strangulation with a scarf then cutting the boy's throat, and God knows what was used to sever the head of the young boy. The pathologist said a long blade, maybe a sword or machete, and done with one blow. Mallen hadn't worked a case like it before. Serial killers usually used the same method every time and normally had a type of victim. The only similarity was that they were all children, but two males and one female. At least none of them were molested, a blessing in a way. How were they chosen? Was it random and opportunistic or was there a method in the killer's madness? Mallen suspected madness was the most likely scenario. If it wasn't, this bastard was pure evil.

Mallen, and even the local police didn't consider Taylor a suspect but some of the villagers certainly did. Three murders of young children. He was the obvious culprit, being an outsider. No one they knew could have been responsible. Theirs was a tight-knit community. It was definitely someone from outside the village in the majority of eyes.

They found young Colin Wilson's head, and his bike, two days later. The bike was propped up against a tree in the woods next to the local common. The village cricket team were playing a Sunday game and one of the visiting batsmen hit a massive six into the woods. Several fielders entered to retrieve the ball and saw the bike. The head was balanced on the white plastic saddle, the boy's mouth wide open in shock or terror. One of the fielders ran from the woods to the cricket pavilion and the payphone inside.

Alan Taylor was watching the match from the far side of the field. He was sitting on a bench on his own and watched the commotion at the other end of the common, near the woods and the pavilion. The game seemed to have been abandoned with a large group of players and several spectators lining the perimeter of the woods. A congregation of four men drinking beer from bottles watched Taylor as he witnessed the scene, muttering to each other in slightly drunken, hushed voices.

Frank was with Martin on another bench not too far away on the other side of Taylor. They had heard of the body discovered in the canal, no surprise as it was the talk of the village. The fact of the missing head was largely unknown and they hadn't heard about it. That part wasn't in the papers or even gossiped about. They hoped it wasn't anyone else dead in there, someone they may even have known well, maybe even one of the lads. Christ, he hoped it wasn't Bridget. He had a crush on her and he knew from her friends that she liked him but he was just too shy to make his move. She was nice looking and intelligent. Just what he liked. Why was he such a wimp? He'd like to take her to the cinema in Watford, *The Man Who Fell To Earth* was on, would she like that? Maybe a comedy instead? He wanted to get to know her better but what if she said no to going out with him? He hated being a teen, he didn't know how to talk to girls unless he was with a group of mates and he didn't want his friends going out on a date with him and Bridget. He supposed it was the same for most teens, finding the nerve to ask someone out for the first time. He was determined to do it this summer. *Soon*, he thought.

Frank was snapped out of his thoughts by an elbow in the ribs from Martin.

"Are you deaf? I asked if you thought it was another one."

"I was miles away. I hope not. Look, the fuzz have arrived. It *must* be another," groaned Frank.

A black Rover, sunlight glinting off its windows and chrome hubcaps, pulled onto the common, not bothering with trying to get into the small car park by the side of the cricket pavilion which was almost full of vehicles anyway. Mallen was the first out of the car, striding quickly towards the group of people near the boundary rope. They parted for him like he was Moses forcing back the Red Sea, all he was missing was a big beard and the long staff in his hand. He wore a grey suit with a white shirt, black and green diagonally striped tie, and very shiny tan shoes. Two other detectives followed him obediently like puppies. All three pushed their way between trees and bushes before they came upon the crime scene deeper in the thick woods.

"Looks like the kid wasn't killed here. Barely any blood at all, just on the saddle and a little of the frame of the bike," said Paddy Mallen through clenched teeth, feeling anger on behalf of the victim and especially the boy's parents. "The killer, or killers, dumped the torso in the canal and brought the bicycle and head up to here and left them. They're taunting us. We still don't have a bloody clue where the actual murder site is yet. My feeling is it's a house close to the canal. They would have moved these here under cover of darkness, pushing the bike up the hill. I doubt they would have risked leaving any blood in a car or van."

"Seems that way, boss," replied Carter, his sergeant, a tall, blond-haired man in his late twenties. The other, Daly, slightly younger and certainly less experienced than his seniors, didn't look too well, staring into the open eyes of the boy's head perched on the bicycle seat. He was trying to control his thoughts by reciting prime numbers in his head. It wasn't working. He hoped he wouldn't look bad by puking in front of his new boss.

"Daly, go and get the lads over here to collect evidence, then get into the pavilion for a swift drink. I'll be over in a few minutes." Mallen knew that it was sometimes hard for the younger men, especially when a child was the victim. He'd been there himself. Daly was grateful to be away from the scene and Mallen went up a few notches in his ever-growing estimation. His last boss on burglaries had been nowhere near as understanding.

Mallen and Carter joined Daly in the pavilion about ten minutes later. The younger detective was sitting at the bar and looked a little more like himself now, a bit more colour in his cheeks. Daly stood and Mallen waved his hand to say 'sit down, lad' and the senior man ordered three doubles of a good scotch for them. Then they sat in the corner next to the bar billiards table. Apart from them and the overweight barman, the pavilion was deserted. Everyone was desperate to see the action as it unfolded out by the boundary rope.

While Mallen and his team were sat drinking their scotch, Mary Phillips had said goodbye to her friend Jenny Randall and walked down the road from the common towards her house on the other side of the high street near the canal. She had been watching the cricket but didn't like or understand the game. The attraction was Tommy Sutherland who was playing for the local team. Mary was nineteen, a little bit young for the likes of Sutherland at twenty-three but it was a small village and there weren't a lot of choices when it came to romance. He had a car, that was a real plus, an MG Midget. None of the boys her age had cars, some didn't even have a job, total wasters. He was a real catch in her eyes.

She continued down the lane, walking at a steady pace beneath the canopy of trees on either side of the long road. She'd seen the police arrive at the cricket field and felt good that they were around. She'd heard about the bodies found in the village. They were all kids and she was a grown-up now so felt fairly safe. It was terrible what had happened to them all. She wondered if the killer was someone who lived in the village, maybe someone she knew, even knew well. There were one or two creepy men around but she supposed the police would have checked them out first. That farmer was a bit dodgy. She'd heard a few things about him. Rumours of people coming from all over for the dog fights at his farm. She thought that was bloody sick. Poor dogs. She was convinced he had something to do with the murders. Why did the police let him go? That head policeman was old but he seemed nice, he looked like her granddad, and the two younger ones with him were a bit of alright. *I bet they have cars,* she thought, and wondered how much policemen were paid. Tommy only worked at the builder's merchants just off the village high street. Mary didn't think he was paid much. She fancied the tall blond copper. Maybe she'll get to meet him, he could come and interview her anytime. She giggled inwardly at being such a tart.

As Mary walked down the hill, past the junior school she went to about a hundred years ago, she heard a crackling and snapping of twigs in the woods. She got a bit nervous and thought she should have gone the other way where there were plenty of houses lining the road. She thought about turning around and going back that way via the common but that would take too long. She was only another five minutes to the fire station and less than one more to the high street. She decided to carry on. It was probably just an animal foraging for food. Her pace started to quicken though, she didn't want to take any chances. *Why didn't I go down the other road,* she chided herself. She started to sing the number one record for the last couple of weeks, just to take her mind off her growing fear. *You To Me Are Everything* spilling from her thin lips. She loved that song even though she was a massive Bay City Rollers fan. That Les was a bit of alright too. He definitely had a car and was paid lots.

Two large hands grabbed her and pulled her into the woods next to the school. Mary tried to scream, but one of his large hands covered her mouth while the other gripped her throat. She could barely move as a crippling panic seized her. She looked into the face of the man who had snatched her. He was very tall and he had a long thin face and the evilest dark eyes she'd ever seen in her life. He was dressed all in black, suit, shirt, and shoes, sort of old fashioned, he even wore thin black leather gloves, the kind posh people used when they were driving. He smiled at her, knowing she was helpless. He pulled her deeper into the woods until he found a small clearing. He forced her to the ground and grinned as she let out a strangled whimper. He constrained her with one knee on her chest to pin her down while he reached into his black jacket. Her eyes widened as she looked at the biggest knife she had ever seen - fully eleven or twelve inches long with a silver handle. The man waved the knife in an intricate pattern in front of her face like some sort of secret ritual. Her hands clawed weakly at his broad chest as she couldn't reach his face. He could see a faint red mist emanating from the girl and he breathed it in gratefully. This was her essence and the reason he attacked. He moved his left hand from her mouth and clutched one of the girl's wrists. She was still unable to scream as his knee pushed deeper into her chest, expelling all the air from her lungs. Her vision starting to flutter like the sun flitting through an umbrella of trees if you were in a car. Different colours and shapes were dancing over her now bulging eyes. The knife flashed, her left hand fell to the ground several feet away. More red mist escaped her, gushing now. Blood showered them both as he quickly grabbed the other wrist. The blade swept again and her right hand tumbled onto the dried leaves next to her. The man gulped the mist forcing its way from her thin body. He had to act quickly to get the maximum he could from her before she died from blood loss or shock. He slashed at her face. Once, twice, three times. Cheeks and forehead, deeply gashed. Her abject fear giving him what he needed. Her ears were next, sliced away from her head, she was close to death but he had to squeeze every single ounce of her essence that he could. Lastly, he drew the knife across both eyeballs. He positioned his face close to the girl's nose and breathed in deeply, the last of the cloudy vapour filling his lungs. Then she was gone. He'd got everything he was going to get from her.

The man got up from the sprawled corpse and walked through the woods. They backed onto the small house he was renting, not far from the school. He was covered in blood but he would be able to get back into the house without being seen. Over the fence at the back and shielded by tall trees on either side of the garden. He removed his gloves and put them in his coat pocket, careful he wouldn't leave blood on the fence. He didn't want to be discovered with just two more victims to complete the cycle. The police were a lot better at investigating crimes now. It didn't take him long to move the three hundred yards that took him to the rear of the property. He scouted around for any sign of anyone else in the woods then put both hands on the top of the fence and easily leapt over, no other part of his bloodstained clothing touching the fence. Once inside the two bedroom house, he stripped and put all his clothes in the bath and filled it with cold water. He soaped and scrubbed the blood from them then hung them on a string he had placed between the handle of the window and a rack used to keep toiletries in so that they dripped any excess liquid into the bath as they dried. He wiped himself down with a large blue bath towel and rinsed that and hung it on the string too. Naked, he went to lie on the bed and it wasn't long before he was asleep. His work done for the day, he needed to rest.


*****


That night Frank was dreaming. It was the same strange dream he'd had regularly. He was grown up and working on a fishing boat. He wasn't sure where. Maybe off the coast of Scotland or Ireland, possibly even America. The boat looked old. Not like the trawlers he saw on TV programmes. It was a different time. The hold was almost full, it had been a great night's fishing with the nets. Cod, Turbot, and Skate as well as Flounders, which the locals called Flukes. He enjoyed the life. Fishing all night in the mostly choppy waters and then falling into his bed, exhausted after the catch was sold at the market next to the docks. Providing for his family made it all worthwhile.

He worked with four other men on the boat, the Mary Jane. Captain Leahy, a stern, giant of a man who owned the boat and skippered it every night without fail. Bobby Kirkland was first mate. He was in his late sixties and kept pondering retirement until he realised he loved the life so much. Alec was Bobby's son, in his forties, he'd been working with the old man since he was fourteen. Eamon McMahon was around Frank's age, early twenties. He was very quiet and had his nose in a book at every opportunity. Frank wondered why he was on the boat given his intelligence. He could have been a doctor or lawyer but Frank supposed Eamon didn't come from the 'right' kind of family. The wrong class for a proper career.

Frank, Eamon, and Alec were hauling the nets in for the final time that night. They were still three hours away from dawn and docking, but Captain Leahy had gone out a little further than normal and it had paid off. Frank's share of the sale would be much bigger than normal. He would buy his wife flowers and his sons, Michael and Sean some new shoes. Both had old newspaper lining their old shoes because they leaked. He'd spend his last penny on those boys and do it gladly. They were his life.

The dark of the night still surrounded the boat. The only illumination came from a single lantern perched high on the mast and another in the wheelhouse and the glow only covered the area of the deck and a few feet around the vessel. The sky was still pitch back, clouds hiding the stars, and would be for at least another hour. The three men could hear a strange roar in the distance. They looked at each other questioningly as they had never heard anything like it before. It was like the wind of a storm but there was no gusting, the roar was a constant pitch and getting louder. The noise reached the wheelhouse and the two most experienced men of the crew.

"Drop the nets," screamed Leahy. "Get below now!"

"What is it, skipper?" asked Alec, confused by the panic in the captain's voice.

"Go! No time to waste gabbing, Alec!" shouted Bobby.

At that moment a giant wave hit the side of the boat at the port bow. The three men on deck were swept into the sea by the immense power of the wave, the wall of water flinging them as if they were made of paper, blown in a stiff breeze. The old boat was pushed for about sixty yards and then started to crack and splinter and then it finally broke up. The captain and first mate never stood a chance and disappeared into the ocean still hanging out either side of the wheelhouse.

Frank could feel the chilly water all around him. He tried to pull himself to the surface but his legs wouldn't move. He realised his back was broken after he hit the water with such a force. Just a slight pain was felt due to the numbing cold around him. He knew he would die but he felt calm. No point in thrashing about with his arms anymore. He had accepted his fate. He thought of his beautiful, red haired wife, Kathleen, and his two boys affectionately as he sank lower, trying to hold his breath for as long as he could. Enjoy the memories while he was still able.

Frank woke as he usually did after that dream, wide-eyed and gasping for breath. He couldn't understand why he kept having that particular dream of drowning. He'd never even been in a boat, let alone an old fishing trawler. Weird how the mind worked, he thought. Why couldn't he dream of scoring the winning goal against Liverpool in the cup final or, even better, taking Bridget out on a date?

*****

Mary was found a few days later by a man walking his dog through the wooded area near the junior school, he liked to watch the children at break time and the dog was a good excuse for him to be there. Albert Knox, a sixty-four-year-old loner, was well known to the police for his voyeurism but they didn't consider him dangerous and largely left him alone. He didn't report the find because he thought the police would blame him. No one ever knew he'd found the body. He never told anyone because of his reputation. He quickly changed direction and decided to stay away from school for a while. He knew he was already shunned in the village but people thinking he was that killer would be even worse. Far worse than that, they'd take his little dog, Trixie, away from him. He'd be shattered if that ever happened.

The body was quite decomposed when a couple of ten-year-olds playing in the woods after school two days later found it. Andrew James and Tim Marshall had noticed the smell first and went to investigate, like Starsky and Hutch, a new show that started on the BBC a few weeks before and they were both allowed to watch it. Tim heard a soft crunch as he stepped on something. What was that? Was it a hand? Then they both saw the bloated corpse of Mary Phillips, although she was fairly unrecognisable by then, nine days after her death. They screamed in unison and they were both still screaming when two teachers from the school came to see what the fuss was about. One of them, Chris Grant, ferried the two boys back into his classroom to calm them down, while the other, Amy Greene, ran to the school office to call the police.

Mallen, with his sergeant and constable, arrived about twenty-five minutes later. Amy took over sitting with the boys while Chris Grant showed the detectives to the spot where the decaying remains of the missing Mary Phillips were found. Mallen paced around the body several times. What kind of monster would do something like this? It was one of the worst crime scenes he'd ever witnessed, even with all his experience he felt sickened. Mallen now realised he was dealing with a complete psychopath. He spotted one hand lying nearby but not the other. He saw that both ears were missing too but no sign of them. Were they taken by animals or trophies for the sadistic killer? The body was severely bloated and a dark pink foam had leaked from the mouth and ran down one cheek and dried. Experience told him the body had been here for over a week and he knew the girl had been missing since the previous Sunday when they'd found the boy's head in the woods not too far away. The forensic guys would confirm the actual day. The killer knew police resources would be elsewhere and stretched to the limit when he attacked the girl. There was little doubt it was the same madman responsible for all four murders.

Mallen was now totally convinced he was only looking for one person despite the different methods used. Psychopaths did not play well together. They struck on their own, wanting all the attention for themselves. He told Daly to go and wait by the entrance to the school for the forensic team to turn up and guide them back to the crime scene. The only children left at the school were the two boys who had found the victim and he'd need to speak to them as soon as possible. He was told there were six or seven teachers still left on the premises. They would have to stay on site until he'd interviewed them too. He decided to talk to the boys first while the incident was still fresh in their minds and then get someone to drive them home. Leaving Carter at the scene he wearily trudged onto school grounds in search of Amy Greene and the boys, trying to quell his anger as he walked. He needed to be calm and in control before he questioned the two boys or they may get scared by him and clam up.

Mallen found them in the first classroom he came to. He could see them both sitting at desks in the front row while Miss Greene was sitting on the large desk at the front talking to them. The boys looked calm enough now, but shock may hit them later on. The trauma of finding the decomposed body would stay with them for years, maybe even a lifetime. He knew he'd probably have bad dreams himself. Mallen entered the corridor off the main entrance which led to the classrooms and a small hall that they presumably used for gym and assembly. The Nativity play at Christmas too. He knocked on the door, opened it a foot, and introduced himself to the teacher. She was a pretty girl of about twenty-five with long blond hair parted in the middle. She was very thin and as she stood up from the desk her colourful tie-dyed smock dress billowed around her. He leaned against the desk vacated by the girl and faced the two boys.

"My name is Detective Chief Inspector Mallen, but that's a bit too much of a mouthful, and to remember, so you can call me Patrick," he said with a warm smile. He was used to interviewing children, he thought their minds, uncluttered with grown-up problems, usually made good witnesses. "I heard it was you two boys who found the poor girl in the woods, what were you doing there?"

"We were playing Starsky and Hutch, looking for the bank robbers, I was Starsky," piped up Andrew, clearly the least timid of the two boys.

"I've heard of them," Mallen smiled. "Sometimes I wish I could wave a gun around and drive a big red car."

The two boys laughed, now a bit more at ease in the company of the veteran detective. It was exactly what Mallen wanted.

"So, Tim, your turn to tell me something. You were paying in the woods, running and shouting and pretending you were detectives, and then what?"

"We were on our way home. We live near to each other, you see," Tim said. "We always play some sort of game, sometimes we're police or sometimes Cowboys hunting Indians. Sometimes we find things too."

"What sort of things?" asked Mallen.

"Those magazines the big boys read, the ones with the rude ladies in," he blushed. "Once, we found a pair of girl's knickers but we didn't touch them."

"Very wise, lads," smiled Mallen. "So, did you see or hear anything before you found the girl?"

"No, we could smell something really bad, like the horrible corned beef my mum sometimes leaves in the fridge for weeks and forgets about."

"I hate that smell too," said Mallen, and scrunched his face up to make the point to the children, building a rapport with them.

"My mum does that too. Do all mums forget what's in the fridge, Patrick?" asked Andrew.

"I think they probably do now and again, although when I was your age times were hard, and I don't think food was wasted as much as it is now. Back in those days we didn't even have a fridge, we had a cold pantry to store things."

"So we sniffed the bad smell and walked towards it," continued Andrew. "We thought it could have been a dead squirrel or something. I feel sorry for that girl though, more than I would for a squirrel."

"I like squirrels, especially the red ones," said Tim.

"So anyway boys, what was the first thing you saw?"

"Tim got there first because he's got longer legs I suppose and he started to scream, then I got there and saw what he saw, the girl, and I started screaming too. Then the next thing I remember is Mr. Grant and Miss Greene were there too. Mr. Grant looked a bit funny like he was going to be sick but Miss Greene was really brave, not scared at all," Andrew looked and smiled at Miss Greene who was standing in the corner listening. She timidly smiled back at him, slightly embarrassed.

"I think you two were very brave as well, and well done for telling me what I needed to know. Do you think you will want to be detectives when you grow up?"

"I don't think so," frowned Tim. My dad wants me to be a bank manager like him, but I need to be better at sums, he says. Andrew wants to be an astronaut… or a milkman I think."

"Astronaut! I'm going to go to Mars one day to meet the Martians and bring back lots of red rocks, and maybe Martians too."

"Mars sounds good, It's a long way. I haven't even been abroad on holiday yet," laughed Mallen. "Thank you very much boys, you did very well and I'm going to ask Miss Greene if she will give you both a special gold star like Starsky and Hutch have. I'm going to get one of my policemen to give you both a ride home. Your parents have been told what happened and how you were safe and helping me and they are waiting for you to get back."

"You're a nice man, Patrick. My brother says that Jack Regan from The Sweeney is a real B-word but I don't know about that. I'm not allowed to watch," said Andrew.

"Maybe when you're older, Andrew," Mallen smiled. "People tell me Jack Regan is a proper hard man and maybe one day there won't be a copper quite like him, even if he is made up."

The boys left and as Amy Greene was already in the room she was the first teacher he questioned. She didn't see much as she stood behind Chris Grant mostly, trying to calm the youngsters down. She was pretty calm herself, considering. Grant was next and told how he saw what was left of the body and said it looked like a girl who he had taught at the school years before, but he wasn't sure. He admitted that he tried not to look too closely at her. The other five teachers all heard the screams and most of them saw Grant and Miss Greene racing for the school gates and didn't feel the need for them all to go. Most were doing their admin and marking before they left for home, and another was in the staff room and saw nothing as she enjoyed an end of day cup of tea before going home to her lonely flat in the village.

By the time he'd finished with the teachers, he was no wiser about this killer than he was that morning. He slowly walked to the crime scene and found the forensic team packing up. Carter gave him an update, saying the killer had possibly used a long knife, heavy enough to sever each hand with one blow, probably right-handed, judging by the angle of the wound on the girl's right wrist and very tall as he'd used his knee on her chest to subdue the victim. Very possibly the same weapon used to decapitate the third victim. Arterial spray from the wrists would have left him covered in blood so it was likely he waited in the woods until the cover of darkness to get back to wherever he was staying. Unseen or it would have been reported.

"Anything from the kids or the teachers?" asked Carter.

"Bugger all as usual. It would be easier trying to find The Scarlet Pimpernel than this bloke. He doesn't leave us too many clues and all I got was apparently kids think Jack Regan of The Sweeney is a bastard."

"He has a sergeant called Carter too."

"Yes, but you're a far better actor, Ray. Come on, I need a drink and it's your round."

They walked to the dusty Rover and saw Daly waiting patiently. "And you're buying the second round!" said Mallen. Danny Daly realised it would be a while before he got home to his wife and son that evening.

*****

The next day there was only one topic of conversation everywhere anyone turned. A fourth murder. Overnight the body, or what was left of it, was identified by the mother of Mary Phillips. She had reported Mary missing a week ago after she hadn't come home the previous two nights. She'd assumed the girl was staying with a friend. The father's whereabouts were unknown so he couldn't be contacted. Frank had heard about it all from a friend called Anthony who lived very close to where Mrs. Phillips did. Ant said the police were there all evening and most of the night, apart from the time Mrs. Phillips was taken away to confirm it was her daughter and then brought back an hour later. It just didn't seem real to Frank and Ant. Not only were people being killed, they were horribly mutilated as well, so the rumour went. And they were all young people too, which made them a bit nervous. It could be a friend of theirs next. Frank again thought of Bridget. She needed his protection.

Mick Sober, despite the name, rarely was. That evening he had been drinking for several hours since he finished work as a labourer on a building site. He was fifty and a big, burly man with hands as big as baseball gloves. He'd heard all the gossip about the murders and the rumours about who had done it. That bastard who lived on the canal, he'd been seen at the cricket match on the day the girl went missing, very near to where her body had been found. He'd see to him even if the police wouldn't. He'd become a bloody hero for stopping the killings, maybe even get a medal. He slurped down the dregs of his eighth pint of bitter and staggered to the door. It was still fairly hot even at ten as he exited the pub and meandered down the hill past the church in the direction of the canal. Ten minutes later he'd reached the bridge which led to the towpath and almost slid down the dusty path in his drunken stupor. A bloody hero! *Everyone will see*, he thought. Sober stealthily walked along the towpath past the other longboats moored there. He knew exactly which one that bastard was on.

Alan Taylor was relaxing as usual on his barge, pipe stuck in his mouth, and reading another paperback, this time it was an old John Wyndham classic. His tastes were mainly Horror and Science Fiction. The police had let him return to the boat two days after he was put up in the B&B. Their work on the barge and surrounding area already completed. He was disturbed when the collie woke with ears twitching and started to growl. He cocked an ear himself and could hear gravel crunching on the path near his narrowboat. He tried to settle the dog down in the confined space but the normally placid dog was getting very agitated. Someone had stepped on the deck heavily. Taylor thought it may be the police again, maybe with a question they'd failed to ask or maybe new information they had to check. He'd heard about the discovery of the fourth body the previous day and was expecting a visit from them. He wearily stood and walked through the galley to the steps that led to the deck. A massive scuffed black boot hit him in the face as he climbed the short set of stairs. Taylor flew backwards and landed on his back, dazed. Blood was streaming from his broken nose and he'd also lost several teeth. The old collie snarled and jumped over him to get to the intruder. It went for the attacker's left arm but a large rock held in the right crashed down on the dog's skull. There was a sharp crack and the collie slumped to the floor, it's skull misshapen. The old dog was dead as soon as the rock struck.

Taylor looked up towards his attacker, a hulking man who would be at home in the wrestling ring up against Big Daddy and Giant Haystacks. Taylor tried to get up but there was another kick to his head. He knew he had to try and stop the kicks and protect his skull. One more and he'll probably be unconscious and then he'd be finished. There was murder in the eyes of the other man and he could smell the stink of beer wafting off him. The other man was out of control and Taylor knew he wouldn't stop. He batted the next kick away and the other man lost his balance, allowing Taylor to get to his knees. That was his big mistake. His head was now easily in reach of the swinging arms of the attacker. A roundhouse left from the man left Taylor stunned then the right with the rock connected and everything went black.

Sober felt good about himself now, he'd stopped the killer and the bloke hadn't even got a punch in. There was a small puncture wound on his wrist where the dog attacked, but the mutt regretted that now, didn't it? He picked the dog up, walked up the short steps to the deck, and dumped the body in the canal, careful not to get covered in blood. He returned to the man lying on the floor in the galley, he checked for a pulse and found one. He was incredibly still alive but well out for the count. Sober picked the smaller man up and threw him over one massive shoulder and hauled him up to the deck. The filth will think he's fallen over and hit his head. I'll be in the clear. Sober threw the man into the dark water easily. Taylor sank immediately into the cold depths. Sober then started to walk home, looking forward to a half-bottle of vodka and congratulating himself on a good night's work. A bloody hero!


Taylor's boss was annoyed when the labourer didn't turn up for work the next day. There was plenty to do and he'd have to do a fair chunk of it himself now. He was used to his workers moving on but most had the courtesy to tell him they were going. Taylor was even owed a couple of days pay so the farmer thought it strange that he hadn't picked it up if Taylor had had enough of the job. No one bothered to check to see if his narrowboat was still there or if he'd been ill. No one cared about outsiders. Especially those who used them as cheap labour.

It was more than a week before Taylor's body was found. A family of four were travelling along the Grand Union Canal from Birmingham to London, all 137 miles of it, in a rented narrowboat. It was their summer holiday. They were docked in a lock, and the parents, Joe and Melissa Graves were slowly turning the cranks on either side of the lock to open the sluice vents so that their barge was lowered down to the secondary level and continue their journey to London. It usually took ten to twelve minutes for the water to vacate the chamber the barge was in. Suddenly their twin daughters, who were left safely on the longboat deck, let out blood-curdling screams. Their parents looked up in a panic as they were getting ready to open the lock gates.

"A man, down there!" cried Annabel, now clutching her sister Susan's hand. Tears were flowing freely.

"Stay there," shouted Joe to his wife on the other side of the canal as he sprinted up a slight incline to the side of the lock chamber and looked down. Squashed between the side of the barge and the lock wall he saw the bloated body of a man of average build, skin tinged green and starting to blacken. He told the girls to get below and then instructed his wife to walk from her position by the lock gates at the front of the barge on the other side of the canal to the rear and climb inside to comfort their panicking daughters. He informed all three he'd find a house nearby and call the police from there and under no circumstances should they come out again until he'd returned. As he hurried away he could hear Elton John and Kiki Dee blaring from the radio in the barge, the screams had died down, replaced by frantic sobbing.


Mallen, Carter, and Daly arrived in the black Rover. The local Plod from Watford had already arrived and barricaded the higher end of the canal, stopping half a dozen more narrowboats from getting near the scene. The family's barge was slowly being manoeuvred out of the lock while four burly policemen were trying to push it away from the body with long wooden poles to prevent any further damage. The body was eventually recovered and laid out on the canal bank.

"That's the chap who found the third victim, sir," said Daly.

"Taylor," replied Mallen. "Bit of a coincidence that, don't you think?"

"Suicide, guv?" asked Carter. "Maybe he was the killer after all?"

"I doubt it. Possibly just an unconnected accident. Daly, grab a Plod, and get them to drive you to where Taylor was moored, check his boat out for anything just in case."

"Yes sir, right away." Daly trotted off to the nearest uniform.

"These sorts of killers don't top themselves unless they are cornered, Carter," said Mallen. "Taylor wasn't the killer. It does beg the question if the real killer murdered him though."

"Doesn't make sense though, does it, guv? All the other four were kids... unless Taylor was a witness?"

"I'm sure if he'd witnessed anything he'd have told us, after all, he probably thought he was still a suspect in the eyes of the police. He'd have wanted to clear himself before moving on."

"Would have been nice to wrap this one up though. That madman is still out there and we don't have a bloody solid lead yet," said Carter.

"He only needs to make one mistake and we'll have the bugger, Ray," said Mallen hopefully.


Danny Daly arrived at the mooring two miles away about twenty minutes later, he was driven by PC Adam Beach in a light blue British Leyland Mini van with white doors, the sun glinting from the chrome headlight rims as they entered a car park next to a children's playground. They had to walk the last two hundred yards from where Beach was parked, across a football field with barely any grass left on it. The day was sweltering and Daly was thankful that his boss, Mallen, had allowed Carter and himself to dispense with their suit jackets and even roll their sleeves up. It was hot this summer, he couldn't remember a hotter one.

Danny Daly was twenty-four, married to Ann, and had a one-year-old son they'd named Gerry, after Danny's dad, himself a retired policeman. The boy was a handful at that age, always crawling across the floor and trying to get into things he shouldn't. A right little terror you had to keep your eye on. Danny realised he was lucky to be settled in his career and home life at such a young age. He was looking forward to young Gerry growing up and buying his old man a pint but that was still a long way off. He smiled as he thought about all the other things he'd experience before then. Taking the boy to football, watching the little man play for his school when he was old enough, his first girlfriend. Plenty of great memories to make. He was sure little Gerry would make him proud one day, maybe even play for Ireland and win the World Cup. Maybe he'd even become a detective and solve a huge crime that had baffled people for years.

They finally slogged their way through the heat to where the barge was moored. Beach waited and watched the area while Daly climbed aboard. Even with his limited experience, he knew something was off. He crept into the main housing of the narrowboat and saw signs of a struggle immediately. Plates and a mug from the galley strewn across the floor, smashed to pieces. Then he saw the blood, difficult to see at first because of the red carpet. There were dozens of flies buzzing about and there was the stench of death about the place. He turned to go and tell Beach to use the radio in the Mini to call in another team when he tripped over something. It was a large rock and it was covered in dried blood. He stepped over it and exited the boat to give Beech his instructions. *Taylor definitely didn't commit suicide, and it wasn't an accident either*, he thought. Beech ran to the police van and used the radio to get a message relayed to DCI Mallen once he'd caught his breath.

The forensic team took over an hour to arrive. Daly was close to melting, standing outside the boat, but that was preferable to staying inside it. His feet were roasting in his shiny black shoes. *This bloody heat can't last much longer*, he thought. He was hoping they could get a good set of prints from the rock and dared to believe they would be on file, otherwise they needed to get lucky with who they pulled in on suspicion. If the perpetrator was the nutter killing kids in the area then it would be a major result for Mallen and, by association, himself and Carter too. This evidence could crack the case wide open. If only they could wrap this whole thing up neatly without another kid being killed. He immediately thought of little Gerry again.

News of the discovery of Taylor's remains in the canal lock soon got around the village. Mick Sober had a sly grin on his face when people in the pub speculated that Taylor was killed by the murderer of the kids. It was a shame he had to keep the truth to himself or they may think *he* was the kiddie killer. He'd be in serious trouble if people knew he'd rid the village of the child murderer, especially as he'd had a record for GBH and was well known to the police for the regular fights he'd had when drunk. He decided on an early night and staggered home after only eight pints. Maybe he was getting too old to be out drinking every night?

*****

The post-mortem on Taylor was conducted that evening. Mallen was in a nearby pub, drinking alone and waiting for the barman to answer the phone and pass on a message to him. The call came just before closing time. Mallen ordered another large scotch and downed it before he'd even paid, left a pound note on the bar, and walked to the local hospital where the Met. Police Surgeon, Matthew Ryan, had finished his work and was waiting patiently for him to turn up.

"What's the word, Matty?" asked Mallen, perked up by the walk in the cooling night air.

"Death was by drowning, he was certainly alive when he went into the water because the lungs were full, also a fair amount of water in the stomach too," said Ryan. "There was a nasty head wound to the left side of the skull causing a fracture which would have knocked him unconscious long enough to get him into the water. Also, some abrasions around the face and neck are most likely from kicks or punches. If he hadn't been thrown into the canal a brain bleed would have probably done for him within a few hours anyway."

"So it was murder in your opinion?" asked Mallen looking for confirmation of the suspicions he'd had since he heard about Daly's discovery of the bloody rock in the barge.

"Without a doubt, beaten about the head with a heavy blunt object plus hands and feet and then asphyxiation after he went in the water. No chance of an accident. The coroner will confirm that on my evidence."

"Thanks, Matty, fancy a drink?"

"Not for me Pat, I have to be up at six tomorrow… and it looks like you've had enough too. Go home and get some rest, mate."

*****

Frank Kelly was up at six for his paper round. His mum was a bit nervous letting him go out on his own at that time of the morning with the streets deserted and tried to dissuade him but Frank insisted. He needed to earn money to build up his cassette collection. He wanted to buy a couple of Led Zeppelin tapes from Britannia. His mate Martin had them all up to *Physical Graffiti* and Frank loved them and wanted his own copies. He was amazed at how long some of the tracks were, a few well over eight minutes, some even over eleven. Hardly any other bands were making songs that long.

It had been light since before five so it felt safe to Frank as he rode his ten-speed bike down to the newsagents where he would make up his load from the papers and magazines laid out on wooden tables in the shed at the back of the shop. Three more kids were there making up their rounds for different areas of the village, there was plenty of chatter about the body found in the canal lock the previous day. They wondered if the killer got him or if it was an accident. Frank was asked by the owner if he wanted to do an extra round for a few days as a couple of kids were stopped from doing theirs by their parents. Frank said yes, grateful for the extra money at the end of the week, he could spend that on another Airfix kit. He had his eye on an Apollo Saturn V rocket but it was a bit expensive. Maybe for Christmas. He'd just had his birthday and got a new Subbuteo football edition, brought out after the World Cup two years previously. Three teams were included, England, Brazil, and Italy and Martin always wanted to be Brazil when they played. Frank didn't mind, he was always England. In the newsagent's shop, there was a 1933 Alfa Romeo car kit he fancied and also a Heinkel HE101 bomber, a German twin-engined beast with a cool looking nose cone. He also liked the HMS Victory model but thought doing all that rigging with cotton thread was a bit fiddly. Maybe one day he'd get that, he liked assembling ships.

Frank left the shop and rode down the high street to Watford Road where his normal paper round took him. Other than a couple of cul-de-sacs it was a straight road and he managed to complete one side pretty quickly. There was an isolated farmhouse about a quarter of a mile further on and he was glad he had his bike to make the journey, it was a bit of a walk with around a third of his load carried in the canvas paper bag with Daily Mirror printed on the side. He didn't like going there in winter when it was still pitch black in the mornings and the snow was on the ground with the cold wind whipping at his face. As he put the Daily Express through the letterbox, ripping it slightly, he saw a tall man dressed in black he'd never seen before walk around the corner of the farmhouse. Frank didn't like the look of him, the thin face, the dark, almost black eyes. He just didn't look right in his old fashioned clothes, he certainly didn't belong on a farm. The man started to walk towards Frank, a strange look on his face. Frank was frozen where he was for a moment then snapped out of it and decided to get away from there. He ran to his bike, which was propped up against the small wooden fence of the farm, swung it around, and jumped on, pedalling as if the Devil himself was after him. Maybe he was.

Frank managed to finish the rest of his paper round, regularly looking behind him at every stop but there was no further sight of the strange man. He rode back to the newsagents and picked up another bag that the owner had made up for him. It was only a small route of about thirty houses and in the opposite end of Kingsford, down by the 'pick your own' strawberry place. It didn't take long to deliver all the papers and cycle home. He kept the incident at the farmhouse to himself as he didn't want his mum to stop him from earning money… and he really wanted those Led Zeppelin cassettes.

*****

Mallen woke with another bad hangover. His drinking was getting out of hand, he knew, but he was in the middle of a very stressful case. He hated child murders more than anything, even more than Liverpool, being a Manchester United fan since his youth. He guessed all Irishmen were United supporters, even though the glory days were a few years previously he was sure they'd return. He wasn't far off retirement and wondered if his drinking problem would improve without the day-to-day stress of being a copper or would it get even worse due to the boredom of no work? There were always the grandkids he supposed, he could take them out for day trips, maybe even a day out at the cricket or football in Belfast. The boys were old enough now. Johnny was the youngest at nine and Mikey two years older. They were probably the only good reasons to retire. He'd miss the work, in truth, but he was sick of turning up to a crime scene and seeing a mutilated child displayed in front of him like meat on a butcher's slab.

He'd been trying to mentor Carter, a man destined for greater things as a detective. He had that intuition that all good coppers have. Young Daly will progress too, his apparent weak stomach will disappear with a bit more experience. A few more years and he'd make a good sergeant for someone, probably Carter. They worked well together and Mallen needed to delegate to them both a bit more. A little more responsibility would do wonders for Daly and he'd shown that when he'd been sent to Taylor's barge and handled things well.

Carter arrived in the black Rover at around eight-thirty to pick Mallen up. Mallen had downed a couple of mugs of strong black coffee and was feeling almost human again, his brain starting to tick over. He had his copper's head back on again.

"Did you see Matty's post-mortem report on Taylor?" asked Mallen.

"Yes guv, I was at the nick around seven this morning," the sergeant answered.

"Careful son, if you do that people might think you're a real copper," Mallen joked. Carter knew how highly Mallen regarded his sergeant.

"One has to make an effort to better oneself, don't you think?" said Carter in a fake swanky upper-class voice, as they got settled in the car.

"Posh twat," laughed Mallen. "Let's pick up Daly and we'll get some breakfast, my coffee has kicked in now."

"Toodle Pip, old chap," Carter enthused and pressed his foot down on the accelerator and sped off down the fairly deserted streets, trying to avoid the school kids dashing across the road at various points.

They picked up Daly twenty minutes later from his house in Barnet, an average two-up, two-down in suburbia. Daly's wife and little boy were waving at him as he walked down the garden path towards the big Rover. Daly turned and blew a kiss at them as he perched himself on the back seat and the car drove off.

"Good looking kid, are you sure he's yours?" joked Carter.

"Piss off, sarge," said Daly and laughed. He liked Carter and put up with his jokes in the spirit they were intended, just banter.

The trio arrived at a transport cafe they had been using near Watford almost every day since they'd been on the case. They walked in and were hit by a wall of smoke as a dozen lorry drivers all looked at them in unison, and maybe malice too. Mallen stood at the counter and ordered for the three of them. Sausage, bacon, black pudding, fried egg on fried bread and baked beans, and 3 giant mugs of tea and returned to the others seated at a wide table to wait for the order to arrive. An old woman trudged to their table with three mugs on a tray in one hand and a huge teapot in the other. Mallen wondered how she could manage it as he'd probably struggle with that teapot if it was full. She managed to fill the mugs without too much of it slopping on the table and walked off back behind the counter. Ray Carter had been filling Daly in on Ryan's post-mortem the previous night. They discussed whether they had another murderer on the loose or if it was the same killer they were after.

They concluded that Taylor being killed by the same man who had been taking those kids very unlikely. As Mallen had surmised the day before, if Taylor had witnessed the killer then he would have said something to clear himself in the eyes of the police. This was a different case, only connected by the fact that Taylor had found the decapitated body of the third child next to his barge.

"What if someone else suspected him of the murders, guv?" asked Carter.

"All we need is Charles Bronson running amok now!" groaned Mallen. "We have enough to deal with without a bloody vigilante knocking off suspects."

"If that's what we have then long odds on it's a local, vigilantes protect their own turf," said Daly.

"Looks like it," sighed Mallen. "Seems a local man, or men, suspected Taylor because he was an outsider, had arrived just before the first killing and also found a body, who needs the bloody police?"

"It's logical if that's true, all the reasons he was a suspect, to be honest," Carter admitted. "Bloody local yokels just jumped to the wrong conclusion."

"Daly, your job for today is looking for a bit of form at the local nick, anyone in the village who has a record, especially for violence," said Mallen, happy for the boy to have a chance to show some initiative.

"Yes sir," said Daly with enthusiasm. Pleased to be given a bit more responsibility by his boss.

"Carter and I will stick with the current case, assuming the real killer is not local then we need to check on recent rentals and house purchases. Anyone new to the area in, say, the last year. If that monster is a local we've got our work cut out lads, he'll be tucked up safe in his gaff."

Their breakfasts arrived at that moment and all three tucked in greedily, preparing for another long day. They could do with a bit of progress on this job, the bodies were starting to stack up.


Frank and Martin were off on a bike ride to the next village, called Flaxton, where a couple of friends lived. Nick Collins and Paul Wilkie. They met at the village field where a large, white single storey community centre dominated, with a football field tucked away at the back. Paul had brought his football and they had a kick about for about an hour. They all played for the same football team in Flaxton and all attended the same school in Kingsford. Frank was tempted to tell them of his experience that morning on his paper round but decided against it. He was still pretty shaken up about it and admitting he was scared and ran away would be a sign of weakness, something that was very uncool for someone their age. They all wanted to be like Fonzie, tough, and cool. They rested in the shade of the giant oak that hovered over part of the football field and shared a pack of ten Embassy cigarettes that Nick had bought from the small shop in Flaxton. Nick's dad gave him loads of pocket money and 25p wasn't a lot to him so he usually bought them for his friends.

They lay there, smoking and talking like they were grown-ups. Discussing the summer holidays and how hot it was and thankful they didn't have to play forty minutes each way in this heat on rock hard pitches. They preferred the ground muddy and Nick loved going in for sliding tackles and taking out the opposition at the same time. He was a proper hard-man defender like Norman Hunter of Leeds United. They were pretty happy they didn't have to go to work either, like most adults. They talked of school and how they didn't miss it, apart from the sports of course. Rugby in the winter term, football in spring and then cricket and athletics in the term just before the summer holidays. Frank was particularly good at throwing the javelin and running the one hundred metres. It was metres, and not yards, now they were in the Common Market with most of Europe and had gone decimal a few years earlier. Frank didn't understand how that worked except British farmers and fishermen seemed to be a lot worse off according to the news he saw on the television. Adults seemed mostly happy with it because there was a vote the previous year to decide if Britain would stay in it and the 'yes' vote won, so he supposed that was how Democracy worked, you accepted a vote even if you disagreed with it. Thinking that way felt like he was a proper adult himself at times. They missed the girls too. It seemed the only places girls were to be seen during the summer holidays were at the public pool in the next town or roaming around the shops in groups, trying on clothes and shoes with no intention of buying. It passed the time, they couldn't do a lot else in this heat. Frank wished the girls would play football with them, even if they were rubbish at it. The boys all decided they would take a trip to the pool in a couple of days, maybe even see Developed Della in her bikini. That would be a treat.

They lazed around for what seemed like an eternity, even in the shade of the oak it was desperately hot. There was already talk of a water shortage and people would be banned from watering their gardens. Frank wondered how bad it would have to get if no one was allowed to have a bath. It had been hot for weeks with little sign of letting up. Could it get any worse? Would it ever end? Frank had read a book by Charles Eric Maine called Thirst where a heatwave just kept getting worse and it was the end of the world, even the oceans dried up and people could drive to America across the Atlantic sea bed. Seemed a bit far fetched at the time but now he wasn't so sure. Could that happen in real life? There was a man on telly a few days ago who reckoned he could predict the weather by using seaweed and some old conkers and he said the heatwave would last another two months at least. Frank thought he was a bit of a nutter though. He hoped the man was wrong in any case. He imagined going back to school and melting in a classroom with thirty other kids trying to hang out of the windows at the same time.

Nick decided to cycle down to the village shop for sweets and drinks and some more smokes. This time the others contributed, 50p each from Frank and Paul and just 20p from Martin as that was all he had. Nick returned twenty minutes later and found all three of them had climbed about ten feet into the oak tree to try and get a bit of respite from the searing heat. Nick said it was a bit pointless buying anything chocolate as it would have melted by the time he got back and said the chocolate mice in the shop were a bit of a soggy, molten mess already and it was cooler in there than outside. He pulled the bag from his bike rack and emptied it on the floor and out fell four cans of Corona orange drink, two packs of Opal Fruits, two packs of Toffo and some Bazooka bubble gum… and another packet of ten fags. Nick shared out the sweets and bubble gum, they were all soft and squidgy but they tasted fine.

Almost two hours later Frank and Martin decided it was time to go home, said goodbye to their friends, reminded them of the pool trip, and hopped on their bikes. They were cycling down a country lane, brown fields stretching on either side of them, no cars on the road and a slight breeze in their faces, when Frank glanced over to his right and saw the strange, tall man from that morning. He was just standing there watching them both from the field as they rode past. Martin was oblivious to the man apparently.

"Race you home!" shouted Frank. He picked up speed again and Martin followed, already panting in the humid heat.


*****


The man was resting on his bed in the rented house, frustrated that he'd missed an opportunity that morning. The boy on the bicycle would have been a good addition and he decided he wanted him as one of the last two victims. He was drawn to him, knew he was from the long line related to Mary Kelly in Whitechapel. He was a witness to the man's strange behaviour and needed to be silenced anyway. He began to doze and memories drifted back to him. The face of every single one of his victims floated through his mind as he drifted off to sleep. The one thing he had managed to blot out over the centuries was his part in the rebellion by the Britons at

Verulamium. He remembered the pain of his execution though. The cold thrust of the spear as it found its way to his heart, the feeling of his life force slowly ebbing away. Waking in the marsh before he was to become fodder for the animals of the dark. More than five hundred victims to keep him alive… so far. Did he consider himself to be alive still, after all these years? The faces, and some names, haunted his dreams and his soul. He wondered just how many more he would kill over the coming years, centuries, even millennia. He often imagined ending it all. Not by knife or pistol or even drowning. He knew that would never kill him. He thought about simply refusing to kill, not taking the sweet fear he extracted from his victims, and just starving to death. He doubted it. He remembered the craving he had before his first kill, he couldn't cope with it then and he doubted he could stomach it now, it could even be many times worse. He'd learnt about certain drugs and potions over the years and the addiction some people had to them. He knew of opium and imagined the addiction to the red mist of fear would eclipse even the withdrawal from heroin. No, he just couldn't conceive of any way to end his life. Even with the exhilaration he got every time he killed, he was so tired. The kills were a means to an end just to preserve him but sometimes he longed for his own end. That was impossible though. He saw no option other than existing like this until the end of time. Young men dream of eternity but the reality of that is far different than they imagine. Had there been others like him, killed by the same spear? Had they wanted to end their immortality too? He didn't think he'd ever know the answer to that.

The summer was the hottest on record and even Consus hadn't seen anything like it. Although heat or cold didn't affect him much he could see the listlessness of the people. They were drained by the hot weather and they prayed for rain to end their torment. There was even a plague of ladybirds across the country, it was almost Biblical. He watched the nightly news on television, there was always something that was affected by the heatwave. Train tracks buckling, reservoirs emptying at alarming rates, even buildings collapsing because of crumbling brickwork. He also saw regular reports about the killings in Kingsford and how the police were constantly criticised for their failure to catch the madman. This man, Mallen, the one in charge, was said to be very experienced and the best the police had. Consus didn't think he was that good. The murder of the man from the canal boat had confused things for the police for a while, he had liked that. They would have discovered by now that it was not the same killer who had taken the children and that teen girl so brutally. Their men would be split between looking for him and the murderer of the bargee. It would give him more time to pick the right moments to find an opportunity for his fifth and sixth victims, one of which would be that boy. He knew that for sure.

*****

Frank continued with his daily paper round, wary when it came to approaching the isolated farmhouse at the end of the road. His bike was pointed in the direction of the village, sat on its kickstand, before he went near the front door, always ready to drop the paper and run. There wasn't a sign of the man there but it would just take one mistake, one careless moment, and he could end up like the other kids who had been killed. He did, however, decide to report the incident to the local police. Maybe it would help catch the killer if that man *was* the killer… as long as his mum didn't find out about it. He needed the money from his paper round. He would be upset if he couldn't buy his little treats for himself every month.

After he'd finished for the morning he rode to the police station. It wasn't big like the one in Watford, just a small office in between two three-bedroom houses where the local constables lived. There weren't even any cells there which was a bit of a disappointment. He'd noticed that when his mum forced him to hand in a ten-pound note he'd found by the bus stop in the high street. He opened the door that led to the office and poked his head in. P.C. Steve Rodgers was there standing over a young man in a dark grey suit who was sitting at the desk looking over some files.

"Ah, young Frank Kelly, come in son, what can I do for you?" said Rodgers.

"Erm, I was chased by a man yesterday on my paper round," said Frank, slightly embarrassed at showing his fear.

"Okay, where was this Frank?" asked the local policeman.
"At the farmhouse at the end of Watford Road, that's as far as I go on the round before I double back and do the opposite side of the road. He may be the one killing all those kids! I'm not sure though, could just be a creepy perv." Perv was the new word they had learnt that spring in the playground after Albert Knox was caught watching the little kids again. He wasn't sure what else pervs do, but watching schoolkids was bad enough.

"Frank, this is D.C. Daly, he's part of the team investigating the deaths of those young people, you came at just the right time to catch him."
Frank looked at the young detective, he had kind brown eyes that put Frank at ease immediately.

"Hello Frank, you can call me Danny. Sit down for a moment and tell me all about it."

"Well, it was early yesterday morning, it would be about seven-thirty by the time I got to the farmhouse. I was hurrying a bit because I had an extra round to deliver afterwards, I want to buy a couple of Led Zeppelin cassettes."

"I like them, better than the stuff my dad listened to. Glenn Miller," he laughed. "Definitely not my cup of tea, or yours I'll bet." Frank liked Danny a lot already. Nothing like Jack Regan, or even that bad actor who played his sergeant. He didn't know who Glenn Miller was so just shook his head in agreement with the young detective.

"Yeah, they are great, anyway, I got to the farmhouse and was just putting the paper through the letterbox when a man walked around the side of the building. He looked funny, dressed in old fashioned clothes like in the war. A black suit but not the same kind as yours. He was quite tall, taller than you are, even taller than P.C. Rodgers, and had a very thin face and dark eyes, they looked black but I've never seen anyone with black eyes before so they can't have been, but they were really dark. He sort of looked like a vampire from those old films my mum lets me watch."

"Like Christopher Lee?" asked Daly.

"No, like that bloke from the really old films, the ones in black and white, even on our colour telly, the foreign one, only much taller, and scarier looking too."

"Bela Lugosi?"

"That's the one, but taller. He was very creepy, creepier than that Legoosey bloke. You won't tell my mum what happened, will you? She'll stop me from doing my paper round and I really want those cassettes."

"No, we'll keep it between us for now, Frank," Daly said, "I do need to tell the rest of the team though, if that's alright?"

"That's okay, as long as they don't tell my mum either."

"I promise they won't, Frank," smiled Daly. "You may have been a big help to us, thanks."

"I hope you catch him, even if he's not the murderer he needs to stop scaring kids and being a perv."

"You're right there. Well, I think P.C. Rodgers and myself need to get to this farmhouse and check the place out. If you see or hear anything else come straight back here and either P.C Rodgers or P.C. Connolly will get in touch with me. Ask your friends if they've seen anything too, even something small may help us a lot."

"I will do," said Frank as he backed towards the door, "See ya!" Frank turned and walked out with a smile on his face, maybe he would be the reason the killer was caught, and then his mum would be proud of him for once. He wouldn't mind being a hero. Maybe it would give him the confidence to ask Bridget out? He walked his bike up the hill to his house, smiling broadly.

Rodgers and Daly walked out soon afterwards and got in the blue and white Morris Minor Traveller that was parked outside. It was a little cramped but it was a nippy little car. They soon got to the farmhouse and parked in the farmyard. The smell of chickens hit them as they got out, the heat made it worse even though it was only a little after nine-twenty in the morning. Daly knocked on the side door of the farm and a stout, grey-haired lady in a green and yellow spotted pinafore opened the door.

"What can I do for you, dears?" she said warmly.

"Morning, Mrs. Wilcox," said P.C. Rodgers. "This is Detective Constable Daly, he's working with me today. This may sound strange but did you notice anyone unfamiliar hanging around yesterday, or even another day?"

"No, can't say I have, but I'm usually pretty busy baking or cooking for the farmhands, keeping my mind on the job at hand. You looking for someone strange then? The bloke who's been doing all this killin'?"

"Just a lead we're following up after a report we got today. Young Frank Kelly was delivering your newspaper and got scared by someone in black yesterday morning, says the man was on your land," said Rodgers.

"Could be nothing, but still needs checking," said Daly, noticing the smell of freshly baked shortbread coming from the kitchen.

"Oh my God, we could have been murdered in our beds! John will need to keep his shotgun handy just in case until you've caught the bugger!"

"Just make sure that your John doesn't shoot any innocent walkers going across his land. Remind him that the path is a public right of way. Don't want to have to put him away, where would I get my eggs from then?" Rodgers joked.

You'll have to get them at old Mrs. Arnott's shop in the high street… and pay nearly double too. Can't be havin' that, can we?" she laughed. "I'll tell John and the lads to keep an eye out for anyone who shouldn't be here."

"Thanks, Mrs. Wilcox, mind if we take a quick look around before we go?" asked Daly.

"Help yourself, love, I have to get back to my shortbread, get them covered and cooling before the flies smell all that sugar," she smiled. "I'll be seeing you this weekend as usual, Steve? I'll pick a few of the biggest eggs for you, my love."

"Thanks. See you then, Mrs. W."

Rodgers and Daly walked around the farmyard and checked the barn and other outbuildings and found nothing. They ambled back to the police car to continue what their priority was for the day. Checking the local residents with a criminal record, looking for the killer of Alan Taylor. He'd update Mallen on Frank's story and the search later when his boss called in. He was enjoying the time spent with Rodgers, hopefully, they could make headway in the search for Taylor's murderer.

First on the list was a Charlie Ryland, a 27-year-old mechanic who had been put on probation for domestic abuse. He'd beaten his then girlfriend because she cheated on him. He also knocked seven bells out of the man she was seeing behind his back, he put the man in hospital for a week. Ryland worked quite near the canal, less than five minutes' walk from Taylor's barge. They visited his workplace, much to the young man's disgust. Sat in the garage offices they questioned him about where he was on the night of Taylor's murder. It turned out he'd had a good alibi, he was out drinking with his boss and a couple of workmates who confirmed his whereabouts very quickly once they were called in. Daly crossed Ryland off his list. It certainly wasn't him unless all four of the garage workers were in on the killing and Daly knew there was no forensic evidence for a group involved in the attack. Just the footprints of himself, Taylor, and the killer. He and P.C. Rodgers moved on quickly to the next possible candidate.

Terry Smith worked at one of the local pubs, The Swan, and was overseeing a delivery from the brewery. He stood at the edge of the trapdoor which led to the cellar and watched the two burly delivery men heft barrels almost the size of a small car off the lorry and down into the cellar. Smith was forty-four and had served two years for the assault of a teenager who had been drunk and attacked him. Smith had taken his 'self defence' a little too far and put the boy in hospital with a broken eye socket, almost blinding him, and breaking his nose. Smith was spared a much longer custodial sentence because he was the intended victim and was injured too. He had been working the night Taylor was brutally murdered and could produce over fifty witnesses to the fact if he needed to. Daly checked the staff rota with the pub landlord who was sitting at the bar nursing a large vodka before the bar had even opened. He confirmed Smith was working that night. He was in the clear.

Third on the list was Mick Sober. They had tracked him down to a remote part of the building site he was working on, a new housing estate being built for the local council. About a hundred two and three bedroomed houses and several two storey flats. Sober was having one of his many 'breaks' from his work, smoking a roll-up and sipping occasionally from a half bottle of rum he kept in the front pocket of his dungarees. He was a giant of a man and was sitting on a pile of pallets when Daly and P.C. Rodgers approached.

"Your mate looks like filth, Rodgers," Sober said with a scowl.

"I'm Detective Constable Daly," answered Danny, trying to keep calm and not rising to the bait. "I'd like to ask you where you were on the night of the seventh, ten o'clock onwards."

"I was at the pub having a skin full as usual then staggered off home and carried on drinking," said Sober a little too quickly, which immediately made Daly suspicious.

"Is anyone able to confirm what time you got home?"

"No, the wife was in bed and I sat downstairs and fell asleep in front of the telly," said Sober with a smirk.

"What did you watch?" asked Daly, intending to check the TV schedule for the timing.

"No idea, I was pissed as a fart," Sober smiled. "Probably some poncy drama on the BBC or something. There's not much choice with three channels, is there?"

Daly didn't like the big man, he was obviously not one of those gentle giants who was a friend to everyone. Sober was a nasty piece of work, evidently dangerous. Danny's gut told him this was the man he was looking for.

"What's all this about anyway? Did someone steal a puppy or something?" Sober mocked.

"We're interviewing any local with a history of violence and you are definitely on a list. I suppose you have heard about the murder of a man on his narrowboat? " answered Daly, looking closely at Sober for some sort of reaction. Guilt or nervousness mainly.

"Nowhere near the canal that night, mate. The bloke deserved what he got if you ask me.

Killing those kids. Bloody outsiders, always trouble. Whoever done him was a bloody hero in my book," he scowled.

"It's been established that Taylor had an alibi for at least two of the killings and had been quickly ruled out as a suspect by investigators. A little too late before word got around it seems," said Daly.

"Probably another outsider that done him," said Sober and winked.

Daly walked away and Rodgers followed quickly behind. Sober was definitely right at the top of his list, but he still had several others to contact and question. They spent the rest of the afternoon tracking down the other possibles. There seemed to be quite a lot of people living in the village who had had a violent past. Most had good alibis and people to back them up, and of those that didn't Daly dismissed them as not being the right type to murder in cold blood. Petty stuff like drunken scuffles and beating their kids were more their style. Not viciously murdering a man without any water-tight reason. Daly was starting to develop an instinct for spotting a bad guy, learning a lot from Mallen who he virtually worshipped. Danny admitted to himself that if he became half the copper Mallen was then he'd be happy with his career when the time came to retire. He imagined himself in Mallen's shoes one day.

"Sober is our man, I'm sure of it," said Daly to Rodgers when they had returned to the tiny police station. "I bloody well know it."

"He's definitely trouble," replied Rodgers. "Always getting into scrapes when he's had too many. He's always the instigator too, he's a bully who knows no one in the village could take him in a fight."

"I'd better get hold of the guv and update him on Sober and also what young Frank saw yesterday. Thanks for your help today, Steve."

"Anytime, it was nice to get out and do some real police work," beamed Rodgers.

"I'll give you a shout if we get to arrest Sober, don't want you missing out."

"We'll probably need another half dozen hefty lads as well," Rodgers joked. "Sober is strong as a bull and you could tell how nasty he is."

"I'll bring the Met. rugby team," smiled Daly. "See you later, mate."

Daly had already called Watford nick from the local police station to find out where Mallen was and was told that his boss and Carter could be reached up at the cricket club in the village. Daly considered asking for a car to come and pick him up but decided to walk. It was only about a mile away. Not too far. Daly told them to give the cricket club a ring to tell Mallen he was on his way.

He walked along the high street feeling pretty pleased with himself. He was sure he had his man. The only problem was proving it, not much evidence to convict Sober at the moment and he doubted if the big man would break down and confess. He was sure Mallen would have a few ideas with all his experience to fall back on. If anyone could dig the truth out of Sober, Mallen could. Daly walked past a greengrocer, the smell of the earth still on the potatoes, and the fragrance of fresh strawberries wafted out through the open doorway. It was the shop which belonged to the father of the third victim, the boy who was decapitated and dumped in the canal and the head left in the woods near the common. He looked in through the door but did not see the owner, just an old woman in a dusty pinafore and dirty hands, long white hair swept back into a ponytail serving a plain looking woman with a green hat and yellow summer dress on. He passed a small chemist which was next to a large house that had been converted into a doctor's surgery. Danny crossed a road which led up a steep hill and strolled past a large waste area which people used as a free car park, the ground was fairly flat, dried and slightly rutted but would be very muddy in winter. He wouldn't be surprised if drivers got stuck now and again when the rain came. If the rain came again that is. He passed the dentist, housed in a large red brick building, and then a carpet shop. There was a newsagent next door and he decided he needed something sweet.

One wall was entirely made up of shelves covered with newspapers and magazines, Daly assumed this was where Frank set off for his paper round. He loved Shoot! Magazine, loved football in general and played on a Sunday for a local team in Barnet. The season had finished a few weeks earlier and Liverpool, who he hated, had won the league title and his beloved Manchester United had lost in the cup final to Southampton. A bloody second division team! He picked up a copy of Shoot! And the grim face of Malcolm Macdonald stared back at him from the front cover. The team photo in the centre of the magazine was Southampton with the cup. What a dreadful summer it was turning out to be. He tucked the magazine under his arm.

Danny moved over to the opposite wall in the long narrow shop and knew he'd have trouble choosing a bar of chocolate for the walk up to the cricket club. So much to choose from; Cadbury's Grand Seville, Ice Breaker which had little chips of mint in the chocolate, Curly Wurly bar, Galaxy plain, and a Needler's lime milk chocolate which sounded disgusting in his opinion, and many more. He settled for an Aero bar which cost 4p. He picked one up and his fingers sank into the packaging, the chocolate soft in the heat. He'd be spending an hour trying to lick the melted chocolate off the tinfoil covering and causing an abrasion to his tongue. He changed his mind, replaced the misshapen Aero on the shelf and took a packet of Spangles, and then asked a young girl, who had probably just left school for good that summer, for a quarter of loose extra strong mints when he got to the counter. The round white mints were in a small white paper bag and he tucked into them as soon as he left the shop, relishing the strong flavour.

His walk along the high street took him past a printer, a general store, a pet shop, and a barber's before he turned left and walked up the hill towards the common and the cricket club. It was hard going trying to climb the hill in the heat so he stopped to take off his suit jacket and threw it over his shoulder to trek the rest of the way. There were houses on either side of the road as he ascended but he saw no one. He assumed they were all at work or lounging in their back gardens, soaking up the sun and getting a tan before the yearly holiday to Benidorm or the Costa Del Sol. He didn't fancy one of those cheap package holidays. He'd rather drive to Margate or even down to Dorset. He'd only go to Europe if Manchester United were in the European Cup final, maybe against Bayern Munich or Real Madrid.

Sweat was trickling between his shoulder blades as he entered the cricket pavilion. The shades were drawn over the windows and the place felt quite cool in comparison to outside in the vicious sun. The smell of stale beer and cheese and onion crisps almost overcame him. He spotted Mallen and Carter sat at a table at the far end of the hall and waved. Daly went to the bar and asked for a pint of Guinness and the same again for the other two which was a pint of Double Diamond for Carter and the usual large scotch for Mallen. Carrying the drinks over on a small metal tray emblazoned with Harp Lager, he nodded to his colleagues before sitting down.

"We got your message from the nick so decided to stay for one or two more," said Mallen with a wink.

"So pleased you did, guv," Daly said with a smile.

"What have you got, Danny?" asked the older detective. Daly surprised at the informality of the senior man although possibly the scotch may have had something to do with it.

"Two things really. I think I have a prime candidate for Taylor's murder, a bloke called Mick Sober, he was far too cocky for my liking and sounded like he was playing with us. He's got a record as long as your arm for violence but never been put away. Fines and probation. He probably intimidated all the magistrates who came across him. Spends most of his spare time in the pub getting pissed when he's not battering all and sundry or skiving off at work on a building site."

"We'll bring him in later. I have a cunning plan. You and I will interview him at Watford nick and if we get nothing from him Carter will casually get chatting to him in the pub and ply him with drinks. Maybe he'll let something slip, you said he was cocky, he may start bragging about how he fooled the police," said Mallen to Daly.

"You're a sneaky bugger, guv, but it's worked in the past though," piped up Carter. "I hope I'm on expenses."

"Of course, although I'd gladly pick up the tab out of my own pocket to get the vicious git banged up. It takes a right bastard to do what he did. Good work, Danny," said Mallen. "What else?"

"The other thing was some kid on a paper round thought he may have been chased by our child killer, I got a description from him and we checked out the farm where it happened too."

"Is the kid reliable or after a bit of attention," asked Mallen.

"Seemed genuine to me, a good kid. He's worried about his mum finding out because she'd stop him doing the round. The description was a tall man in dark, old fashioned clothes, a thin face, and black eyes, a tall Bela Lugosi type. I don't think it's imagination," said Daly.

“Should be easy to spot if he exists. Thing is, no one else has seen anyone like that, have they?” said Mallen with a frown.

“Even if the description is slightly exaggerated I believe he does exist, the boy seemed genuinely frightened. I asked him to see if any of his friends had seen anything and he’ll get back to one of the Plods at the local nick. By the way, that Rodgers is a good bloke, he’ll be useful for any more local info if we need it,” offered the young detective.

“Right, so we have a plan of action in the Taylor case. We’ll pick this Sober up and take him to Watford, grill him for a bit, and if we get nothing we release him. Then Carter goes to work on him this evening. If we can wrap this up tonight then we’ll be at full strength for the child murders.”

“Yes, guv,” the younger men said in unison.

“First things first though, get them in Carter,” smiled Mallen.


*****


At just before five-thirty Mallen and Daly were waiting outside the entrance to the building site. Sober was easy for Mallen to spot as he towered over everyone around him. They stepped out of the car and approached the giant.

“Mr. Sober, I’m Detective Chief Inspector Mallen and I gather you’ve already met D.C. Daly? I’d like you to come with us for a chat.”

“I ain’t done nothin’ filth!” spat Sober.

“Not the sort of attitude I like, Mr. Sober. It won’t take long and you’ll be released very shortly. I’d just like to clear a few points up, and Daly here says you have your thoughts on the murderer of Alan Taylor, maybe you’ll be able to help us catch him.”

A smirk appeared on the face of Sober. He thought he had the upper hand, they didn’t suspect him for knocking off that kiddie killer! The large man nodded and Daly opened the rear door of the Rover for him. Sober just about squeezed onto the back seat of the big car. Mallen almost grinned at how smug Sober looked. He’d used reverse psychology in the past to trap suspects into feeling over-confident.

They arrived at Watford's main police station about twenty-five minutes later. Sober had been silent in the back of the car, very thoughtful about the yarn he was going to spin them. *Stupid filth, you’ve got nothin’.* He’ll try and lead them in the direction of another bloke on the building site, another thick Mick like Mallen. Probably got IRA connections, that bloke. Serve him right!

Sober span his web of lies about his workmate Sean Sullivan, a middle-aged carpenter from Sligo. Sullivan had never done anything to wrong Sober, the big man just didn't like him. He didn't like any Mick. Sullivan was an outsider too and Sober tried his best to convince Mallen that there was no way a local man had killed Taylor or even the little kids murdered recently.

"Always trouble when they come to work here, they never fit in and don't last long," he said. "Even if it's not Sullivan I bet the killer of the bargee has already moved on. No, not a local man has done it."

Mallen didn't believe a word the big man had said but nodded sagely at every point Sober made, giving him a false sense of security that Carter could take advantage of later.

"Well, thank you for your help, Mr. Sober, said Mallen "We'll certainly be having a look at this Sullivan. I'll get someone to drop you off home in a minute unless there is somewhere else you intend to go?"

"Wouldn't mind stopping off at The Swan in the village," said Sober.

Mallen now knew where Carter would find him. Get him pissed and he may talk to the sergeant. Meanwhile, he and Daly had other things to check out.

*****

A little later, after Carter had checked in with Mallen, the sergeant stood outside The Swan. He knew that the police car from Watford had dropped Sober there. Carter rehearsed his story before he went in. One sniff of suspicion from Sober and it would all be over, the plan blown. Carter checked his wallet to see if he had enough cash for the evening and went inside.

The pub wasn't too busy but it wasn't too quiet either, he'd be able to have a conversation with the suspect and hear what he said but the background noise would make it difficult for anyone else to hear what was said between them. He immediately spotted Sober at the bar, couldn't really mistake him given the description that Daly had provided. Carter stood at the bar next to the giant man and sighed loudly.

"Long day, mate?" asked Sober.

"Bloody long, and this heat doesn't make it any easier. Been a crap day too, to be honest, and I need a drink. One for yourself?" Carter offered.

"Don't mind if I do, been a bit of a strange day for myself too."

"Oh, nothing too bad I hope?" asked the sergeant.

"I don't really want to talk about it," said Sober.

"Fair enough, mate. I lost a big contract today. Spare parts for a chain of garages, plugs, filters, windscreen wipers, general stock like that. Would have made a bundle in commission."

"Unlucky son," said Sober and then gulped down half of the pint Carter had bought.

"Yeah, would have paid for my winter holiday in the sun," lied the copper.

"Haven't you seen enough of that bloody sun over the last few months?" laughed Sober.

"Different kind of sun on the slopes," lied Carter again. "Nice and cool outside on the slopes and nice and warm in the evening in the lodge drinking. And you should see the birds too, mate, German, Swiss, French, Italian, even a few Yanks, all sorts of gorgeous girls… and they don't go there for the skiing if you know what I mean?" he winked at Sober.

"Could do with some of that," drooled Sober. "Another pint?"

"Why not? I've got nowhere special to be," said Carter with a friendly smile, playing his part.

Three pints later and the conversation had drifted from football to politics, then women and back to football again. Carter noticed the slightly glazed expression of the face of Sober and suggested they have a little rest at one of the tables. Carter ordered a pint each, a couple of bags of ready salted crisps each, and a pair of large Irish whiskeys to wash them down with. Carter knew the salt in the crisps would make Sober a little thirstier and ready for more drinks soon. He pretended to be a little drunker than he actually was and hoped Sober was as pissed as he looked and would start to babble and ramble pretty soon. Carter had taken his pint to the toilet a couple of times and poured most of it in the urinal to make sure he didn't drink too much. He had to try to keep up with the big man somehow.

"So what pissed you off today mate?" Carter slurred.

"Bloody filth hauled me in about these kiddie killings that have been going on," slurred Sober.

"I read about those, bloody shocking, hope they get that bastard soon," replied Carter.

"Yer, I told them a bloke at work, a stupid Mick, was good to nab for it. They'll probably pick him up for it tomorrow. Some outsider who lived on a narrowboat was killed too. Someone must have thought he was the kiddie killer but the filth told me he was in the clear, whoever killed the tosser made a mistake."

"I suppose whoever killed him would be feeling pretty guilty by now. Imagine taking revenge on someone, thinking you're doing the right thing, and then finding out you killed an innocent man? That's got to play on your mind a lot, eating away at you, you'd never get over something like that." Carter was intentionally using the word 'you' now, trying to coax a mistake out of Sober.

"Well, he looked bloody guilty to a lot of people, ask anyone in here. Anyone could have made a mistake, couldn't they?"

Carter excused himself, On the way to the toilets he saw a payphone in the long, dimly lit corridor. He looked to see that Sober hadn't followed and made a quick call to Watford nick, asking for Mallen. The senior detective was found in the canteen and was told that Sober had virtually confessed and needed picking up. He had to be interviewed again in his drunken state. It was the best chance they had to get him.

Thirty minutes later Mallen and Daly had arrived in the Rover and were followed by a van load of six burly uniforms, the biggest Mallen could find in the canteen at the nick. Carter had continued to keep Sober topped up with alcohol while he waited for the cavalry to arrive. He was fairly drunk himself by now and had a bit of fun with Mallen, keeping up the pretence as a car parts salesman and trying to stop the 'pigs' taking his new friend off. Mallen winked at him and Daly grinned. Had the plan worked though?

Sober tried to resist being put in the van but the amount of drink he'd consumed meant he was as docile as he was ever going to get and it was only an indignant, token resistance against the half dozen big coppers, the booze and the heat of the day sapping his strength, his guilt doing the rest. Mallen was pleased but he knew he only had a couple of hours before Sober would start to recover his wits. They took him straight to the nearest interview room in Watford nick and started to cajole a confession out of him. Mallen acting like he was a friend and sympathising with Sober for making such a tragic mistake. He didn't mean to kill Taylor, it was the drink and the frustration of the police not doing their job, he suggested.

Sober broke down in tears and said that he didn't mean to kill Taylor, he just wanted to rough him up and get a confession out of him for the child killings. It went too far, he admitted. He was sorry. He wanted to be a hero, not just some idiot on a building site for the rest of his life, doing donkey work.

It was a great result and the three detectives celebrated well into the early hours, deciding on a late start at about noon. One major problem sorted, still clueless about the main one though, the child killings by a person or persons unknown.

Word soon got around the village the next day about Sober's arrest and confession to the killing of Taylor, the outsider who lived on the canal barge. No one was really surprised. Sober was known to be violent and vindictive with a drink inside him and the majority of villagers avoided him. Most people were happy and relieved that Sober will probably be put away for a lot of years. A welcome respite for all those who frequented the various pubs in the village.

A week later the general optimism that the killer of the four children (although Mary Phillips could hardly be classed as a child) had moved on was growing. There hadn't been an attack for close to two weeks. They prayed their particular nightmare was over, even if he did continue in another area. The detectives were still about though, interviewing dozens of people, trying to find a lead. They had empty houses searched, sheds and garages, and farm outbuildings too.

Even the woods looking for a campsite of some sort, however basic. There was no sign of the man anywhere. There were no strangers in the village that anyone knew about, or had noticed.


*****


Martin Frost was at a loose end. Frank was feeling a bit under the weather after being stung on the ear by a wasp. They had both been pouring jugs of water into the holes of a manhole cover knowing there was a wasps nest inside. They didn't think the wasps would swarm. Martin was lucky. He'd managed to get to his feet quickly and get far enough away but Frank wasn't that quick, he realised he'd been standing on his shoelace and nearly tripped. The wasps were on him in a flash and he was lucky to be stung only once. He ran down the road holding his ear, trying hard not to stand on his undone shoelace again and go flying, trying hard not to cry.

There was no one else about so Martin decided to take a ramble across the farmer's fields, maybe make a camp in the row of tall ferns that divided two of the fields. Possibly take a trip up to the pond too. He'd stolen a pack of ten Rothman's from his dad and there were six left in the pack, also a box of Swan Vesta matches. He could relax and smoke a few of the fags. He knew he shouldn't really call them fags because that meant something else in American. He found that out from watching Kojak but he still used the word. Maybe he could call his smokes queers or nancies, sort of like a code to fool his parents and amuse his friends. That would definitely get a laugh out of Frank. He chuckled at his own joke as he wandered along the stony path which led to the fields. It was a scorching hot day, not a cloud in the sky that he could see. A puff of fine was dust kicked up by his feet. About half a mile away he could see the farmer had been baling straw for the winter feed of his animals and Martin headed towards the the mountain of bales. It would be a good place to sit down and have a smoke. He had to be careful not to catch them on fire though, that would mean *big* trouble.

There was a one strand electric fence designed to keep the cows away from the straw bales. Martin and Frank often dared each other to touch the wire but they were too chicken, worried they may cry. Martin decided it would be a good time to actually try it, in private so if he did cry no one would know but him. He stood at the fence and his finger floated above the wire for what seemed like an eternity before he finally touched it. A jolt of pain flew up his arm and seemed to stop at his funny bone. It didn't hurt that much after the initial shock but he was numb up to his elbow and his arm tingled as it regained it's feeling. He laughed because he expected a lot worse. He could dare Frank to do it and maybe have a bet too. He no longer feared the shock from the wire and would touch it again if there was an incentive to do so. He ducked under the fence and walked up the incline.

He reached the bales of straw, stacked up in the middle of the field. He pulled one down from the stack and sat on it and lit up his first fag of the day. Sucking down the thick grey smoke into his lungs. The sun was beating down on his face and arms and his black plimsols burned his feet. He took his white t-shirt off and tucked it into the waistband of his jeans and kicked his footwear off. Proper Wranglers the jeans were, cost a packet and miles better than the ones they had down the market over in Watford. He got these from a Littlewood's catalogue and was paying fifty pence a week for twenty weeks to his mum. He decided to lie down on the bale and take a rest before he carried on to the pond a mile away. His back was getting scratched slightly from the rough straw and his legs were dangling off the end of the cuboid bale. He started to get a little drowsy in the hot sun, he closed his eyes and let the heat of the day flow over him, seeming to come in waves as a slight breeze flitted through the heavy, humid air.

Martin had been dozing for a while when something clamped over his mouth and nose. His eyes shot open and immediately closed again as the bright sun flashed overhead. He was blinded and unable to breathe. Another large hand pushed his chest down and pinned him to the bale with incredible strength. He struggled and the sharp edges of the straw started to draw small rivulets of blood all over his back and neck. Blind panic started to hit him. He knew it was the man they were looking for, the child killer, and he realised unless he managed to shake himself free he'd have no chance to escape, he just needed to get to his feet and run. His lungs were already burning and he doubted he had much time left to save himself. He tried to struggle, tried to sit up but the power of the man was immense. The sun looked bright red through his closed eyelids but that was starting to fade, first turning to grey and then to black as the life left Martin Frost. Another victim of the callous murderer.

Consus had finished breathing in the fine red vapour he'd extracted from this one, his fifth of this cycle. This boy's friend would be the sixth even if it took weeks to find the right opportunity, he'd put up with the craving if he had to. He'd have to think of something special to end the life of the boy who had escaped him before. Maybe as spectacular as Mary Kelly in Whitechapel, the last of his victims back in 1888. Consus quickly laid Martin's body face down in the field and then stacked the bales to cover him again. He slowly walked back to the path, there was no one around to witness his fifth killing.

*****

Martin was missing and had been for the last three days. Frank knew, just knew for certain, that he'd been taken by the child killer. He was devastated. He dragged himself out of the house and down to the small police station for any news of his best friend. P.C.Rodgers was there on duty.

"Have you found any sign of Martin?" Frank pleaded.

"Nothing yet, Frank," said tall, thin copper, sitting at his desk going over a ream of paperwork. "He went off on his own without telling anyone where."

"If only I hadn't been stung by a wasp, I'd have been with him," said Frank ruefully.

"Don't blame yourself, son," said Rodgers, trying to calm the boy down. "It wasn't your fault he's missing."

"We'd have been together, we'd be safe together. He's been taken by that man, I know it!"

"I know you feel guilty that you weren't around, Frank, but we're doing all we can to find him. Maybe he's hurt himself and can't get back home."

"We both know he's not coming back, even if he's hurt he could die of thirst or something."

"Please try and stay positive, mate. We'll find him, hopefully, safe and sound."

Frank left the small police station and returned home, climbing the stairs to his bedroom and lying on his bed. He wasn't in the mood for any music so just lay there thinking of Martin and trying to work out where he would have gone. Frank thought that Martin would either have gone on a bike ride or over the fields for a bit of peace and quiet. He needed to go and look for him. Frank ran back down the stairs, out of the front door, and across the road to check if Martin's bike was still there and he saw it propped against the fence outside the back door. That left only one option. Martin had gone walking over the fields, maybe as far as the pond.

Frank rushed back home, picked up the binoculars he got for his birthday a few years previously, and then filled a small glass bottle with water from the cold tap and walked up the hill in the stifling heat and onto the stony path which led to the farmland. He reached the electric fence and was careful to duck under it and then moved up the slope. In the distance he saw a mountain of straw bales ahead and slightly to his left. He lifted the binoculars which were on a strap around his neck and looked through them. *Nothing there,* he thought. He carried on in a straight line, skirting the bales by a good fifty yards, all the time searching the ferns and hedgerows separating the fields for any kind of evidence they'd been damaged or disturbed in the past few days. All the while he was calling for his friend. Eventually he'd got to the pond. Legend had it that a witch was burnt at the stake nearby and her remains were dumped in the pond, but he didn't know if that was true or not. He knew it was very deep so if a witch *was* down there she would be a long way down and would probably never be found. Maybe this hot weather would evaporate all the water, like in that book, Thirst, he had read, and the pond would dry out and she'd rise again like a zombie in that George Romero film he'd seen on TV a few months ago. They would have to shoot her in the head to stop her eating brains. Problem was, no British cops had guns apart from Jack Regan in The Sweeney, but he was on telly so that was probably made up.

He walked the perimeter of the pond, tried to look into it's depths with the binoculars, but he saw nothing. The water was as dark as it always had been. If Martin had fallen in wouldn't he be floating? He wasn't sure. Maybe it had something to do with how much a person weighed? Fat people, like Ian Hootkins at school, would probably sink, but Martin was skinny and probably weighed about eight stone dripping wet. He'd have floated, Frank surmised. He sat at the edge of the pond, hot sun on his face, hugging his knees tightly, and cried for his lost friend. He knew he'd never see Martin alive ever again.


*****

There were four search parties, each led by one of the three detectives and the other by P.C. Connolly. Danny Daly was in charge of searching the farms, fields, and the wooded area nearby. He had six other men with him, a mix of local volunteers and Plods from Watford nick and he relished the responsibility. It was hard going in the heat. The stench of the farms was overpowering and there was no respite from the blazing sun in the open fields. He was burning up and wished he'd brought a bottle of water with him. Only the woods offered any shade, but it was still humid under the cover of the trees. They'd found nothing, no clue or sign that Martin had been there at either farm. They had searched the woods, found the remains of a badger and a couple of porn magazines, hopefully unconnected, he thought. They only had two fields and the pond to go. He dearly hoped the boy was not in the pond. According to the locals with him, it was quite deep, even in these drought conditions.

They neared a stack of straw bales in the middle of the next field, still waiting for the farmer to collect and store in his barn. They were neatly stacked and the men started to move them. Daly recognised the stench of decomposition. They discovered Martin in a hollow in between the bales, lying face down. Daly sighed, checked the boy for any signs of life, however remote the chance of that was. Martin was stone cold, protected by the heat of the day by the housing of straw. At least it wasn't the pond, he thought thankfully.

He sent one of the Plods to report to P.C. Rodgers who was co-ordinating things from the village police station.He could then contact Mallen who was at the other end of the village. The senior detective was checking the collection of large private houses there, owned by the more affluent residents of the village, including a third rate TV actor who coincidentally played a copper badly in a popular series set in London, a broadcaster on BBC radio, and a couple of footballers who played for Watford in the Fourth Division. Their manager also lived in the village but he was up by the junior school, the area searched by Carter's party.

Mallen eventually arrived at the scene in a Landrover borrowed from the farmer. It would be a while before the forensic boys arrived and Matty Ryan, the Police Surgeon, was also on his way to officially pronounce death, the local G.P. unavailable due to a full surgery of patients with severe sunburn and infected insect bites.

"I was hoping the boy would turn up alive," he said to Daly.

"I think we both knew deep down what the outcome would be, guv," replied Daly. "At least the family will know for sure. Not much consolation, I know, but better than not knowing for years on end like some of the families in past cases."

"Talking of which, are you up to breaking the news to them?" asked Mallen.

"Yes, I'll stop off and get Rodgers if that is okay, they could probably do with seeing a familiar face."

"Yes, that's fine, Connolly should be back by now and he can take over there."

Daly took the Landrover back to the farm, Ryan would need it when he arrived. Mallen stayed with the body with the remaining Plods while the local volunteers drifted off back home or to work, they all felt angry that another local kid had been murdered and the police were no nearer catching the killer. Daly walked the two hundred yards from the farm to the police station, told Rodgers the latest development and they took the short road uphill on foot to the house of Martin's parents who had been waiting patiently for any news with a WPC who was constantly making tea. They took it badly, of course. The father sat down in shock, trying to make sense of it all and the mother ended up on her knees in the front room wailing for her son, rejecting all attempts by Daly, Rodgers and the WPC to offer comfort. There was a knock at the door and Daly answered it. Frank stood there in tears. Daly didn't want the boy to see the parents in the state they were in so took him over to the short wall at the front of the garden and they sat and chatted quietly. Frank had seen Daly and Rodgers arrive at the house and knew it meant only one thing.

"We'll get him, Frank, I promise," said Daly. "I'm sure we're getting closer all the time and Mr. Mallen is the best there is, we're lucky to have him heading up the case."

"If it wasn't for that bloody wasp I'd have been with him, Mr. Daly. Do you think he suffered?" asked Frank. "I couldn't bear it if he did."

"Well, we'll have to wait for the post-mortem but I couldn't see any injuries, no blood, so I really hope he didn't suffer much. He would have been scared but maybe not much pain in the end."

"I want to kill the bastard who did it," Frank spat.

"I'm sure a lot of people feel the same but we need to catch him and put him on trial, Frank. Revenge is wrong, especially if it's inflicted on the wrong person without any evidence, just like what happened to the guy from the canal boat. Some people thought he was the killer but they were wrong and an innocent man died. Do you see that, mate? We need to find him and prove in court that he did it, that's the way justice works."

"I know you're right, Mr. Daly… Danny, but I hate him for what he did. My best friend is gone forever."

"I do know how you feel, Frank. My best friend died when I was not much older than you. Not murdered, but died in a road accident. He was on a moped and thought he was like Barry Sheene and took a bend too fast and hit a small patch of oil. He slipped off and collided with a lamp post. Put me off ever getting a motorbike. So I really can understand your loss, mate."

Frank knew Daly made sense and thought of the satisfaction he'd feel looking into the eyes of that monster as he was sentenced to life in prison. Shame there was no death penalty anymore but life in prison would have to do. He liked Daly a lot, wished he had a dad like him or even an older brother. Frank's dad had left when he was a toddler and he worked overseas now but Frank didn't know where, he could be anywhere. His dad never kept in contact. Not even at Christmas or for his birthday. Frank didn't miss him that much.

Daly walked Frank home just across the street. He left him there with his mum and went back to Martin's parent's house. The WPC had made more tea and the mother had calmed down enough to be quietly sipping the strong, sugary brew. Daly tried to say all the right words to the parents. He'd broken the bad news to people before when he was in uniform. After traffic accidents mostly, but never to the parents of a murder victim, it was more experience for him, he supposed. He told them, as he'd told Frank, that he didn't think Martin had suffered a lot. He was relieved that Martin hadn't been viciously mutilated like the Phillips girl or decapitated like the lad Taylor had found in the canal. Small mercies, he thought. It wouldn't bring the boy back but identifying the body wouldn't be as traumatic for the parents this time.

Frank lay on his bed listening to some of his tapes. Queen blasted out from his cassette player. *March of the Black Queen* currently, one of his favourites. He just couldn't believe it. Martin dead! He had expected the news to come but hoped it wouldn't. He had to help the police find the killer, but what could he do that they hadn't? He decided to spend as much of his spare time as he could cycling around the area, keeping a lookout for anything out of place, anything unusual or suspicious. He turned off the Panasonic cassette player, ran down the stairs, and went out the front door. Frank jumped on his ten-speed bike which was leaning untidily against the fence near the door and rushed off down the road. He decided it would be pointless watching the high street - too busy and anyone suspicious would be easily spotted by other people. He rode down Church Lane, past the thousand-year-old church, and then past his old nursery school, the old brick building looking as shabby as it was when he went there for lessons, now deserted in the summer holidays. He toured the area around the new trout lake, accessible through a small industrial area housing a transport firm, a mechanic and a couple of warehouses. He saw a few people fishing, hidden from the sun in the shade of some ash and elm trees.

Frank then moved on towards the canal. He turned right onto the towpath and followed the rutted track for about a mile. The ducks scattered away from the bank as he approached on his bike, quacking their displeasure at him. He just about avoided another cyclist coming from the opposite direction and he studied the man closely until they passed each other. He was tall and dark but a lot older than the man he'd seen at the farmhouse, not as thin either. He wondered how the real killer had got around the village. Did he have a car or a bike or did he just walk? When he arrived at the lock where Alan Taylor's body was found, according to gossip, he turned right again and then left onto the main road to take a look at the farm at the end of his paper round. He saw Mrs. Wilcox in the yard, sweeping the loose gravel to one side of the entrance. She looked up and waved and he waved back at her but rode away again. Frank doubled back down to the train station at the bottom of the valley. He rode around the station car park a few times, admiring the almost new E Type Jaguar that was there, a beautiful cherry red convertible. *It must belong to someone who works in London,* he thought. He was beginning to feel frustrated and despondent now. No sign of the dark man. He had to be hiding somewhere in the village, *but where?*

Frank cycled along Station Road, noticing nothing out of the ordinary. He saw a younger school friend, Mark Davies, and stopped for a chat outside the corner shop, first going inside for a can of lemon & lime fizzy drink. He told Mark that Martin had been found dead. Mark was visibly upset at the news as he liked Martin and looked up to the boy who was a year above him at school. Frank left again and continued to ride on in the heat. He rode past another industrial area, there were car garages, a petrol station, warehouses, an industrial laundry, and a builders merchants, all looking busy despite blisteringly hot weather. On and on he moved through the extremities of the village, mentally ticking off each area as searched, frustration growing. There must be something, somewhere!

He tried another part of the village, rode past Bridget's house, and then doubled back at the end of the road and passed it again, wondering if she was in and if he should knock on the door and summon up the courage to ask her out. He chickened out again. She'll go out with someone else at this rate if he didn't ask her soon. The summer holidays were the perfect time and they could spend a lot of time together. He also fantasied about keeping her safe from the killer. Maybe tomorrow will be the day he'd ask?

Consus watched the boy ride twice past the house opposite where he was renting and wondered who lived there. Another friend probably. He couldn't wait for an opportunity to take him, although it was probably too late to stop him from giving the police a description of him after the incident at the farmhouse when the boy had escaped. Consus could bide his time, the boy will be the last this time and he would enjoy it immensely. He needed to corner him in an enclosed space, give himself plenty of time to extract the maximum amount of fear from the boy before he mutilated him. Then he would hibernate again. He wondered what 1998 would bring, what new innovations.

*****

More than a week later the police still had nothing to lead them to the killer. They were not going to make the mistake of thinking the child murderer had moved on though. They had uniforms roaming the streets, brought in from Watford and also London, as well as Rodgers and Connolly, the local lads. All very visible. Frank was still riding his bike around every day, always looking, searching for the killer. No one felt safe in the small village anymore, even with a massive police presence. The majority of kids were quarantined by their parents, desperate to avoid them being the next victim. Everyone was sure there *would* be another victim.

The funeral had taken place for Martin Frost. This did attract a large number of people. Safety in numbers, everyone thought. Undercover officers were mingled in with the mourners, but even a blind man could see they were out of place in this village, not looking like a part of any of the families mourning Martin. After the service in the Norman church, Frank and his mum stood with Martin's parents as the coffin was lowered into the ground, tears flowed freely. Frank thought Martin was the best friend anyone could have. They'd never had a fight or even a major disagreement in all the time they knew each other. The local vicar, a very thin, balding man of around medium height was wearing what Frank thought looked like an ankle-length frilly dress. The clergyman stood over the grave and spoke:

"Man, that is born of a woman hath but a short time to live and is full of misery. He cometh up, and is cut down, like a flower; he fleeth as it were a shadow, and never continueth in one stay.

Forasmuch as it hath pleased Almighty God of his great mercy to take unto himself the soul of this child here departed, we therefore commit his body to the ground; earth to earth, ashes to ashes, dust to dust: in sure and certain hope of the resurrection to eternal life, through our Lord Jesus Christ; who shall change the body of our low estate, that it may be like unto his glorious body, according to the mighty working, whereby he is able to subdue all things to himself."

They shall hunger no more, neither thirst any more; neither shall the sunlight on them, nor any heat. For the Lamb which is in the midst of the throne shall feed them, and shall lead them unto living fountains of waters: and God shall wipe away all tears from their eyes.
Now unto the King eternal, immortal, invisible, the only wise God, be honour and glory forever and ever."

Frank didn't understand most of the words, he'd never been to a funeral before. All he knew was that he would never see his best friend ever again. He didn't believe in a Heaven or a "God", only what he could see, hear or feel. And today he felt like shit. He wondered if he would ever get over the loss. Most of the mourners returned to the church hall after the service, the rest drifted away back to their own lives. Sandwiches and soft drinks were laid on in the modern-looking annexe. As people filed into the new building, the undercover officers remained in the graveyard, making themselves even more obvious and out of place. Mallen knew the police presence was pointless, but it was protocol now. He knew he was dealing with a highly intelligent man and not one stupid enough to attend the gathering at the church. He knew the killer would stay away.

*****

Several days later Frank was out on his bike again. He was determined to check every square inch of the village for signs of the killer. Near the canal was an area of allotments. Villagers grew their own fruit, vegetables, and flowers on a tiny bit of land rented to them by the local council for a couple of quid a week. In the corner of the flat land was an old shed with flaking light blue paint where everyone kept their tools. The allotment area was deserted, no one willing to expose themselves to the grilling heat of the day, preferring to do the work in the relative coolness of the evenings that summer. Sometimes there was even a slight breeze.

Frank knew he had to check out the shed. He circled it at first, weaving his way around the stack of wheelbarrows and bags of soil to the rear of the small building. Then he tentatively tried to enter. The shed was not locked. The light pine door creaked as it opened outward towards him which was slightly unnerving. There was a dry musty smell like old earth and carrots. The dusty floorboards squeaked as he trod lightly on them, investigating every corner for any clue. The door slammed loudly! Frank spun around. Consus was standing there, blocking the exit.

"You murdered Martin, all the others too!" said Frank coldly.

"Yes," Consus hissed in a voice that chilled Frank's entire being.

"Why? Why kill all those kids?" yelled Frank, hoping a passerby would hear.

"I need to survive," said Consus.

"How can murder help you survive?" shouted Frank again. "It just doesn't make sense. Who are you?"

"My name is Consus, I was a Roman, stationed in Britain. I need to feed on my victims before they die to preserve my immortality. Six victims and then I return every twenty-two years and repeat the process again. You will be the sixth this time. I saved you until last. You could say we have *history*," said the immortal, enjoying the private joke.

"No!" Frank shouted and threw a rusty trowel at the man. "I'll kill you!" Frank backed away and picked up a gardening fork with a green plastic handle and a bent tine and thrust it towards the towering man. The tines punctured the man's chest, Frank pushed deeper. Consus stayed upright, smiling smugly at the boy.

"You cannot kill me, you fool. I told you, I am immortal. I was killed and came back to life. I don't know how and I certainly don't know why, but here I am, and we all have to make the best of our circumstances. Don't you agree, young man?"

Frank pulled the fork from the chest of Consus, thrust again at the man's head, his eyes. If he could blind the killer he could maybe get away. Consus batted the weapon away this time with one of his large hands and walked slowly towards Frank, like a prowling tiger preparing for the kill, making it impossible for the boy to strike again while still cutting off the exit. Frank didn't know what to do. The man was still between him and the door. There was no other way out. The shed had no windows, there was only a small, cracked and cloudy perspex skylight in the roof and no way of opening it, or even reaching it. Consus pulled out a knife, the same one taken from the daughter of General Festus, the one he'd used on the six Ripper victims in Whitechapel.

"No more talk!" he said.

The door burst open, Danny Daly came flying through it and flung his arm around the neck of the child killer, bundling him to the ground.

"RUN!" he shouted at Frank, loud enough to wake the dead.

Frank needed no second invitation, he took advantage of the struggle between the detective and Consus and rushed past them and out through the battered door. He had to find a call box and get help. He ran, not for his life, but the life of the policeman. He ran harder than he'd ever done before. He sprinted down the canal towpath to the bridge and scrambled up the embankment to the road. Frank spotted the phone box outside the corner shop and took a deep breath for the final dash to make the call for help, his lungs were burning in his chest. Luckily when he got there no one was inside. He pulled the heavy red door open and lifted the receiver.

The door shut slowly with a squeak. Frank dialled 999. No one answered. He saw that the wire to the receiver had been cut. The phone was useless. Had it been vandalised by kids? Bloody idiots.

The next nearest public call box was in the high street. Frank knew he hadn't much time to help Detective Daly. He hoped Danny could hang onto the man until assistance arrived. Frank was fit but running at full pelt uphill for another half a mile was a lot different than jogging or the cross country runs they did at school in the winter. It took him over five more minutes to run up the slope to the phone box outside the post office. He grabbed the receiver and was relieved to hear the loud buzz of a dial tone. He dialled 999 on the rotary face of the phone again, almost dropping the heavy black handset due to his shaking hands. Luckily he didn't need a coin for the emergency services because he didn't have one. He stuttered into the mouthpiece when he was asked which service he required.

"P-p-police," he eventually got out. "The killer! Mr. Daly has got him in a shed on the allotments. You have to hurry! Please!"

Frank gave the operator the location of the allotments and a brief description of the man and the situation as cars were immediately dispatched to the scene from Watford. Frank thought their journey would take another ten minutes at least, even at top speed with sirens blaring.

He prayed it wasn't too late, even telling himself that he would believe in God if the nightmare was truly over and the killer was finally caught and put on trial like Donald Neilson, the Black Panther who had been at large for several years and whose trial was reported in the papers that month. Neilson started as a burglar and graduated to the armed robbery of post offices. He'd killed several postmasters in Yorkshire and Lancashire. The money Neilson got from the post offices wasn't enough for him. He decided kidnap was what was needed for more money, a big job, maybe leave the country after he got paid the ransom. He abducted Lesley Whittle from her house in the dead of night and hid her in a deep drainage shaft beneath Bathpool Park, near Kidsgrove in Staffordshire. After a few weeks, the police found her in the drainage shaft, dead, hanging by the neck from the cord used to subdue her. Neilson was caught in December 1975 when he took two policemen hostage at gunpoint in a car. One of them deliberately slammed on the brakes of the car and the pair struggled with Neilson and with the help of a passer-by they managed to overpower him and make the arrest. He confessed to the robberies and killings and said the death of Whittle was an accident, knocking her off the ledge she was on by mistake. He'd been given five life sentences at Oxford Crown Court just days previously and the reports were still fresh in Frank's mind.

Frank pictured himself reading about the trial of this local killer and even being a witness to the heroics of Mr. Daly. Maybe he'd be in the papers too, a hero and a celebrity. It seemed almost over. He could start to live his life again. He felt angry that his best friend was dead and that he was an intended victim too, but he felt a lot safer now that Danny Danny had caught the killer.

The police cars swooped down the hill towards the bridge over the canal. A dozen officers, some armed, ran down the towpath towards the area of the allotments. They approached the shed cautiously. Sergeant George Roper had seen it all in his twenty-six-year career but what lay behind the door would immediately make him decide on retirement. After calling out to Daly and getting no response he gently pulled the shed door open. He thought it strange that the shed would have a wall painted in red while the rest were light blue, but then the coppery stench hit him - it was blood. It was almost everywhere. He cautiously stepped inside, ready to pounce on anyone trying to leave but saw quickly that no living person was in the small wooden building. He saw Daly hunched over against a wall of the shed, or rather, what was left of him. He had been butchered. He was surrounded by a lake of blood on the floorboards, his own presumably, and various body parts lay around him, unattached from his torso. Roper rushed from the shed and lost his breakfast.

Less than forty minutes later Mallen and Carter arrived. Mallen's face was ashen even before he saw the remains of Daly. He liked the boy, he was almost like a son despite only knowing him for just under a year. He blamed himself, of course. Mallen had told Daly to keep a close watch on the Kelly kid. Daly would have volunteered to look out for the teen anyway. He knew Frank had been searching the village on his own and Daly following in an unmarked car was not only for the kid's protection but on the off chance he may even turn something up, a major clue as to the identity or whereabouts of the child killer. Mallen needed all the help he could get. He told Carter to go and get Frank. The boy had been told to wait by the phone box he'd called from in the busy high street.

Carter arrived at the bright red call box a few minutes later. Frank was being comforted by two old women. He hadn't told them what had happened but they knew something had upset him and didn't press the boy too much. Frank was glad to see Carter and ran to the car. He was greeted by the long, sad face of the police sergeant. He knew that Daly hadn't managed to arrest the killer. He burst into tears at the thought it wasn't over yet.

"I'm really sorry, Frank. I'm sure Danny did all he could."

"Can I talk to him? I want to thank him for saving my life," said Frank between sobs.

"That won't be possible, mate," said Carter.

Frank got the meaning straight away and covered his face with both hands and wailed, not caring about the growing crowd watching him.

Carter took Frank home and they waited for Mallen to join them. The weary-looking senior detective arrived and sat down next to Frank on the green sofa and put a comforting arm around him. Frank was out of tears. He was angry again. He told them about the last few days. How he'd been out looking for some sort of clue to help the police. How he'd been cornered in the shed by the dark man. Frank told them the man had said his name was Consus and he'd also been told that the murderer was immortal, killed and risen again. Then Frank said that Consus told him he would be a victim too. The boy told the policemen that he tried to fight back and stuck a garden fork into him before Mr. Daly burst into the shed and told him to run and get help.

Mallen put the tale of immortality to the back of his mind, dismissing it as just shock and imagination. The garden fork injury too. No one could do what that sick bastard did to Daly with deep wounds to the chest. It was just bloody impossible. Frank described the killer again. It matched his earlier description when he was chased by the sinister man at the farmhouse on his paper round. Mallen was in deep despair. Nothing more than he had before, and he'd lost a good man in Daly too.

Carter drove Mallen to the pub. Neither man spoke much, both deep in thought and regret. Mallen decided that it was time to retire after this case was finished, or when, rather than *if*, he was removed. He was responsible for Daly's death just as much as the killer, he'd been following Frank Kelly on his orders. It wouldn't be long before the brass replaced him anyway, maybe a matter of a few days. Making up some excuse about his failing health like they usually did to get rid of failures. Saving face for the sake of good PR. Damage limitation. Mallen tried to look back on his career, all the successes. The high profile cases he'd solved. All erased after today's tragedy. A good young detective eviscerated by a madman on his watch. Mallen grieved for Daly and the void in the lives of his wife and young son. The boy who waved from the doorstep every morning. He'd do all he could for them both. He thought Carter would too. He was nearer Daly's age and had been closer.

*****

Consus was furious. He wanted the boy but that policeman had saved him and then got what he deserved. Consus had gone into a frenzy in the small shed. His knife whipped around, blood flew in wide arcs from the long blade. There was some of the red mist coming from the policeman but not enough. He was the sixth of this cycle and Consus knew he could get no more until another twenty-two years had passed. Why had he told the boy the truth about himself? It was arrogant of him. He knew that there was no point in trying to silence the youngster, he would have already told his story to the police. How much would they believe from the boy, though? He also knew that the boy would have protection now as he was a key witness. No matter. He'd be back in his cave very soon. He needed to clean his black clothes of the blood. Luckily the house he'd rented was close to the allotments and he'd returned there without being seen. He stripped and put his clothes in the bath, even his shoes and the knife, and after running the bath to halfway to cover the clothes, washed himself down and lay naked on the bed to rest. It took him a while to calm himself enough to be able to sleep for a few hours.

Frank was in bed, drowsy because he'd been sedated by the local GP. A policeman was downstairs protecting him, given endless cups of tea by Frank's tearful mum. The scenes in the shed whirled around in his head. The man, Consus he said his name was, coming at him with a long knife. Frank picking up the fork and plunging it into the man's chest. It didn't seem to affect the killer at all. He remembered the awful sucking sound as he pulled the tines from the man's body. Trying to go for his eyes with the old gardening tool. Failing, giving up on escape, waiting to die, scared stiff of the man and what he would do. Then the policeman, Mr. Daly, had burst in, like a hero he'd saved Frank and ultimately paid the price for his selfless bravery. Frank felt so guilty. He'd liked Mr. Daly a lot, like the big brother he'd never had and Danny was now dead because of him. No - not because of him, he realised. Because a crazy killer was roaming the streets, living somewhere in the village. A sick man who thought he had to kill to stay immortal. The nutter should be in a mental hospital. But the fork sticking out of his chest? It wasn't possible, was it? Did it really happen at all? If it was real Frank hoped and prayed that he'd done some real damage to the man and he'd die later, in extreme agony, holed up wherever he was. He wanted to look down on the man's body and feel satisfaction that he'd avenged the deaths of Martin and Mr. Daly, as well as the other victims. Frank began to fall asleep, luckily there were no dreams that evening.

*****

Mallen was called to the Met. headquarters the next day. As he had thought it was 'suggested' he took a leave of absence for a while. Mallen knew his career was over and he was almost glad, the death of Daly weighing heavily on him. He'd had enough now. He was told DCI Winston Richards would be taking over. A West Indian who had risen through the ranks because it was good PR and he ticked all the boxes. It was all good for recruitment, he was told in the past. Richards hadn't had much of a career to date. Carter had a lot more experience than he did and more achievements too, but was overlooked for promotion yet again. Maybe it was being associated with Mallen himself that was holding Ray Carter back? Mallen may have been regarded as the top man, but he knew he wasn't well liked in some circles. He wasn't a Mason, after all.

Mallen left the huge offices in the heart of London and returned home. He planned a trip to Belfast to visit his grandkids and immediately called his daughter to tell her. He opened a new bottle of single malt, thoughts whirling through his brain about just what the killer was. Was Frank telling the truth? Was the killer even human? Mallen drunkenly dozed off in his chair after half of the scotch was gone.

DCI Richards had arrived at Watford nick. He found Carter in the canteen, nursing another cup of tea. Carter had been told to wait there until he received further instructions. As soon as he saw the tall West Indian enter the room he realised the truth. Mallen had been replaced. He felt angry that a hero and legend like Mallen had been discarded because of something he had no control over. He wondered how much longer he could stick the job himself. Daly hadn't been sacrificed by Mallen. He'd been doing his job like they all were, it could even have been him trailing the kid and ending up lying in that shed. Daly's death was front-page news all over the country and public opinion was turning against the police. It didn't matter how many successes there were, like the recent Black Panther conviction, as soon as something went wrong it was a disaster according to the media. Now Mallen had been replaced by a 'quota copper' and the only motivation Carter had now was finding Danny's killer.

Richards spent the rest of the day getting familiar with the case files and Carter was bombarded with inane questions. Richards wanted to be up to speed before he visited the area. He particularly wanted to re-interview Frank Kelly. The boy had had two encounters with the killer and had survived. Maybe he'd been deliberately targeted for some reason? Maybe the boy had something to hide, something he wasn't telling.

Carter was sick of Mallen's methods being questioned by the new DCI. Who was this bloke anyway? He knew he had much more experience and should be heading up the manhunt for the killer now as he knew the case inside out. By the time this idiot was ready to get out there, the killer would be untraceable again. Carter knew his frustrations would eventually make him say something out of order to his new superior. He was just itching to get out there, do some proper police work instead of babysitting someone who should be chasing up parking fines.


*****


It was the next day when Consus was ready to retreat to his cave. His clothes were clean and dry, his shoes had been stuffed with old newspaper to soak up the moisture. He walked to the next town along the back roads and through the surrounding woods. He knew it was only a three-mile walk along the main road but took the detour to avoid being spotted by the roaming police cars and that worked out almost double the distance. Consus arrived in the town centre mid-morning and headed for the taxi rank outside a large bank. He moved swiftly to the first car in the queue, a light blue 1973 Ford Cortina, and sat on the rear seat behind the driver. He looked closely at the ID tag displayed to the left of the man. It was of a fat, white, ginger man by the name of Michael Emmet.

"Where to, mate?" said the driver.

"West Wycombe, the high street there," replied Consus.

The car pulled away and after a couple of corners was headed along a long road with only a few twists and turns. The driver tried to make polite conversation but Consus remained silent, ignoring the man. Emmet eventually gave up, he was only trying to pass the time, people were getting ruder. Consus stared blankly out of the window as the car sped past fields, lanes and the occasional petrol station. He knew he'd be safe soon. Forty minutes later the taxi pulled up opposite a pub in West Wycombe high street. Consus paid the man with cash he'd taken from the policeman he'd killed and took a shortcut between the houses up to the caves.

The caves were now a tourist attraction and had been for several years. He paid for his admission, pushed through the turnstile at the entrance, and moved silently through the chambers to his special alcove which was out of bounds to the normal paying public. He made sure he was not being watched by anyone and then ducked under a stout rope into the narrow crevice that led to 'his' cave. Consus breathed in the familiar mossy aroma and stood with his back to the smooth, grey-brown section of the wall. His last thoughts were: *I'll find you again, boy*, thinking of Frank Kelly as he melted into the rock which then began to solidify again and give him sanctuary for the next twenty-two years.

Over the next two months, there were no more attacks. The police eventually found the house that Consus had rented and had now vacated. They were two weeks too late in finding it. The letting agent had been unable to contact the renter, the rent unpaid. He went to visit in person and found the place deserted and let himself in. The blood-stained bath made him contact the police immediately from the house next door, one of the few in the street which had a phone, judging by the lack wires leading from the pole outside to sporadic houses. Carter wondered how this house had slipped through the net when they checked the rental properties before. The case was officially left unresolved.

Life went on, the villagers were relieved the murders had stopped and didn't seem to have started elsewhere. There had been a series of knife and hammer attacks on prostitutes in the Leeds and Bradford area by a man which the media had dubbed 'The Yorkshire Ripper'. The police could find no real connection to the Kingsford Killer, as the media called him. The drought continued all through August and into September. Southend Pier burnt down and a posh bloke called James Hunt won the Formula One world title for Britain. Frank Kelly returned to school. He hated the reasons for his celebrity status and just tried to quietly get on with things. He immersed himself in his lessons and, in particular, sport. It was rugby season that term but he couldn't wait until the new year when they switched to football. 1976 had been the worst year of his life. He still lived in hope that the killer had hidden away and died from the wounds Frank have given him. Frank never had the courage to ask Bridget out on a date. Something he would regret for years to come.

Mallen retired later that year, a broken man. He'd never lost one of his lads before and felt totally responsible. Mallen had instructed Daly to follow the boy, keep him safe. It was down to him. He chose Daly because he knew the young detective liked the boy. He only wished Daly had been able to phone in before he tried to tackle the evil killer but the nearest phone was at least half a mile away and Frank would have been dead at the hands of the killer by the time help arrived. Daly did the only thing possible. He was sure that the young copper hadn't acted alone for any glory or recognition, he just wanted to save Frank Kelly. He would have made a bloody good sergeant in a couple of years, three at the most. It was such a tragedy. Mallen hoped Carter wouldn't be stuck with Richards for too long and would get to work with someone with more experience and a lot more 'nous' and then eventually get his promotion now he wasn't associated with his old boss anymore. It could take a while though. No one involved in the failure to catch the killer won any plaudits. Mallen decided to move back to Ireland. England, and especially Kingsford, held too many bad memories for him. He sat down to write a letter to DCI Richards about his thoughts on the killer. He still wanted to be some help. For Daly.

# PART THREE

**1998, Aviemore, Scotland.**

Frank was fairly happily married and had been for several years. His wife was called Maura, a wild lady of Irish descent with bright green eyes and flame-red hair and a temper to match. She was still beautiful after two kids. Michael was ten and Mary eight. Two little terrors who luckily took after their mum in looks. Frank's dream of being a writer or film director never came to pass. He worked for the AA as a mobile mechanic. It wasn't a bad job and he had a bit of peace and quiet in-between jobs and he got to meet a lot of different people every day and loved driving in the wide open spaces of Scotland. It paid the bills comfortably. His internet connection at home wasn't great but at least he could get the news about his old home of Kingsford and the surrounding area. He knew it had started again. A series of killings like in 1976, the year his best friend had been taken by that monster, Consus, and the policeman too. It was in the Tring area this particular year, this cycle of murders. The police investigating had no idea these new killings were linked to the ones in 1976 in Kingsford or 1954 in Hastings. With this new internet thing, news and events were available to him without having to trawl through dusty books in libraries like he used to. He knew that the same killer was responsible. Every twenty-two years a spate of six murders then nothing. No killer was ever caught. He just disappeared and started his spree again a generation later in a different place. There were usually several suspects but Frank knew the police weren't even close to catching the killer. They were looking for a man, a human being. Consus was not human anymore. He was sub-human, immortal. The man had proven that by surviving the normally fatal injuries Frank had inflicted with the garden fork in that shed where Danny Daly had died.

Frank had a list of years in his battered green notebook. Before Hastings, there were six more in 1932 in Kilburn, London, including two children of five and six. 1910 was Buckingham, three little kids and two teens included in the six this time. Taking it back another twenty-two and there is a year that really stood out. Whitechapel in London. The infamous 'Jack The Ripper' murders in 1888. Frank had travelled back down south one weekend and tried to tell the police back in Hertfordshire of the connection. They laughed at him and warned him not to waste their time, but assured him they would be on the lookout for a man at least 110 years old slicing up people after escaping from a care home. Frank wanted to tell them the killer was much older than that but he'd been ridiculed enough for one day by these idiots. He returned home on the train the next day and silently drowned his sorrows with a good single malt. Maura was concerned about him and his growing depression. She wished he would talk about what was worrying him. Was she to blame? Was he having an affair and feeling guilty? Is that where he was that weekend? Was this the beginning of the end for them?

Frank was frustrated at the lack of time and effort the police were affording him. He was almost a victim of Consus himself until the policeman sacrificed himself so Frank could escape. Frank tried to get help but he was too late. If only the police had got there in time to save Mr. Daly and catch the killer. Nothing was heard of the killer after that day. He'd disappeared altogether, but now he was back. How the hell could Frank stop more killings? There had been three dead so far in Tring and there would be three more before Consus retreated yet again. No one would listen to him. If only that policeman was still around. He knew the truth in the end. Daly had overheard what Consus had told him before the detective burst through the door of the shed. The killer thought that Frank should have some sort of explanation before he was sacrificed. Frank had thought since that the murderer was trying to unburden himself of the guilt. More likely he was just bragging. Either way, Frank knew his name and where he had come from. A Roman centurion called Consus who had somehow become immortal. It was all he had really, unbelievable as it sounded.

*****

Gerry Daly was twenty-three and now a copper. Just a lowly uniformed Plod in the west of London, but he hoped it would lead to bigger and better things. He wanted to be a detective just like his dad. He still lived at home with his mum. It was cheap and convenient for work and gave him the opportunity to save for the future. His mum was still haunted by the death of her husband, Danny, and had never remarried or even had a serious relationship with anyone else. At twenty-three, Gerry was career-oriented and rarely found time to socialise out side of the job. He had the odd girlfriend but nothing too heavy. He realised that the social side of the force was essential for him to get on in the job and he mixed with senior officers mostly, picking up valuable experience through their advice and stories.

Ray Carter, was now a DI. His progression had been slow, the Kingsford failure of Mallen and the team holding him back. He had always kept in contact with Gerry and his mum. While not trying to be a father figure to him, he made sure he was always there for Gerry if needed and was a big help and inspiration in his choice of career. Regular trips to football matches watching Chelsea followed over the years and when Gerry was 18, Ray took him for a pint or two once a week. They had talked about the current murder spree in Tring but neither made the connection to Kingsford all those years ago. Neither were involved in the current investigation. Carter was based in Essex heading up the Armed Robbery division and Gerry was just a Plod walking the beat, chasing the odd mugger and arresting drunks after the regular pub fights most nights.

Consus was angry. He had vowed to make Frank Kelly one of his victims this time having missed two opportunities in the past. He had travelled back to Kingsford and made some discreet enquiries about his 'old friend' and was told that Frank had left the area and moved to Scotland. Consus knew that if he strayed too far from the cave he experienced crippling vertigo and couldn't travel more than around 200 miles from his haven. He'd tried to travel further several times over the years but had to turn back each time. Scotland was a safe place for the boy who had escaped him twice. The first three victims had been easy, a young blond woman walking home from work, snatched in an alley and strangled. The first red mist for a generation flowing from her in abundance, she must have been utterly terrified. Maybe she had something to live for?

He'd found from reading the newspapers and from television that most people didn't have the same regard for life as those in the past, not even their own lives, it seemed. He thought it may be something to do with the coming millennium. He'd heard stories in 1008 about a similar mass depression eight years earlier, especially after the Catholic Pope, Gregory V, had died in 999. People thought the world was going to end. There were many suicides even though it was a mortal sin. No one had any care or empathy towards anyone else in the years leading up to the year 1000. By the time he'd returned to the world in 1008 things had settled down again and he could carry out his work in relative 'peace'.

He'd discovered that the girl actually did have something to live for. That very day she'd had a positive pregnancy test and was on her way home to tell her boyfriend the good news. Consus had killed two souls with one murder. Would that mean he could take only four more this time? Intriguing thought. He was interested to find out. Did the foetus even have a soul yet?

The second kill in 1998 was a boy of four, abducted from his back garden while he played with small metal cars on a concrete path. Consus had grabbed the child and ran to a nearby building site, abandoned for the day as it was early evening. He held the boy tightly in the shadows of a half constructed house and stared into his eyes and the vapour gushed from the child without him having to commence the killing. Consus sucked it all in, every last drop, then ferociously twisted the boy's neck, snapping it. He thought for a moment if he really needed to kill the child after taking the red mist, but he was used to killing and now he enjoyed it. He really was a monster, without heart and definitely without any feeling for his victims or their families.

The third was a little more satisfying. A teenage girl walking home from a friend late in the evening was bundled into an open garage next to a housing estate and mutilated after she gave up the rejuvenating cloud to Consus. She didn't scream. He'd closed the garage door afterwards and she wasn't found for over a week, despite a search by family, friends and the police. Everyone was relieved when her casket at the funeral remained closed.

The fourth was Kate Harby, she was in her forties, very fat, if not morbidly obese, probably not far off a heart attack. Her dark hair was tied back and she was wearing a baggy top and trousers straining at the seams. She was home alone in her flat. There was a knock on the door. She was expecting a delivery, more shoes to add to her collection. She walked towards the door with a steaming mug of coffee in her hand. As soon as she released the latch the door flew inward, hitting her full in the face, shattering her nose and covering her with scalding liquid. Consus pushed his way in and closed the dark wooden door, looking at his next victim crumpled in a heap on the carpeted floor of the small hallway, her head lying just inside the bathroom on white tiles. He stepped over Kate and then dragged her towards the bath. She would have been too heavy to move for a mortal man but Consus had an added strength which was more than useful to combat her vast weight. He still struggled to lift and cajole her over the rim of the bath though. She was still very dazed from the blow of the door but was slowly regaining her senses. She looked up from the floor of the bath into the eyes of the man and tried to scream. Another blow to the face stopped her in time. She tried to rise but her immense bulk made it difficult in the slippery tub. Consus produced his long knife from his coat and the red mist started to flow. He began to slice as he bent over his victim. Starting at her head he cut at her scalp and peeled it back. The woman again tried to scream but panic took over and her throat constricted. Consus ripped at the scalp, revealing a bloody cranium. The remains of her nose was the next to be cut away, she then started to lose consciousness so Consus slapped her hard twice on the cheek and her eyes snapped open again, full of terror. The vital vapour was now gushing from her and Consus gladly sucked it in. He slashed at her huge stomach, cutting through the layers of fat until her entrails began to slip from the wound and into the bath, staining the sides. She died horribly and in excruciating pain as Consus sniffed the last of the mist, rivers of blood flowing towards the bath's drain. He washed his hands under the cold tap, dried them on a pale green towel and exited through the front door again.

The next kill was Jane Martin, a thirty-two year old secretary, long blond hair tied in a ponytail and wearing a pastel green blouse and black pencil skirt over her slight frame. She had arrived home in her brand new red Nissan Micra, a present to herself for her birthday two weeks previously. She exited the small car and looked proudly on the new Nissan. It was the first new one she'd ever bought. She'd worked hard and saved hard too. Jane was divorced and lived alone in a rented two-bedroom house on a quiet estate. The ex-husband long gone and working abroad the last she'd heard from one of his friends. *Good riddance to bad rubbish,* she thought. She was happy being single now. She had plenty of friends and often went out dancing at a couple of nightclubs or for group meals in the local Chinese or Indian. Most nights she sat at home reading or watching TV. She never watched the news or read newspapers so was largely unaware of the spate of murders in the vicinity.

Jane's first stop, as always, was the kitchen to put the kettle on. Her friend, Alyssa, had gotten her into herbal tea and she put a raspberry and lemon teabag into her favourite mug, a good sized green one covered in daisies, and waited for the kettle to boil while looking through the post that had arrived sometime during the morning. She ignored several brown envelopes for the moment, knowing they were bills, and opened a letter she knew was from her friend Julie in America. It started with great news about Julie's daughter, Terri, getting engaged. Jane was immediately cheered up and decided she'd make the trip over for the wedding. As soon as she had a date she'd book the flight to Michigan. She was in a really good mood now that she had something significant to look forward too. Not only a wedding celebration but the opportunity for a holiday on her own. She's been away for the odd week to Spain and Portugal with a few friends but she'd never travelled alone. It was a bit scary but also liberating. She could finally prove to herself she could be independent.

The doorbell chimed. She was slightly annoyed because she'd not yet sat down for her daily after-work ritual of her relaxing mug of tea. She hoped it wouldn't take too long answering the door and getting rid of whoever it was. A tall man stood in the doorway as she opened up. He was dressed smartly, yet old-fashioned in a way. He had short black hair and looked quite pale, in spite of the summer weather. He had very dark eyes, almost as black as his hair. The man introduced himself as Detective Sergeant Johnson and asked if he could come in for a chat. Jane didn't even think to ask to see some identification and obediently let the man in, asking if he would like a cup of tea or coffee. He politely declined so she showed him into the front room and offered him a seat on the dark grey single chair of the suite and she sat on the two-seater opposite him, wondering why the policeman was there.

Her body was found the next day after her boss called several times when she failed to turn up for work. He eventually left the office to visit her and then called for an ambulance when he saw her lying on the floor through the large front window. The ambulance crew broke in through the back door when they arrived and confirmed Jane was dead. The police were called, the post mortem the next day said the cause of death was strangulation. Jane would never take that trip to America for the wedding.


Consus stalked his last victim of this cycle, a young student called Mel Cross from a nearby college. He was following her through a park between a housing estate and a shopping precinct, presumably on her way home. She was tall and fairly plain looking as a lot of studious types were, dressed in slim fitting light blue slacks and a darker blue blouse, black shoes and a loose fitting bright yellow scarf around her slender neck. Mel was listening to Wham on her CD Walkman, the small headphones drowning out the noise of the traffic nearby. She entered a dark alley, a shortcut behind the parade of shops, Consus followed. She must have been deeply absorbed by the music because she didn't notice the man gaining on her. He soon caught up with her and wrapped his large hand around her mouth, stifling any scream. He pushed her up against a large aluminium waste bin and whispered in her ear that he was going to kill her. The crimson mist oozed from her and he took it all in. His other arm snaked across her windpipe and she struggled fiercely as she choked. When it was over he lifted her easily and dumped the body in the bin.


Consus was disappointed not to have Frank Kelly amongst his victims this time but vowed to get him eventually if it took yet another twenty-two, forty-four or even sixty-six more years. Frank Kelly would die horribly at his hands. Four days after his last kill he took a bus to West Wycombe. He inwardly chuckled at the thought that the other passengers were oblivious to his identity and were probably terrified they could be the next victim of the unknown killer. He knew they wouldn't realise, of course. He'd taken the six victims he needed this time and looked forward to finally finishing Frank during the next cycle. The dark green bus passed the Dashwood Mausoleum set high up on the hill, he looked at it and smiled. The twenty mile bus journey over, he strode up the steep hill, paid for his admission to the caves, and found his own hidden haven again.

The police in Tring, like in Kingsford, were never close to catching their man. They assumed he had moved on, possibly abroad, to evade capture. Little did they know he was only a few miles away in his cave at West Wycombe. The panic died down after a few weeks and things in the Tring area got back to normality. People, and especially children, were safe again. Frank, in Scotland, had another list of victims in his old notebook.


# PART FOUR


**2020, Kingsford, Hertfordshire.**

Frank was now fifty-eight. A lot had changed for him over the last couple of decades. He was now happily divorced and didn't talk to the ex-wife. He rarely saw Michael and Mary. They were now thirty-two and thirty and had their own lives to lead as well as their own families. He'd thought he would love being a granddad but he saw his grandkids even less than his own two. They were all still in Scotland and Frank had returned to his old home town after his divorce. He was still with the AA but at least these days he was finding a little time to write now he was alone and had a lot of spare time on his hands. He knew what he'd write about too. The evil monster in the guise of a man who came back every twenty-two years to wreak havoc and then hide away until he was ready to kill again in another twenty-two years. The tale the creature told him before he was going to murder Frank was truly horrifying… and fascinating too. An immortal Roman who had to kill to survive. Frank wished he knew where the killer hid for those twenty-two years he was inactive. Then he'd have a chance of stopping him for good. He doubted he'd get any help from the police as in 1998.

The first kill of that year was a young student. Consus or 'Jack' was back in Kingsford. He had unfinished business there. Frank Kelly. Simon Linscott had just got off the 500 bus that took him from Watford College back to Kingsford, about a twenty-minute trip usually, but roadworks had extended it to almost double that, which irritated him. He was getting hungry and couldn't wait until he got home for his evening dinner. He was seventeen and quite short and round. Long brown hair covered his head and flowed down the back of his black leather biker's jacket. He exited the bus with three other people but they went in the opposite direction along the almost deserted high street. Simon walked quickly up the hill near the bus stop, as quickly as his short legs could carry him, and cut through a short alley that would take him to the estate he lived on with his parents. He'd been at the college for about a year, his parents didn't really have the money to send him to university so the local option was best. Simon didn't make friends easily, so being closer to home was better for him as several of his former classmates from school went to the same college.

Approaching the end of the alley he was confronted by a tall, slender man in black. The man was smiling at him, almost grinning. *Looks like a right nonce, this one,* thought Simon, even though something about the man made him slightly nervous. He tried to sidle past the towering man and had almost succeeded when he was grabbed from behind, a long arm cutting off his airway. A red mist that only the man could see seeped from the top of Simon's head and the man breathed it in gratefully. *Christ, how do I get out of this?* Simon jabbed his elbow into the man's ribs like he did when he was bullied at school but it did not affect the tall man at all. He was very strong considering his thin frame. Simon tried again and thought he felt the grip around his throat loosen slightly. He kicked back and landed a heavy blow on the man's shin, that didn't work much either. Simon twisted and then almost got away but then he saw the blade. Ten inches of steel was waved in front of his face, the mist then gushed out of him in waves. The man greedily sucked it all in. Simon felt a little pressure on the side of his chest and then pain when the knife was pushed in deep between his ribs. He couldn't breathe as both lungs filled with blood, pierced by the long knife. The man then pulled the blade downward towards Simon's stomach, angling it slightly away from the body to avoid Simon's pelvis. There was a wet sucking sound as the knife exited the wound, followed by most of Simon's innards. Simon could see them all splash onto the path as his head slumped forward and the life slipped out of him. The man let go of the body and it hit the ground hard in a bloody heap. The man calmly walked to the end of the alley and faded into the thick bushes, satisfied with the first dose of 'his' mist of fear.

Detective Inspector Gerry Daly entered the short alley from the same direction Simon Linscott had barely an hour earlier. The body had been found by a little old lady, Olive Smith, as she went to visit a friend not far from the scene. She was still receiving medical attention for shock and he was amazed she had the presence of mind to stagger to her friend's house and call the police after she discovered the butchered corpse of the boy. *Can't have been easy, I'm surprised her heart didn't explode,* he thought. Daly turned to his sergeant, James Weatherby.

"SOCO come up with anything yet, Jimmy?"

"Just a lot of blood and guts so far, no weapon, no prints, possible partial footprint in some moss but that could be anyone who used the alley," replied Weatherby.

"Have Plod contacted the parents?" asked Daly.

"They're doing so now, they'll be in a right state, I doubt we can interview them until tomorrow," said Weatherby.

"Poor buggers. Right, there's not much we can do until the SOCO boys are finished, I spotted a pub just around the corner, looks a bit poncy but it will do." Daly, like most coppers his age, had developed a dependence for a drink. He'd seen and experienced a lot in his sixteen years as a detective. He'd been a DI for around six of those years. Weatherby had been his sergeant for the last four.

Daly left the car in the short road which led to the alley and they walked to the Duke of York and spent the next couple of hours sipping scotch and eating a decent cod and chips. Weatherby thought Daly was right - it was a touch poncy, not their usual type of haunt. A little later Daly had a call on his mobile. The techs at the scene had pulled the partial shoe print and found something unusual. According to their database, the heel was of a style of a shoe made in the early fifties. Didn't help a lot unless the killer was in his eighties at least or fond of retro clothing. He made a mental note to check on anyone who was a Krays fanboy. He could search the crime database for pretty much any keyword now. It was a long shot but they had nothing better as yet, the weapon used may give him some idea… if they could find it.

Frank Kelly heard about the murder the next day from a friend of Olive Smith. He'd known it was coming but who would believe him this time? Twenty-two years on from the spate of killings in Tring and now that monster was back in Kingsford. *It's started,* he thought. He pulled out his old, battered green notebook and made the first entry of 2020.

**1. June 4th - Simon Linscott, 17, male, Great Elms estate, gutted with? Loc: Alley leading to the estate.**

Large knife by the sound of it, he thought. It won't be the same method every time though, different enough to confuse the police into thinking there are two or three killers at first. He considered contacting the police but knew he'd be ignored as a nutter as he was in 1998. If he was to stop Consus he'd have to do it alone. It was the reason he'd returned to Kingsford after all these years.

Daly and Weatherby arrived at the home of Mr. and Mrs. Linscott at around ten in the morning. They left their unmarked black Audi at the top of the road. The path in front of the Linscott's house was full of reporters, mostly local but he did recognise a couple from the daily rags he never read, he'd met them before. *The vultures are circling,* he thought. They not so gently pushed past, ignoring questions shouted at them by the reporters and walked to the front door which was opened by a WPC. She was Family Liaison and assigned to give support to the parents and keep the wolves from the door. The last thing Daly wanted was for the family to be intimidated by the press before he got a chance to talk to them. He wanted them to be focused enough to give him the facts. He'd had a lot of experience dealing with grieving parents and he was very patient with them. He'd dealt with many child murders in London but most of them were gang-related stabbings and the odd shooting. This was different though. He needed to know a bit of background. Maybe the attack was personal, it was certainly brutal enough. Daly introduced himself and Weatherby to the parents who were obviously still in shock. They had identified the body of their son the previous late evening.

Daly doubted the kid had enemies vicious enough to do something like this but he needed to make sure. Any tiny bit of information could be crucial, even if the parents didn't think it was relevant. The WPC entered the living room where they were seated with a tray filled with mugs of tea. Hot and sweet, like she was taught. She put the tray on a table between Daly and Weatherby, who were seated in two comfortable leather chairs, and the parents who were perched on a matching three-seater couch opposite the policemen.

"I know this is a very difficult time for you, but I do need to ask these questions," said Daly sympathetically. "We need to find whoever did this to your son. Not only for you but for any more potential victims. Sometimes people will just snap and repeat their actions until they are caught." Spree killings were very uncommon in Britain, unlike America, but there were the odd one every few years and Daly had investigated them before.

"We understand," replied Mr. Linscott, a thin, almost emaciated, figure of a man who had dark thinning hair and a gaunt face and wore thick old-style glasses with jet black frames, he was clad in black trousers and white shirt with a light green cardigan which had large brown buttons at the front. One was missing. Daly noticed his brown shoes were very scuffed, but not of the style the forensics people had found. Mrs. Linscott was the total opposite of him, a large, full-faced lady with a mass of curly ginger hair and dressed in a dark dress with a floral pattern on, daisies, they looked like. Her eyes had very dark shadows beneath them and she'd obviously not slept at all the previous night. She remained silent but listened to every word attentively. Daly had a feeling that she was the real dominant personality in the household and reluctantly allowed her husband to do the talking on this occasion. Daly wondered why. It was in his nature to pick up on personality traits.

"Tell me about your Simon," Daly asked the man in a calm, soothing voice.

"He was pretty ordinary really, apart from having very few friends locally. They all seemed to be online, Facebook mostly, I think. I can't remember the last time he'd invited anyone over. Not for years, maybe four or five. He was studying Graphic Design at the local college, it was expensive for us at over £6000 a year but he had his heart set on it and was really committed, so we didn't mind the expense as long as he was happy. We thought the university would be better but the fees, as well as food and accommodation and other expenses, was just too much for us. The design stuff and gaming online were all he cared about really. He wasn't the athletic type, so he was never out playing football with his mates as I did at his age. I just can't think who would do that to him. He was a nice lad, just a bit insular. I'm sure no one hated him. Not that I know of, anyway." His wife sniffed into a linen hanky. *Was that a glare she shot her husband just then?* thought the detective.

"We're at a very early stage in the investigation, so obviously not that much to report back as yet, but we did find an unusual shoe print at the scene, probably unconnected, but I don't suppose you have noticed anyone who dresses like they were from the 1950s? Around the estate? Maybe walking in the village? Maybe even an old car?" Daly knew he was clutching at straws.

"No, I'd have certainly noticed an old car as I'm interested in them, made before all this electronic stuff they put in them now, I used to have an old Ford Prefect when I was younger," Linscott said, more enthusiastically than Daly would have liked, considering his son was brutally murdered only fifteen hours ago. *What is it with this guy? What don't I like about him?* he thought. Mrs. Linscott was still very silent but Daly was sure her husband would be on the receiving end of something later. Harsh words or even a slap or two. The liaison officers would be there working shifts for the next few days until the reporters found someone else to badger, so hopefully, the wife could restrain herself a bit longer.

"I'd like to take your son's computer with us, maybe there is something on there that will help, possibly someone making threats, bullying him on social media, that sort of thing," said Daly.

"Of course, I'll show you up to his room," offered Linscott.

Daly followed Linscott up the narrow, carpeted stairs while Weatherby and Mrs. Linscott sat in silence downstairs, Weatherby constantly taking notes. Daly entered the boy's room, the walls were painted black, *typical teen phase*, he thought as he unplugged the monitor and power leads, the mouse and keyboard were wireless. He tucked the workstation under his arm and moved carefully down the stairs again, nodding to Weatherby that it was time to leave.

The desktop computer revealed very little upon inspection, no threats at all. Simon Linscott seemed like a normal teenager, at least more normal than his parents, which Weatherby had also picked up on. The boy had several dozen friends on Facebook, a mix of boys and girls all around his own age, and a few of his old teachers from the local secondary school he'd left the year before. There didn't seem to be any hints of romance with any of them, male or female, just keeping in contact and posting cat memes and game videos mainly. No one felt like a threat in Daly's experienced eyes. He didn't like the father though. He didn't like the way he'd acted either. Daly knew shock and grief can hit people in different ways but something was very off about the father, he seemed to be hiding something and even enjoying the attention too. He'd like to know what the man was covering up. He'd have the house watched as soon as the Liaison

WPCs left in a couple of days. He wasn't sure if it was anything to do with the murder but maybe it was, although instinct told him the father wasn't the killer - too timid. He'd love to clear this case up quickly.

*****

The second murder took place on the next Friday. Amanda Peabody was taking her dog, Sabre, for a walk across the local fields and was thinking she'd had enough for the day. It was almost three in the afternoon and the heat was building, getting humid and oppressive. She should have gone earlier when the temperature wasn't so high. She hadn't seen a soul for about half an hour and the old dog was panting like he'd run a marathon. Amanda was forty-two and sturdily built. Her dark brown hair was tied back in a ponytail to get some air to the back of her neck. She wore a flimsy yellow blouse and matching yellow shorts and a pair of old white trainers that were a few years old but still comfortable, perfectly worn in. Walking the dog was the only exercise she was getting these days as her husband Brian didn't seem interested in her anymore. She felt lonely all the time and had virtually no friends since she moved to the area from Bedford over two years before. She was quite a timid person and Brian always said she was scared of her own shadow. He was probably right. She worked in a call centre for one of the big banks. Being on the other end of the phone was a lot easier for her than meeting people face-to-face. They couldn't see her and that made her far more comfortable. She hadn't made any friends at work, preferring to go for a walk during her lunch break. There were people she got on with but she didn't talk to them much, just the odd word as she waited for the vending machine to pump out awful coffee that tasted of chemicals.

Amanda turned left onto a short tree-lined path, the partial shade welcomed on such a warm day when the dog tried to pull her into the trees, sniffing at something interesting. Suddenly the dog was lifted into the air and she heard a cracking sound as the dog's neck snapped. She was almost pulled over as the dog's weight fell to the ground. Standing in front of her was a tall man clad in black, he was dressed in old fashioned clothes like he was from a Sherlock Holmes film. He smiled at her. She was frozen, couldn't move due to her fear.

"Good afternoon, madam," he said as he crouched and removed the dog's lead from its collar. "You arrived at a most opportune moment."

"D-don't hurt me," she stammered, "I'll scream."

"And who exactly will hear you?" he said with a leer.

The man lunged at her and caught her by the wrist with hands covered in thin leather gloves and pulled her towards him. She tried to struggle but his immense strength and iron grip made it almost impossible. The red mist started to emanate from her every pore. She was terrified. The man breathed the vapour in, lapped it up like sweet nectar. He pulled her even closer and used his free hand to wrap the dog's lead around her neck. She pulled at his black hair, tried to scratch his face and eyes, now in full panic mode. She couldn't catch her breath through fear and when the lead tightened around her neck she knew it was hopeless. She wondered if Brian would mourn her or if anyone but him would turn up for her funeral. The leather noose tightened even more, her head throbbed and her eyes bulged, her face beginning to turn purple as daylight flitted through the tree-tops onto her panicked visage. More and more of the crimson vapour was being squeezed out and greedily taken in by the man in black in front of her. As she died she had a flashback to her wedding day, fifteen years previously. Brian and she were so much in love, she was surrounded by her friends and family, big smiles on the faces of everyone as they posed for photos in the grounds of the church. She was all in white, the bridesmaids dressed in emerald green, and Brian handsome in his new light grey suit with a carnation in the buttonhole. She was so happy that day, how could it all end here in the woods at the hands of a complete stranger? The man let her slump to the ground next to her dog, the lead wrapped around her throat, cutting into the flesh. He walked further into the woods, back to the property he was renting not too far away.

Brandon West found the body of Amanda Peabody two days later. He was twenty-seven. Very short at just over five feet and still looked like he was in his early teens. He was thin and had long brown hair pulled back and secured by a hair clip. He wore light grey jogging bottoms, a white sleeveless shirt and new white trainers with no socks. He worked in a warehouse distributing magazines on the night shift and had finished work an hour before. Brandon was on his daily walk to de-stress and help him sleep for the next eight or nine hours and was caught short, as they say, and went to relieve himself behind some bushes. All thought of urinating forgotten as he was confronted by the body of Amanda covered in flies. She was a neighbour of his and he already knew she and the dog were missing. The police activity around her house had been evident for the last thirty-six hours. Her husband, Brian had told the police he was at first worried that she had left him but none of her clothes or prized possessions were gone and that was when he had started to panic. As he was a neighbour Brandon had already been visited the day before by the police doing their routine door-to-door enquiries. He'd been woken four hours into his sleep and was slightly groggy when he told them he'd not seen her.

Brandon stared at the body trying not to lose his breakfast. Amanda's purple face stared at him, eyes wide open, mouth full of flies, the dog lead was still wrapped tightly around her neck. The heat of the day made the small copse feel like a greenhouse, the buzzing of the insects around her corpse was almost deafening in the enclosed area. The smell was almost unbearable too. He took his cotton handkerchief from the pocket of his jogging bottoms and held it over his nose and mouth, the respite was only slight. He stood frozen there. *How could someone do that to her? She was such a nice lady.* After a few minutes, the shock seemed to abate a little and he knew he had to call the police. He pulled his new Samsung smartphone from his pocket and dialled 999. No signal, it must be the trees blocking the call. He moved out of the copse onto the track alongside a cornfield and dialled again. This time he got through and explained that he'd found a body in the woods. After a few questions from the woman on the other end of the line, he was told to wait where he was and officers would be there as soon as possible. Brandon knew he would be waiting for a while as the only access was a very steep hill, a rutted track used by the farmer's tractor and Landrover mostly, so was cut up during the wet weather and had dried into deep ruts of solid earth for the duration of the summer. Even though it was only June he longed for the rain and snow. He would have been walking around the local roads instead of finding a body in the woods.

Twenty minutes later a white Range Rover with a flashing blue light made it's way warily up the hill, the driver careful not to lose control on the uneven track. Brandon was sitting at the side of the trail, the crop of corn at his back, trembling slightly. He knew it was unlikely but in his mind he thought that he would be their main suspect as he'd found her. Logically, it was unlikely he'd have called the police if it was him but fierce doubt still gnawed at him. Two uniformed men got out of the large four-wheel-drive and walked briskly towards him. He noticed one of them was the same officer who had knocked on his door the previous day. He rose and showed them to the spot in the trees where he had found Amanda. One of the officers had the same signal problems with his own smartphone as Brandon did and walked out of the copse before dialling again. Smartphones had transformed communications for the emergency services in recent years, as long as there was a signal of course, no one restricted to radios anymore. The other policeman led Brandon out of the wooded area again and sat him in the back of the Range Rover, mainly to escape the smell of decomposition himself as well as detaining a possible suspect.

It was over an hour before DI Gerry Daly and Sergeant James Weatherby arrived. They had left the black Audi at the farm at the bottom of the hill and had to be ferried up in the Range Rover. Daly could see a nervous young man sitting quietly at the side of the narrow track, lost in his thoughts it seemed. He exited the four-wheel-drive while Weatherby checked on the ETA of the SOCO team from the car. The small man rose wearily to his feet as Daly approached him.

"You found the body?" asked Daly firmly, watching closely for any reaction out of the ordinary. Brandon nodded meekly. "Tell me what happened, son."

"W-well," he stammered, obviously nervous of the detective. "I finished my night shift at the warehouse, Ellis Freight down in the industrial estate, at just after eight and went home for breakfast before I took my usual walk ahead of going to sleep. It's been so hot recently it's been a problem falling asleep and have been taking a longer route to tire myself out more. I don't usually come this way but it was such a nice morning I thought being around a bit of nature would be more relaxing. I didn't expect this," he pointed to the copse.

"I've been having problems myself," smiled Daly, trying to put the witness at ease. "How did you find her?"

"I've been drinking a lot of water due to the heat and needed to go, you know? So I nipped into the trees for a quick leak and saw her there. Strangely I haven't felt the need since, is that normal? Anyway, I saw her and called 999 as soon as I realised she was dead."

"Did you touch her? Check for a pulse or anything?" asked Daly.

"No, I know that you shouldn't disturb anything, seen that on cop shows on TV, Inspector Morse and Midsomer Murders mainly, and it was obvious she was dead. So many flies were on her, in her mouth too. I didn't even go too close because of the smell either." Brandon started to pale again.

"Okay, that's good, I assume one of the officers has taken your details down, we'll need you for the inquest of course. Can you make your own way home or do you need a lift?"

"I don't live too far away, I can walk. I doubt I'll get any sleep today so I'll call work and tell them I won't be in tonight because of what happened. I feel like getting good and drunk."

"I don't blame you, Mr. West. If you are sure you don't need a lift you can go now. Someone will be in touch about the inquest," said Daly.

"Thank you," said Brandon as he turned and walked past the copse, trying not to look in that direction. He turned back to Daly and said, "She was a nice lady, this is such a shame."

Daly was joined by Weatherby and was told it could be a while before SOCO got there. The location wasn't ideal for road traffic and nowhere to get a helicopter in without destroying crops. Daly and his sergeant moved towards the copse. The odour of decaying flesh already hitting them. The hot weather was accelerating the decomposition process and would make it difficult to establish an accurate time of death. They both pushed their way through a short bush and into the main clearing of the wooded area. One of the two officers who were first on the scene was standing guard over the body, seemingly used to the smell now. Daly took out his little pot of Vicks Vaporub that he carried for these sort of occasions and dabbed a little on his top lip and passed the container to Weatherby who did the same. Daly crouched over the body of the dog first. He could tell by the angle of the head that its next was broken.

"Must have been someone quite powerful in the arms and shoulders to snap the dog's neck like that, fast too," deduced Daly. "The woman must have been in shock to have stood there while that happened and then watch him take the lead off."

"Yes," answered Weatherby. "All those films where the victim screams and runs are usually bollocks. The first reaction is always to look and assess what is happening, decide on the fight or flight response."

"You and your horror films, Weatherby, they'll give you nightmares you know, Jimmy."

"This is the stuff that gives me nightmares… the real world, guv," Weatherby said with a sigh.


Word soon got around, thanks to Twitter and Facebook, of the latest murder. Frank knew straight away that the killer of Amanda Peabody and Simon Linscott was the same man. Different methods as usual just to throw the police off the scent, but he knew it was Consus. He thought about going to the police but they wouldn't take him seriously. There was one ray of hope. The copper in charge was called Daly. Was he related to the one who had sacrificed himself so that Frank could live back in 1976? It was a fairly common name though. What were the chances? Frank added the name of the latest victim to his old notebook and also made a note of Daly and the tenuous, but possible, connection to Danny Daly. He needed to talk to this Inspector Daly, but how? And would he be able to convince him of the connection to Tring and the previous killings here forty-four years ago and the history of this killer too? Would he be laughed at as all the others had done? Like his own wife and children had done. He suddenly felt angry and not for the first time.

**1. June 4th - Simon Linscott, 17, male, Great Elms estate, gutted with? Loc: Alley leading to the estate.**
**2. June 9th - Amanda Peabody, 42, female, Blackstone Avenue, strangled. Loc: Copse at top of Berrybush Farm Lane.**

*****

Consus was resting in the rented flat. He wondered how the blundering police were doing regarding the investigation of the woman's' death. Had they worked out both were done by the same person yet? Had they looked at the connection between these and the murders in this village forty-four years ago? He knew the police now had computers which could look for connections between crimes in a matter of minutes. He'd watched a lot of crime shows on television when he rested. There had been a lot of progress over the years and this thing called DNA would help them. He had to be careful not to leave any trace when he killed, make it as difficult as possible until he got to the sixth victim - then it wouldn't matter. Without the television dramas, he would never have known to wear gloves for the two killings so far. Even though they were not bloody from the latest attack he'd washed them in the small kitchen sink and they were clean and dry again, ready for the next time he would kill.

Daly was back at Watford nick. He was using the crime database, looking for any connection between the latest murders and anything else in other areas. His heart almost stopped and the cold feeling of shock came over him. Kingsford. Seven murders in 1976. He read on, almost knowing already what he'd find. Five children including a teen, a man murdered after mistakenly thought of as the killer… and a policeman. The murderer of the man, a travelling worker who lived on a canal barge, was caught and sentenced to life in prison.

Daly had always known that his dad was killed in the line of duty, a real hero according to his mum as he was growing up fatherless, but the full details were always kept from him. He always assumed it was undercover work and the circumstances were too sensitive for the full story to come out. But now he was getting to the real facts.

Detective Constable Daniel Daly was killed saving the life of a young boy called Frank Kelly. *So he was a hero,* he thought. Murdered by an unknown man, thought to be the well known Kingsford Killer, the last case of the equally famous Detective Chief Inspector Patrick Mallen. Daly read on. The mass murderer had killed the five youngsters and this Frank Kelly should have been the sixth victim. Danny Daly had tackled the killer and gave the boy enough time to escape and raise the alarm. The policeman had been badly mutilated, assumed to be the result of a rabid rage at the young lad escaping. It was almost like the kid was somehow targeted by the man. This was difficult for Daly to read. The truth about the death of his father revealed to him.

He took a break to get a strong, black coffee from the canteen and when he returned he carried on reading through the reports. He thought it was possible there may be a connection between these current murders and the ones from 1976, however unlikely. The killer from forty-four years ago would have to be in his sixties now at least if he was a teen back then. Probably even older. He couldn't really see a sixty to eighty-year-old overpowering anyone let alone a large teenager like Simon Linscott who may have fought back. He had to check on the man who had been jailed for the killing of the bargee even though he wasn't a real suspect in the murders as he was already in custody when the fifth and sixth victims were killed. According to the report, he'd be ninety-four now, even more impossible he was involved this time. He still needed to be checked though, maybe it was a relative? Did he have any sons to carry on for him? But why now? He'd get Weatherby to check.

There were arrests back in 1976, although none were kept in custody for too long, especially after other murders occurring while they were being held. Mallen apparently didn't have anything solid on anyone, not officially anyway. Daly tried to put himself in Mallen's shoes and found he had a lot of sympathy for the man. Forensics were in their relative infancy and they had a lot fewer tools to work with in those days. No computers, everything was written or typed up in a file and things could have been missed by tired eyes. Fairly poor communication too. Officially the 1976 murders were still an open case but it was unlikely they would ever be solved now - even by the dedicated cold case units they had investigating old crimes. He continued to read and then suddenly froze. The post mortem photos of his dead father would have put Jack the Ripper to shame. There was very little left to recognise of the father he waved goodbye to every morning when he was a tiny child. He logged off the database and found the nearest pub.

An hour later he was joined by Weatherby who had been checking out Mick Sober, the murderer of the bargee, Taylor, after Daly had called him from the pub. Sober was released in 1994 after serving 18 years of his life sentence, moved to the north of England and had died two years after his release. No kids or other family in the area, his widow had died in 2009. Another dead end thought Daly, amazed he could still think after the quadruple single malts he'd been downing since instructing his sergeant earlier. Weatherby pulled Daly up by his arms and led him to the waiting car outside. The sergeant drove to Daly's home, a modest one-bedroom flat in Marsham, and dumped him fully clothed, apart from his shoes, on the bed to sleep off his drunken stupor, then left him alone and drove home.

Unfortunately for Daly, his sleep was not dreamless. He woke in a panic. The dream was still vividly clear in his mind. He had been there watching his dad being mutilated by a man who was hidden in the shadows. The place looked like an old wooden shed. Daly saw the flash of a knife and the policeman fell to his knees clutching his throat. There seemed to be a faint redness emanating from him as he dropped. It wasn't arterial spray, it was too hazy, almost transparent. The dark figure stooped over Daly's father and breathed in the mist like it was the vapour from a diffuser. Then there was a flurry of activity, the knife flying in arcs across the body and face of the prone man. Daly hoped his father had already died from the throat wound, wished there was no more pain for him. He sat on the side of the bed and wept with his head in his hands. His brain was throbbing from dehydration. He staggered to the bathroom intending to get a glass of water but threw himself to the carpeted floor in front of the toilet and vomited until he was empty. He pulled himself up to stand in front of the sink and gulped water from the tap, not even bothering with the glass, and then brushed his teeth with his eyes closed, avoiding looking at himself in the mirror. Daly made his way to the bed and stripped, then lay on top of the duvet. He was roasting hot. He prayed the dream (vision?) wouldn't return. Not ever.


Cassius Darwin was up to no good… as usual. Tall and skinny, he always stood out in his Hertfordshire surroundings. He'd never fit into village life since he moved from London where he grew up in the slums of a once-great city. Cassius was one of a handful of black people who lived in Kingsford. It was 4 am and he'd broken into a large house on the outskirts of the village. The owners, a retired 80s rock star and his trophy wife, were away in Los Angeles at their other home for the summer, producing a band called Melonhead. Darwin had filled his rucksack with the few items he knew he could sell to fuel his drug habit. The framed gold discs on the wall the rock star received for classics like *'Sacrifice Your Daughter'*, *'Septic Town'* and *'Evil Toads'* would be worth a few quid but he'd never be able to get rid of them without getting caught. The alarm had been easy to disable. His only real job was as an engineer for a firm that fitted them so he knew how to de-activate it very quickly and easily. Now he made his money as a thief, living from day to day, his sole purpose was finding ways to pay for his heroin addiction and the reefer he smoked almost constantly.

He left the sprawling mansion and walked slowly through the huge back garden, trying to remain in the shadows of the odd tree, and then into the surrounding woods with the full rucksack slung casually over his shoulder. Almost everything about him was casual. He was listening to rap music through his earbuds so was oblivious to the sounds of the night… and good taste. A tall, dark shape stepped in front of him.

"Watchoo want, blud?" said Darwin, taking out one of his earbuds.

"I've come for you!" said the man, smiling menacingly.

"Well, you found me, mofo!" Darwin slipped a knife from his pocket and stabbed the man in the neck. It wasn't the first time he'd done that, it was how you survived on the streets of London. Consus smiled at him as he stood staring into the other man's eyes, mocking him.

"What the…?" Darwin never got to finish before Consus grabbed him by throat with his large leather-clad hand. Darwin couldn't understand why the other man wasn't dead and seemed to have the strength of ten. For the first time in his life he felt afraid, scared shitless, in fact. The thin crimson vapour oozed out of him, slowly at first, and then gushed as he realised he was going to die instead of his attacker. His throat was being crushed with seemingly little effort from the other man. He stabbed the torso of the man, again and again, the force of each thrust lessening as he slowly asphyxiated until the knife dropped from his hand and he was stone dead. Consus used his strength to throw the man against a tree, cracking his skull like an egg shell. Consus went through the man's pockets and found a roll of ten-pound notes. They would be needed to fund his trip back to West Wycombe when he'd killed his sixth victim this time. He slowly walked away through the woods. He'd had his fill of the red mist for that night. On his walk back to the rental house he thought of Frank Kelly, his obsession.

Later that morning Frank was relaxing in his kitchen, going over the notes in the old green book yet again, trying to look for the slightest clue. In the background music was blaring out. Black Star Riders, White Lion, The Climax Blues Band and Steel Panther relaxing him while he worked on his obsession. He had a map of Kingsford spread out on the table in front of him, held down by a steaming mug of coffee. The locations of the 1976 murders marked by red pen. The 2020 ones in green. He was trying to work out the most likely place where the killer could be staying. The house Consus had stayed at in 1976 was marked in blue. What was scary to him was that Consus rented a house directly opposite from where Bridget lived. She was very lucky she wasn't a victim herself. He couldn't have coped if she was taken from him as well as Martin. A shiver ran down his spine at the thought.

There was no obvious pattern from the locations of the 1976 murders in relation to that house. He would have expected it to be somewhere in the centre of the pattern but it was outside, almost at the far west of the village. He supposed a house or flat in the high street would have been too conspicuous. The actual house backed on to the woods which would have given him covered access as well as an escape route if the police had found him. Obviously there had only been two murders that he knew of so far so it was pointless trying to find a pattern this time. He carefully folded the map again and placed it inside the back pages of the notebook, leaned back and closed his eyes. The soothing prog sounds of ex-Marillion front man Fish flowing through the speakers. He didn't have to be at work until two pm so turned the music off and went to lie down to think and maybe snooze a little. He set his alarm for one o'clock.

*****

Three days later a man, Chris MacDonald, walking his dog found the fly strewn remains of Cassius Darwin. Maggots writhed in the crevice in his head and his empty eye sockets as he lay slumped against a tree. Once MacDonald had gathered himself he'd managed to stagger home and called the police to report the body. Thirty minutes later the police had found the corpse and called Daly.

Daly shrugged and spoke to Weatherby.

"From the contents of that rucksack, the local boys will probably pin all the unsolved burglaries on him. What do you think regarding our killer? Do you think it's the same man?"

"Got a feeling you're spot on there, guv," said the sergeant. "Secluded area, no witnesses, no forensics as yet, but they've got a large area to cover still. Could take a while."

"Let's find a pub Jimmy, I've got something I want to run past you. Then you can either back me or go to the Chief Constable of the Met. and have me suspended or committed."

"Err... Okay guv," said Weatherby, worried the stress of the case was getting to his boss. It was starting to get to him too, if he was being honest.


Daly and Weatherby drove to The Horseshoes, a large pub in a country lane not far from Kingsford. Daly told his sergeant to find a table away from prying ears and went to the bar to order a large scotch for each of them. When he returned Weatherby looked up at him warily, not sure what to expect next from his boss.

"So what's troubling you, guv?" he asked, slightly concerned.

"Did you know there was a spate of murders in Kingsford back in 1976?" Daly asked.

"It came up when I was checking out that Mick Sober the other night. A collection of mainly child murders and he killed someone he suspected of them, the real killer was never caught."

"Right. Do you know who the last victim was, Jimmy?"

"Not without checking the database, guv, what's all this about?"

"Did I ever tell you about my dad?" said Daly.

"No, not much really, other than telling me he was a copper too," replied Weatherby.

"He died when I was a baby, in 1976. He was the last victim of the murders back then."

"Jesus! So that's what's getting to you? The proximity to where he died?" surmised Weatherby.

"Not quite. I believe that the 1976 killings and the ones now are somehow connected," confessed Daly.

"That's bollocks," exclaimed the sergeant, "Same killer forty-four years later? It's almost impossible, the killer would have to be about seventy at least, mate."

"I know it sounds a bit far fetched, but there are a lot of similarities, Jimmy."

"I'm listening. Not calling the big boss yet, guv," Weatherby smiled. He took his mobile phone from his jacket pocket and placed it on the table then held up his empty hands as a sign he trusted his superior... for now.

"Okay. 1976, the long, hot summer your parents have probably mentioned to you several times. Five murders of young children and teens. In between all that was the murder of the bargee Sober had wrongly suspected of the crimes. The killer then cornered another boy of fourteen in a shed at some allotments, a Frank Kelly, and the boy was saved by my dad, DC Danny Daly. The killer took his revenge on my dad for helping the kid to escape. You don't want to see the post mortem snaps, mate. I saw them when I checked the database. They'll chill you to the bone."

"So that's why you went on that bender the other night? Sent me off to check on Sober and drank yourself into oblivion? So falling down pissed I never even risked buying you a kebab to choke on," said Weatherby.

"That's it. It hit me hard," sighed Daly. He took a gulp of his scotch and winced.

"I'm not surprised. You never knew how he died then?" asked the sergeant.

"I was told he died in the line of duty, being a hero. That's all I ever got out of my mum. Christ, she would have had to identify him after the attack." Daly looked green. He took another large sip of his scotch, relishing the burning sensation of the liquid as it made its way down the inside of his throat to his empty stomach.

"So what's the connection with these killings forty-four years later?" said Weatherby, puzzled.

"Call it copper's instinct, Jimmy," said Daly. "I really don't know how, it's almost impossible it's the same guy, but I'm sure the murders now are connected to 1976. Maybe a relative continuing a legacy, or something like that."

"Like Son of Frankenstein?" quipped Weatherby.

"I'm serious, Jimmy. Strange shit happens. Like that thing with Mark Mason last year. Like your predecessor Gibson and the spider in London. Maybe some evil family gene triggered a couple of generations later. This guy, or family, or whatever, could have even been operating in other parts of the country in between the sets of attacks in this area. But how the hell could we make the connection when the methods of killing were different? They were in 1976 too, you know. Mainly suffocation and strangulation but a large knife or machete were also used on three, including my dad. Maybe it's some cult like the Manson Family back in the sixties, different methods because of multiple killers? Much harder to connect."

"Now that's starting to sound a lot more plausible, guv," said Weatherby. "A killer cult that has been going for decades but never detected. No connections made because there were different killers, different MO and possibly moving from one area to the next. Any physical evidence wouldn't have matched to anything else. So who the hell could be doing it? Killer Moonies, shacked up on a farm somewhere? Away from mainstream society? Some religious nut jobs, brainwashed for years?" asked Weatherby.

"Exactly," said Daly. "It's the best we have so far, the only hypothesis."

"Okay, I'll put the Chief Constable on hold, no booby hatch for you yet, guv," joked Weatherby.

"Thanks, Jimmy - I'm touched," smiled Daly. His first real smile for weeks. "What I want you to do is get on the database. The killings in 1976 stopped at six, never continued after my dad for some reason, maybe six is a significant number, a possible religious connection? I know 666 is in the bible, and your bloody horror films too, but does it crop up anywhere else? Check it out. I want you to search for other unsolved murders of six in a tight area, anywhere in the country. Go back as far as World War Two if you need to. If this is some sort of murderous cult then it may have gone back a lot longer than the seventies, the personnel always changing, breeding new and willing killers. Grab plenty of coffee, it could be a long night for you."

"Where are you going to be?" asked the sergeant.

"I'm going to visit my mum," Daly said with a frown, knowing it would not be an easy visit.

*****

Daly pulled up in the Audi and left it in the Waverley Nursing Home car park, there were only two more cars there and he parked well away from either. He was well known at the home and several of the carers exchanged a few pleasant words with him as he walked to the lounge where his mum was sitting watching daytime TV with a blank expression. Daly thought that millions of others, even without mental health issues, mostly students, were doing the same. The same blankness on their faces. She'd been in the home for several years, Daly couldn't look after her as he was away from home maybe sixteen hours a day or more, but he tried to visit her whenever he could. He found this place for her through a friend who had similar circumstances to deal with. His mum had been suffering from progressive dementia for about ten years and it made Daly sad to see her mind slipping away from him even more every time he visited. But at least she was well cared for by professionals. A better life than he could provide for her at his home and safer for her too.

"It's nice to see you, Danny, is it time to go home now?" she asked hopefully.

"It's Gerry, mum," how are you?"

"I don't think I know you, are you a doctor?"

"No mum, I'm a policeman just like dad... Danny."

"I knew a Danny once, he was a policeman too."

Daly was getting frustrated. She was a lot more confused than she was last time he visited, four or five weeks previously. He needed to ask her questions though, he hoped he'd get some answers from her.

"I need to ask you why you never told me how dad died. Why was it such a big secret that he was the victim of a serial killer?" asked Daly.

"It was bad," she said in a rare moment of lucidity. Daly hoped it would last a few more minutes. "I saw him. Cut up, not my Danny anymore. I tried to spare you, protect you."

"Did he ever talk about the case in Kingsford?"

"Kingsford, yes, Kingsford where he died. He always talked about a boy called… Fred? Francis?… Frank? Yes, Frank. Thought he was the key to it all."

"The key to what, mum?" pleaded Daly.

"Can I go home now, Danny?" she said with the glazed look returning.

Daly knew that was all he could get. He knew she meant Frank Kelly, the intended sixth victim. He had to track him down and talk to him. The key to it all? What had he meant? He stayed with her for another thirty minutes, just staring at her, lost in his thoughts, until he decided to find Frank Kelly.

*****

Frank was having his usual recurring dream, he was on the same trawler late at night. But it was somehow different this time. The deck was bathed in the light from the mast, as ever, but there was a very faint red glow surrounding it. He wasn't hauling in the nets anymore, the sea was very calm, an eerie feeling hit him suddenly. He was looking for his crewmates, Bobby, Alec and Eamon, Captain Leahy too. He called out and got no response. It was still bitterly cold but Frank was sweating. Where was everyone? He scanned the unbroken water, not even a ripple visible. He silently walked around the entire circumference of the deck. It was deserted. He stepped up into the wheelhouse, no one there either, not a sign of anyone. Frank then knew he had to go below, he was dreading it, a bad feeling coursing through him. As he walked down the eight rough wooden steps he could see a fine red mist floating towards him. He walked on and the mist cleared. His heart almost stopped in terror at he saw what was before him. His crewmates, his friends, were sitting on the floor, leaning up against the cupboards in the galley. They were all dead, blood seeping from their eyes, and their mouths were open in a wail of horror. He was alone on the boat with four corpses. Or was he? Someone had to have done this to them. They must still be aboard, no way to get off. He moved past the bodies of his friends, trying not to look down at them. He shivered as his boot touched one of them as he crept past, he had no wish to see who it was. He was expecting a hand to reach up and grab the leg of his thick trousers. He moved slowly towards the cold store where the catch was kept, only accessible by a hatch on the deck. A gap of fewer than two feet was on either side and he squeezed through the opening on the right, difficult in the heavy jacket he used for above decks. His breath puffed out ahead of him as he moved towards the bow. The dark man was sitting there, smiling. Why was he here, how did he get on board? The trawler always had a safety check before they set off. Vital because their lives were at stake every time they left port. He could not have been aboard when they left. The man opened his mouth to speak…

…Frank woke with a scream, alone, sweat streaming from his entire body. Why was his dream different this time?


Consus saw a news report about the murder of Cassius Darwin the next day on TV. Cassius? A Roman name? He wondered why black people named their sons after Romans when they were so opposed to slavery. After all, the Romans were the biggest slavers in history. It was a mystery to Consus. It didn't make sense but sometimes very little of the modern world did. He remembered the slave trade of the past, between roughly 1700 and 1800, a terrible time for those transported, most on their way to America. It didn't make any difference to him what the victim's name was, or who he was. He extracted what he needed from the man, same as the others, that was all that mattered. He needed three more before he hibernated again, he preferred not to think of it as hiding. Hiding was for cowards. No - he was resting, rejuvenating. There was so much more to learn about this time period though. Knowing about all the advancements could make all the difference to his survival. He was fascinated by the headway made in forensics and police procedures. He had to stay one step ahead of the police to avoid detection before he was finished. He dreaded the thought of prison and needing to kill the criminals to get his vital fix of the mist. They'd be men with little fear unlike those incarcerated with him in the past. Those men had feared for their lives, knowing their time on earth would be short. They valued every single day they were alive, even in jail. He'd never get enough now. Criminals were different, more hardened, they scoffed at their own mortality. And how would he return to his cave anyway? Let himself get murdered and then fake his death and dig himself out of a grave again? Did they still bury those who die in prison or were they all cremated now?

He remembered back to 1646. A bad year for him. He'd killed three young girls and was careless enough to get captured. He had spent many weeks in jail awaiting his trial. His hunger for the mist was excruciating and he was forced to kill another man in his cell, a common thief called Jacob Carpenter. The mist from the thief had satisfied his yearning for a short while. They came for him a three weeks later. The trial and sentence a formality. He was taken straight to the gallows, hands tied behind his back with a thin sisal rope. He was forced up half a dozen crude planks, the steps up to the gibbet. He stood calmly looking out at the assembled crowd awaiting his execution. They threw rotten vegetables at him, most missed. He was made to stand on a rickety wooden stool. He felt the thick, rough rope being placed around his neck by a man halfway up a ladder propped up against the wooden frame of the hanging platform. He smiled at the crowd. A grin of contempt. They all jeered. He showed no fear. The stool was kicked from under him and he fell less than two feet. The fall did not break his neck as he expected. This was good for him. He could feign suffocation easily. He'd witnessed it often enough in his victims. He was still swinging in the breeze when the crowd drifted away.

Two days later they cut him down. They carried his inert body to a small cart and transported him a mile away to the unhallowed ground he would be buried in. He was interred in a shallow grave with no religious ceremony. He was a criminal and would soon be descending into the depths of Hell in the minds of the two men who had dug the grave and the cart driver. He waited several hours, or what seemed like hours, it may well have been days. He had no idea how long he was in the grave as he could not see the sun or moon. Consus slowly clawed his way out of the still loosely packed damp earth. It was night time. He ran through the darkness and hid in the woods.

He'd made his last two kills over the coming days and returned to his cave, re-emerging another twenty-two years later, fresh for another set of kills.

*****

Frank Kelly was reading the news report online the next day on a local newspaper's website. A criminal killed whilst fleeing through the woods after he perpetrated a robbery at the home of Steve Walker, founder of the eighties rock band, Angel Dust. Frank was a fan of the band, his favourite song an album track called *Evil Minds* from the Babylon Nights LP. Walker was apparently in LA at the time and was obviously not a suspect. The report listed the victim had throat and head injuries. Somehow a news source had got hold of the post mortem report. He assumed someone had been paid for a copy. Easily done with cameras on phones now. It was Consus again. He was absolutely sure of it.

**1. June 4th - Simon Linscott, 17, male, Great Elms estate, gutted with? Loc: Alley leading to the estate.**
**2. June 9th - Amanda Peabody, 42, female, Blackstone Avenue, strangled. Loc: Copse at top of Berrybush Farm Lane.**
**3. June 19th - Cassius Darwin, 23, male, Unknown address, choked/head trauma. Loc: Woods south end of Kingsford.**

Three more chances to stop him but he was no nearer to knowing where the killer was than the police. He had to speak with this Inspector Daly. Somehow he had to convince the detective that his knowledge was vital in helping to track down the killer. He had just put an Angel Dust CD in the player and started it off, the blistering intro to *Rabid Badger* shrieked from the speakers. The doorbell rang. Frank cursed. He still had plenty of research to do and didn't need any interruptions other than the music. He walked hurriedly to the door, hopeful of getting rid of his visitor quickly and carry on with his work.

"Frank Kelly?" asked a man in his forties, dressed rather scruffily in a lightweight grey suit, standing in the foyer of the flats. Frank wondered how the man had got past the security door.

"Yes?" answered Frank. The man at his door looked like a bank manager, apart from the wrinkles in his jacket.

"My name's Detective Inspector Gerry Daly. I think you may be of some help to me."

Frank's knees suddenly gave way and Daly was quick to catch him before Frank's head hit the wall of the short hallway he was standing in.

"What's all this about Mr. Kelly? It's not the usual reaction I get, even from women," smiled Daly reassuringly.

"It's just... Shit! I was just thinking about how I could contact you and here you are. I can be of help… if you're willing to listen, Mr. Daly."

"I'll listen to anything at this point if it leads to the killer, I assume you've heard by now that there has been a third death?" asked Daly.

"I was just reading about it, inspector. Come in, we can't do this on the doorstep. By the way, I don't suppose you were related to Danny Daly, the policeman killed in 1976?"

"He was my father, I know he saved your life. I read the original reports a few nights ago and your name came up. That's why I'm here. According to my mum, my dad thought you were important," said Daly, hoping to find out exactly why.

"Christ, this gets weirder all the time and what I have to tell you is pretty weird too, and maybe even unbelievable," Frank said, trying to hide his anxiety.

"Tell me what you know and maybe you'll be surprised what I believe," said Daly with a faint smile, or was it a grimace? Was that desperation showing on the detective's face? Frank wasn't sure. Frank was pretty desperate himself. Could they help each other stop the killer?

They both sat at the kitchen table. Frank had made coffee for the pair and they sat opposite one another. Each weighing the other up while sipping the hot liquid slowly.

"Okay, I'll start, shall I?" said Daly, taking a very deep breath. "We have a serial killer. There have been three victims so far, as you know. Different methods, no evidence at all. I do have a theory though. I believe that these murders are linked to the six here in 1976. Sounds mad, doesn't it?"

"It does sound mad, but they are," said Frank calmly, now recovered from his near faint in the hallway. "I tried to warn people in 1998 too but no one listened, cost me my marriage and now my kids think I'm a deluded nutter with an obsession. I rarely see them or the grandkids these days."

"1998?"

"There were six murders in 1998 in and around Tring, a couple very brutal but mainly suffocation or strangulation as usual. Just like 1976. This man strikes only six times every twenty-two years and then disappears until the next cycle begins. I was working and living in Scotland at the time and tried to help but was dismissed as a lunatic by the police here when I came down for a weekend. I tried to help and got nowhere. They just refused to listen."

"How can it really be the same man, Mr. Kelly? We're working on a theory that it's some cult using newer members to commit the murders, maybe travelling around the country and now returned to the area."

"It's the same man because…" Frank hesitated and took a deep breath. "He's immortal!"

"Oh come on, Mr. Kelly!" exclaimed Daly.

"I'll show you, I have a list of six murders every twenty-two years stretching back to at least 1888."

Daly took the list from Frank. Read it carefully. 1998 Tring, 1976 Kingsford, 1954 Hastings, 1932 Kilburn, 1910 Buckingham, 1888 Whitechapel, London. The names of every victim listed, every method of killing, every exact date and location under the heading of each year. It was all laid out in front of him in black and white. He recognised some names from 1888.

"Are you seriously trying to tell me this bloke is Jack the Ripper?" Daly laughed, wondering if Frank was dangerous.

"You'll find that for every year listed there were six victims, no evidence whatsoever, no real suspects, or none they could hold for any length of time. No one was ever caught and convicted, and it was exactly the same in 1888. Precisely a twenty-two-year gap between each series of murders. Yes, I do believe this killer was Jack the Ripper, and I do believe he is immortal. He told me so himself. There can be no other valid explanation. I know I don't sound very rational but you have to believe me. He said his name was Consus. Or that was his original name. He obviously uses a different name each time he comes back and rents a property to stay in while he does the killings. The police found the house he was renting in 1976 but missed him by a few days. A guy from the letting agency went to visit about unpaid rent and found bloodstains in the bathroom. They matched the blood type of your father. That should be in the police reports."

"It is."

Daly looked at the long list again and quickly did the calculations. Twenty-two-year gaps, every time. Daly didn't believe in coincidence. There had to be more to this, he decided.

Frank told Daly about what had happened before Daly's father arrived at the old shed Frank had been trapped in. Consus had told him how he had died and been brought back to life. How he needed to kill to stay alive, or more accurately, to exist. Consus saw no need to lie to him as Frank was about to die himself… for the only time. Frank told Daly the immense weariness he felt coming from the immortal. No guilt though, the murders were just a means to an end. Like a shark killing to survive.

Frank said that he'd been obsessed with Consus for the last forty-four years, researching the sets of murders coming every twenty-two years working back from 1976. About trying to tell the police what he knew and being laughed at in 1998. What confused Frank though, was why

Consus had come back to Kingsford. This was the first time he'd ever returned to a particular area. Tring was fairly close, but far enough away that the police never made the connection that it was the same man.

Daly listened without questioning or interrupting Frank. Letting the man talk. And the more he talked, the more Daly could see the connections between each set of murders. But why six every time? Why not more if the killer enjoyed the mutilations as much as it seemed? Was the man in Kingsford in 2020 really the monster from 1888 known as Jack the Ripper? There were more than six credited to Jack by some Ripper historians but most believed there were just the six. It seemed too ridiculous to consider though… and yet somehow plausible if he could believe in the immortality angle. And all the dates fit, and the mindless mutilations were almost the same. Frank had done his homework incredibly well over the years, almost obsessively, no wonder his marriage broke down.

Daly's mobile buzzed in his pocket. He could see Weatherby's name on the screen. Frank got up to make another cup of coffee for them while Daly spoke to his sergeant. Weatherby had been doing the checks for unsolved sets of six murders as he'd been instructed by his boss.

"It looks like the cult angle is the way to go, guv. These murders go back years, a longer time span than just one man, or maybe even a family could be responsible for."

"How many series of murders have you found?"

"Six lots so far." Weatherby reeled off his list, Daly matching each year to the schedule Frank had given him perfectly.

"Notice they are all after gaps of twenty-two years?" said Daly, definitely intrigued.

There was silence for a few seconds as Weatherby looked at his own list and did the mental arithmetic.

"Bloody hell, I didn't notice that. So that really does confirm it's a cult, killing to some sort of pre-ordained cycle. Maybe some pre-apocalypse thing like those American cults in the seventies and eighties?"

"It could be something much worse than that, Jimmy. Meet me back at The Horseshoes, there's someone I want you to meet. Be there in an hour."


Weatherby arrived at the pub in his blue Toyota Avensis and saw Daly's dusty black Audi already in the car park as he entered the building. He saw Daly with an average looking man, slightly overweight, in his late fifties sitting at the same table they had been at earlier. Daly pointed at the pint already waiting for him. Weatherby sat down and was introduced to Frank.

"Jimmy, this is Frank Kelly. He was the intended sixth victim of the killer back in 1976, the one my dad saved. He's been researching these murders since then and could be a lot of help to us. Let's face it - we have bugger all tangible so far, mate."

"So do you think this is a cult that has been operating for decades, Mr. Kelly? Confusing the police with different methods in several areas? Different killers. No one making the connection until now?"

"Not quite, It's the same source every time but it's not a cult. Just one man."

"That's bollocks," said Weatherby, surprised. "I have a list going back to 1910."

"And mine goes back even further," replied Frank with a sad look. "I need you to keep an open mind just as D.I. Daly has."

Weatherby looked at Daly who was looking so serious the sergeant immediately dismissed this as a wind-up and went straight to mental illness affecting the pair of them. He kept quiet and gulped down his full pint and rose to get more drinks, giving him a chance to think. When he arrived back from the bar he sat down after placing a metal tray of drinks on the table, Daly spoke calmly once again.

"Look, Jimmy, I had the same reaction when he told me what he'd got, but if you keep an open mind and don't dismiss everything without a bit of thought, a great deal of it actually makes sense. So just listen to him for a few minutes, will you? Make your mind up after you hear this… please?"

"You're the boss," said Weatherby with a half scowl on his face wondering how the boss could actually justify any of this bollocks.

Frank pushed his list towards Weatherby, it slid easily across the dark polished oak table. Weatherby picked it up and read slowly, noting even more detail than he'd been able to pick up from the police crime database.

"Where did you get all this?" asked Weatherby.

"Well, I basically did what you did, looked for sets of six unsolved murders using the internet. I looked at each year and got all the information from local news reports. As soon as I found a cluster of killings it wasn't difficult to access the old newspaper files from the area, sometimes for the cost of a subscription as most were online, but I did need to visit a few local libraries to access a microfiche a few times where the records weren't digitised. As you can see I've been very determined and spent countless hours on this over the years, a lot more time than you were given. Probably more than the combined hours of the police in these cases, discounting 1888 of course. That was a mammoth effort and the police came up with virtually nothing. Spending more time trying to stop mobs like the Vigilance Committee lynching various suspects and even coaxing male officers to go undercover dressed as prostitutes in the hope of luring him out into the open.

Weatherby was at first confused by the mention of 1888, the year sounded very familiar but he never made the connection until Frank's comment about officers dressing as whores to catch a killer. Jack the Ripper. He sank the rest of his pint, he was speechless. Daly actually believed all this, or at least a large part of it otherwise he wouldn't allow his sergeant to be here listening to it. *He's really lost it,* he thought.

"I thought it was only this guy who was the nutter, guv, but you're losing it too! Bloody cracked from the strain. It's total shite, it's got to be!" He rose and turned to walk out of the pub.

"Just… listen, Jimmy," implored Daly with a sigh. "Please give me five more minutes. I believe that every single one of these crimes going back to 1888 and possibly even beyond are connected. The only bit I can't get my head around is an immortal killer. The *only* bit!"

"It's mental, no one is immortal!" exclaimed the incredulous sergeant. Several of the bar patrons turned and looked at him as he stood there.

"But what if it's *not* impossible?" Frank interjected quietly, hoping the whole conversation wasn't carrying to the other customers. "There are thousands of mysteries yet to be solved by science. Just because it hasn't been proven yet doesn't mean it is empirically not possible. One day we'll find life on other planets, it's not impossible but very likely according to most astrophysicists, but it hasn't been proven yet. Maybe they will even find evidence of some God or other supernatural being? The fact is nothing is impossible until someone proves that it is."

"Jimmy," said Daly. "Let's not rule anything out, please. Your mum is religious, isn't she?" Weatherby nodded. "She believes in an afterlife, and a God and everlasting whatever," Daly continued. "Would you call her a nutter? She believes all that with all her heart and with absolutely no proof at all. Where is the proof that the Jesus she loves was the son of God, performed miracles or even came back after death? Or even existed? Yet over six billion people believe that he or she or some other god exists. More than half the population of the planet believe in some sort of supernatural too. Maybe the real truth lies somewhere in the middle? I don't know. There are always countless possibilities and everyone can't be wrong about what they believe in. I'm with Frank here, if there is the slightest possibility that just one man in all of history has somehow become immortal then we can't rule it out, whatever the odds. And until we can prove otherwise we have nothing else, mate."

"Fair enough, boss. I don't like it but if it helps catch this bastard I'll go with it for now, until we find something either way."

"Good lad," said Daly. "Who knows what will turn up."

"Catching him is no good, we have to destroy him and make sure he *can't* come back," said Frank. Weatherby groaned and downed the rest of his drink.

"Jimmy, if you're in, you're in, no half measures on this, mate," said Daly. "If all this turns out to be true then we may have no alternative. It will probably mean my career but I can arrange things so it won't look like you are too involved. I just need your help for a while. Let's get this bastard!" Weatherby sighed and nodded again.

"So what's our next move, Mr. Daly?" asked Frank.

"There is a reason why I'm more susceptible to belief in the supernatural, than Jimmy here," he told Frank. "Last year I was involved in a case concerning a guy called Mark Mason and what appeared to be a reincarnated witch from the fifth century. A demon was apparently killing on her behalf until she was almost fully formed enough to do the last one herself, the intended was Mark's girlfriend. I wasn't there at Marsham Stones at the end, never saw what happened, but that case, and Mark, convinced me there was more than just facts and figures and things you could prove one hundred percent."

"The local guy who wrote that book? I read it," said Frank. "I thought it was fiction?"

"Yes, well he was convinced by his publisher that if he turned the account into fiction it would sell. It was the only way he could get the story out there. Anyway, there was a lot of help from a history professor, a bloke called Jim Anderson. His mentor, Stuart Pearson, was killed by the demon in Kent. Jim may be able to provide us with some information about this Consus. He has contacts all over the place. If he can confirm this Consus existed it would be a good start. I'll set up a meeting with him tomorrow."

"So what do we do until then?" asked Weatherby.

"I'm all for getting rat-arsed if you want to know the truth, said Daly. "This could be the biggest fight we could ever face in our careers, and there is a revenge incentive for Frank and myself too. His best mate and my dad."

*****

While Daly, Weatherby and Frank were settled for the rest of the evening in the pub drowning themselves in beer and scotch and some bar food, a painfully thin girl called Annabel Watts was in her back garden, spending the night in her new tent. She was only eight years old and her dad had finally agreed to let her sleep alone outside in the relative coolness of the garden. She'd been complaining about how hot it had been in her bedroom despite a big fan on a stand blowing in her direction every night since the current heatwave had started several weeks previously. Her mum had died the summer before and as she had no other siblings, knew her daddy doted on her and would eventually give in to her on just about everything. She was very small for her age and her hair was so blond it was almost white. She looked a couple of years younger than she was which made her dad even more protective of her. They were all each other had in the world now. No other family. She dreaded losing her daddy too, worried about what would become of her. She had no aunts, evil or otherwise. Her daddy knew she would be safe in the back garden, a high wooden fence protecting the property.

Annabel had spent the early part of the evening reading her Harry Potter book by the light of a small battery-operated lamp. She imagined herself as Hermione but she would have liked Ron instead of Harry if it was her. Ron was cute and funny and the boy who was Harry in the films was dull and creepy and she didn't like him much. She'd turned the lamp off and was listening to the bats flitting around the large garden, hoping that none of them would find their way into the tent. She'd hate to be face to face with one but she did love to watch them from her bedroom window as dusk fell. Were they really blind? Did they suck blood from little kids like that girl, Hillary, from school, told her? She didn't like Hillary, she was a bit of a bully because she was bigger than most kids her age. She smelled funny too. Annabel giggled. As she slowly dropped off to sleep she was thinking about giant bats taking over the world and she and her dad having to hide in shops because bats lived in their house. She couldn't even go to school because the bats were there too, having lessons about how to catch people easier and to suck blood. The police had all run away because they were scared of the bats, but her dad wasn't scared. She knew he would keep her safe. He was so brave.

Annabel heard the zip to the front of the tent opening. She guessed it was her daddy coming to make sure she was all right out there on her own. She decided to play a joke on him and pretend to be fast asleep until he got really close to her and then she'd frighten him. She could feel him getting closer as he crawled silently towards her. She stifled a giggle as he crawled nearer and nearer. When she felt the warm breath on her cheek she opened her eyes and shouted "Boo!"

It wasn't her daddy. It wasn't a giant black bat either. It took a couple of seconds for her brain to register that and by the time it did there was a huge gloved hand clamped over her mouth and nose, it smelt like that brown stuff daddy painted the fence with. She couldn't scream for her daddy to hep her. The man was big, he hardly fit into the tent. Annabel struggled the best she could but her slight frame barely moved under the weight of the man. She tried to bite the man's hand but she couldn't open her mouth wide enough. Reams of red mist escaped her. The man sucked at it in greedily, enjoying the vapour rushing into his lungs, the sweetness of it coating his tongue and throat before it disappeared. Annabel stared into his eyes, there seemed to be a very faint red glow in them. She had never seen anyone whose eyes glowed before. Please daddy, come and help me, she pleaded in her head. She was so terrified, she couldn't move. She felt the burning in her narrow chest because she couldn't breathe. As her eyesight dimmed and coloured flecks invaded her limited vision, she thought she could hear her mummy calling her to come home as she used to at the playground across the street. She missed her mummy so much. She hoped her daddy wouldn't be too sad. Goodbye, daddy.

*****

The next morning while nursing a massive hangover, Daly got the call about a missing child from the Ash Grove estate at the southern end of the village. She'd apparently been sleeping in her tent all night and was gone when the father had called her for breakfast at 8 am. Weatherby parked his Toyota in front of Daly's house and switched cars. He was equally hungover. A couple of Plods were already at the scene when Daly and his sergeant arrived. There had already been a thorough search of the estate. Sheds, garages and other outbuildings and a door to door in search of anyone who had seen the girl since the day before. No trace of her at all. The pretty little red-haired liaison officer Daly had met at the Linscott's had arrived and was doing her best to calm the father and explain to him the various procedures that the police would be going through in the detailed investigation of his daughter's disappearance. Daly knew in his heart that the poor little girl would be the fourth victim of Consus and the only thing he could do was find the body as quickly as possible, hoping there had been no mutilation of the girl. He recalled the post mortem pictures of his own father on the police database and felt sick. He didn't want the father of the little girl to go through what his mum had when she had to identify the body of the murdered detective. Daly was keeping his options open though, and decided that the disappearance could be unrelated to Consus and the father was a possible suspect. He hoped not. *Never rule anything out,* he thought.

He suddenly wished he could talk to the legendary Paddy Mallen, or his sergeant, Carter. Their thoughts on the murders in 1976 could have been invaluable. Thoughts that would have never made the official reports. Mallen had died from liver disease more than thirty-five years before. He'd retired soon after the brutal death of his detective constable and failure to catch the child killer who had seemingly vanished into thin air. He'd virtually drank himself to death after that, living alone, secluded in a flat on the remote west coast of Ireland. Carter had died of cancer several years ago after rising to Detective Chief Inspector in the Met. Just as Mallen had thought he would. Carter had had a great mentor, the best. Just as Carter had been a mentor for the younger Daly. Maybe I should try a bloody medium to contact them? I'm willing to try anything and believe even more, he thought and smiled grimly to himself.

Later that afternoon Daly and Weatherby had picked up Frank, who was even more hungover and taken the day off sick, and arrived at Jim Anderson's house in Paddenham. They left the search for the little girl in the hands of two junior detectives and a dozen Plods. Daly parked next to the massive black Lincoln Continental belonging to the giant history professor. The trio were greeted at the door by a beaming Anderson. Frank was amazed at how huge he was. The big man brushed both walls of the hallway with his shoulders as he led them into his small office at the rear of the building.

"Nice to meet you, professor, I remember you getting a technical assistance credit in Mark Mason's book about the witch. Inspector Daly tells me that it was a true story," said Frank.

"It was all too true, I'm afraid," replied the rotund man. "People died at the hands of the demon Anrok on behalf of the witch, including Mark's best friend and my own best friend and mentor," Jim said with a sigh.

"I visited the stones at Marsham again after I'd read the book and there is a new stone there. It's incredible," replied Frank.

"Can we get on with it, please?" asked Weatherby irritably, still not comfortable with the whole immortal scenario and didn't want to hear about demons and witches on top of it all.

"Of course," said Anderson and grinned at the sergeant. "Tell me what you've experienced so far, Mr. Kelly."

"For a start call me Frank, only people trying to sell me stuff call me Mr. Kelly," he smiled. "Well, I'm not sure how much Inspector Daly… Gerry has told you, but I'll try to make it short. Back in 1976, that scorcher of a summer we had, there were several killings of children and young people, including my best friend, Martin Frost. Five victims, before I was the intended sixth. I was saved by a policeman, who, in turn, became the sixth victim. That policeman was Gerry's father, Danny, part of the team trying to track down the killer. The killer's name is Consus. For some reason, he decided to unburden himself with his story before he killed me. I suppose if he hadn't taken that time I wouldn't be here.

Anderson nodded for Frank to go on.

"What he told me I just couldn't take in at first. He said he'd been a man who had died and come back to life, he didn't tell me how though. He said he needed to kill six people so that he could survive and be able to return several years later to repeat the cycle. He told me that at first he felt guilty for taking innocent lives, especially the children, but as the centuries wore on he started to enjoy it, relished it. It was his new way of life. So I was saved by Danny. I moved away from the area a few years later and got married, had kids and was thankful that I'd survived. I didn't believe that the killer, Consus, could come back again. I thought he was just a nutter telling me a story, maybe one he truly believed in his mind that he was immortal. Sadly I was wrong."

"So he came back?" said Anderson. "What else did you discover? I understand from Gerry that you have done a hell of a lot of research."

"It was 1998. I was living and working in Aviemore, Scotland at the time. It was the early days of the internet and I kept up with the local news from down here. Mostly the websites of all the local newspapers. The Watford Observer mentioned a series of events in Tring. There had been another spate of six murders in the area that year and no killer had ever been caught, they didn't have one suspect in the case and then the murders abruptly stopped. It reminded me of Kingsford back in '76. I knew Consus was back. I remembered him saying that he killed six and then would return but I had no idea how long it was in between his sprees. I tried to tell the police that the Tring killings were connected to the Kingsford ones but I was ignored."

"I remember both sets of murders, I was only a little kid in 1976 but everyone was in a panic, even out here away from Kingsford. And when the Tring ones occurred I was at university at the time but still got news from home, courtesy of my parents," said Jim.

"So I researched as much as I could for groups of unsolved murders going back year by year and ended up with several hits," Frank continued. "Six deaths, all different and usually unconnected because of the different methods the murderer used, the police never even realised the link in some of those years, thinking they had six different killers, none of the victims were known to each other, dead ends."

Frank handed Anderson the list of murders. 1998 Tring, 1976 Kingsford, 1954 Hastings, 1932 Kilburn, 1910 Buckingham, 1888 Whitechapel in London. Anderson immediately picked up on two things.

"Twenty-two years between them all, nothing else matched in any other years?" asked Jim.

"No, nothing, the closest was a trio of unsolved murders in Oxford in 1957, and they were all stabbings, no variation," said Frank.

"Whitechapel in 1888?" I assume the obvious has jumped out at you too?" said Jim raising his eyebrows above the rims of his glasses.

"The Ripper." Frank was relieved there was no mocking tone from the professor. It made a welcome change.

"So, what you are saying is we have a serial killer called Consus, that definitely sounds Roman to me. He died and came back to life somehow by unknown means. He kills six people every twenty-two years and then… what? Hides away? Retreats somewhere? Leaves the country? And then he returns and the cycle repeats. Interesting. Why twenty-two, I wonder? It obviously has significance or the periods would be more random, twenty-seven one time, fifteen the next, then fifty. It has meaning, I'm sure it's significant."

"Yes, you are right, it has to mean something or it would be random like you said," said Daly who had been listening to it all quietly, memories of the 1976 case files flooding back to him. The post mortem pictures of his father and the similar crime scenes in 2020. "I think there was another one today. A little girl snatched from a tent in her back garden overnight. I'm sure she's the fourth of this cycle."

"Shit, that cuts down on the time we have left to find this bloke!" said Frank angrily. "Two more and he's gone for another generation."

"Right," said Anderson. "I'll dig up whatever I can on this Consus, check if he was a real person, who he was and possibly how he died. I have a few friends who are experts on Roman Britain. The name does sound very Roman so that's the best place to start. I doubt I'll find anything about him after his death though. I'm sure that any immortal would be keeping a low profile, afraid of discovery, changing his name regularly. What really interests me is how he died, the circumstances. It could be the key to finding out how he's become immortal and also maybe stopping him."

"Thanks for not treating me like a mental defective, Jim," said Frank.

"I'm intrigued by the whole thing to be honest. You don't get too many stories or legends about immortality these days. There have been people who were thought to be immortal in the past, alchemists like Nicolas Flamel and the Count of St. Germain. Then there are Merlin and Sir Galahad from the Arthurian legends. No one knows if they were actually real people though. I have my suspicions they were but that's a discussion for another time. There was even Tithonus in Greek mythology, who was granted eternal life and then transformed into a grasshopper apparently. It's all very interesting if true and I love a mystery, Frank."

As Daly, Weatherby and Frank got into the black Audi, Daly's phone rang. After a thirty second, almost one-sided conversation Daly hung up and said, "They found the girl." All three travelled in silence back to Kingsford, immersed in their own thoughts.


After dropping Frank back home, Daly and his sergeant went on to a set of council garages in north-east Kingsford, well away from the initial search area. The little girl had been bundled into a corner of one of the open garages, partially covered with a soggy green tarpaulin covered in mold. The garage was rented to a man who was on holiday in Ireland at that time, according to his next-door neighbour, and the garage had been left open while he was away, which had been almost a week. The girl's body had been found by a teenager who had been playing football on the adjoining playing field with his friends and had nipped into the first open garage to relieve himself. He spotted a Harry Potter slipper poking from the dirty tarpaulin and he accidentally urinated on it. Then he lifted the canvas sheet slightly to see what was underneath and had then run home in tears to call the police. He'd heard that a girl was missing from the estate almost two miles away and knew at once it was her.

"How the hell did our man move her from her garden to a garage miles away without anyone seeing him?" asked Weatherby.

"Even at night there would be cars going through the high street and most of the journey would have been along the main road, and he would have had to cross that road to get up here too," said Daly. "Maybe he flew," he half-joked.

"Wouldn't be surprised the way things have been panning out, guv," sighed Weatherby.

"Christ, how do we get to this guy, Jimmy? I assume there won't be any evidence again once the forensic boys have finished. We have no idea where he's holed up. The only description is from forty-four years ago when he tried to kill Frank, and that may have changed over the years. No witnesses this time around. We're dealing with a man who has supposedly been evading capture successfully for centuries. What chance have we got?" said Daly, the frustration starting to get to him. The more he found out, the more he realised the killer was intelligent enough to know what the police would be looking for. Where did he get that knowledge? Could the bastard read minds too? It was getting surreal.

"Especially when we won't get much help because we can't reveal to the brass which way the investigation is headed," replied Weatherby.

"Four victims so far, two left. We may only have days to find him, Jimmy," Daly punched the closed wooden door of the garage next to the one containing the girl.

"We can't watch every single kid in the village, boss, but I think the only chance we have is catching him in the act. But when and where will he strike next?"

"It's not just kids we'd need to watch, he's taken a lot of adults in the past too. The Peabody woman was in her forties. More over the years according to Frank's list. I'm sure he prefers to kill children but it depends on the opportunities he's presented with. Four thousand people in the village. Every single one a potential victim. Christ, I'm tempted to get a few more bodies in and get them to act as bait. Tell the brass a cock and bull story just to get the manpower."

"Didn't work for the police in Whitechapel, did it?" said Weatherby. "It just made the police seem like a laughing stock at the time. The Ripper just went on killing and then disappeared."

"Are you warming to the idea that it was the same bloke then, Jimmy?"

"You believe it, guv. I just take my lead from you," he laughed. Weatherby turned and was confronted by the dead girl's father. The man swung angrily at him. Weatherby ducked and pushed the man against the same wooden garage door that Daly had punched, restraining him as gently, but firmly, as possible.

"I'm sorry, mate. I wasn't laughing because of the death of your daughter. We're in a spot and we need to let off a little steam now and again or we'd all top ourselves. I promise we'll do whatever is humanly possible to get this bastard for you and the families of the other victims."

"Forensics are here, Jimmy," said Daly quietly. Weatherby released the man, who was comforted by the pretty WPC Liaison who had driven the man to the scene, and walked slowly towards the Audi. He sat in the passenger seat and took two deep breaths, his frustration and anger threatening to bubble to the surface. Daly opened the driver's door and planted himself behind the wheel. They sat quietly for a couple of minutes.

"That went well," said Daly with a wry smile. "At least you didn't batter him, mate."

"It was like slow motion, I saw him swing and had time to think that it was his grief attacking me. Can't blame him at all. Anyone else would be needing stitches though. We've got to get this bastard, immortal or not - this has to stop!"


Daly had called Frank later to confirm what they all thought; the little girl was indeed the fourth victim. She had been sliced up in an as yet unknown location and moved to the garage in the dead of night… somehow! The search was now on for the location where she was killed. The police were grasping at straws now, hoping that even the tiniest piece of evidence would lead to where the killer was hiding in between the brutal murders.

**1. June 4th - Simon Linscott, 17, male, Great Elms estate, gutted with? Loc: Alley leading to the Great Elms estate.**
**2. June 9th - Amanda Peabody, 42, female, Blackstone Avenue, strangled. Loc: Copse at top of Berrybush Farm Lane.**
**3. June 19th - Cassius Darwin, 23, male, Unknown address, choked/head trauma. Loc: Woods south end of Kingsford.**
**4. June 21st - Annabel Watts, 8, female, Ash Grove estate, multiple lacerations/ blood loss. Loc: murder scene unknown.**

Daly was called that evening by Alan Jarvis, the police surgeon conducting the post-mortem. The girl had died from asphyxiation, probably in the tent, and was then taken elsewhere to be mutilated. Daly was thankful she was already dead by the time the killer had started to cut at her frail body. Small mercies were a lot better than none. He supposed the killer could not risk disfiguring her in the tent. So where did he take her? The search of the area had drawn a blank. Had he taken her to his place and mutilated her there and then moved on to the garage to dump her? Where the hell was his place? Was the tarpaulin in the garage used to wrap her? If not then surely there should have been a trail of blood to follow from the garage back to the scene of the mutilation. Daly poured himself another large scotch and sat back in his leather armchair, closed his eyes, and tried to put himself in the place of the killer. Try to think like him.

What are the thought processes of a man supposedly two-thousand years old? Were they any different from a modern-day predator? The priority for both is survival, first and foremost, evading capture to carry on killing. He knew that a modern killer would eventually be caught. They would make a mistake or leave evidence or DNA, but his killer had left nothing… ever! Also, if the theory about needing to kill six people was true then what would happen if he couldn't complete the cycle? Would he die? Daly gulped down his drink and refilled the cut crystal glass then sat back again, the soft leather moulding to his contours. He sipped as he thought. He agreed with Frank that Consus had to be destroyed, ended. If he really was immortal it was no good putting him behind bars. Where the hell did he go before he returned a generation later? Another part of the country to lie low? Maybe abroad? No, he'd need a passport for that. Unless he swam the bloody channel. Daly groaned at the thought. Things were bad enough without the immortal having super-human strength and endurance too. Did the man ever get sick or injured? Daly started to doze.

*****

The next day Daly got a call from Jim Anderson, the history professor.

"Hi Gerry, I've been spending a bit of time on this Consus with the help of a friend. Consus did indeed exist. He was a Roman centurion executed for Treason in 62 A.D. The interesting thing is if you go back twenty-two years from 1888 and keep going back, eventually you get to that year which does support the theory that the gaps between the murders have been very consistent and rigid, that's assuming that he was brought back to life in that year too. So let's assume he was, maybe it was only hours or days between his execution and his resurrection. Coming back to life any other year really wouldn't fit the pattern unless it was in 84 A.D. Every single set of murders fits. There will be more years before 1888 too but most records will have been lost for the earlier ones but I'll keep digging. I'll go back each set period and see what I can find from those other years before the Ripper murders. Frank will be a lot of help with that in his spare time too. We can cover the ground in half the time."

"Good work, Jim," said Daly, hoping that they had the time to do the research before the fifth and sixth murders of this cycle occurred. "Keep me up to date with anything significant, cheers mate."


Consus was ecstatic. He'd found out that Frank Kelly was back and living in Kingsford again. He would make absolutely sure that Kelly would be the last victim this time around. He'd found Kelly on the electoral roll, knew he lived alone. Consus had learnt how to use the internet in 1998, just basic things, but 2020 was another dimension to him. He could search for virtually anything he liked. He researched police procedure and detection, forensics, maps of the area. He kept up with the news reports of the case easily, amazed that most of that information was freely available to the news websites. He could even book a taxi, or an Uber, whatever that was, online for his trip back to West Wycombe. He enjoyed the technology of 2020 and wondered just what the future would bring. He fantasised for a moment about travel to the stars but was quickly brought back to earth with the knowledge that he couldn't stray too far from the site of his death at the hands of General Festus, or his cave.

It should be easy to break into Frank's flat and wait for him in a dark corner. Waiting so patiently for him to return home. He'd be able to take his time over this sacrifice, like that woman in Tring last time. Kelly wouldn't escape this attempt. He'd silence him and then go to work. He'd slice off all his extremities then gut him, take his organs out, maybe leave them on the grave of one of his victims from 1976. Yes - Kelly's best friend. That would be a nice touch. Ironic. They may even make the connection between the killings now and the victims back then. There was one more to find before he finally got to Kelly. He could hardly contain his excitement. He knew it was Frank's destiny to end up as a victim, he knew he was drawn to him.


*****


Jim phoned Daly two days later. He told him of some police records he'd found covering a spate of unsolved murders in Beaconsfield in 1844. As always, there were no arrests, but they were apparently very close to catching the killer. He'd somehow escaped after being chased to West Wycombe. Consus had disappeared in the caves there. Jim's information came from a letter sent by Charles Mansbridge, a parish constable at Beaconsfield, to an Inspector William Kense of the Metropolitan Police at Scotland Yard. Jim read the letter to Daly:


*18th September 1844.*
  *Rose Cottage*

  *Jerrold Lane*

  *Beaconsfield*
*Sir,*

*As you know from my previous reports and correspondence, we have no clues as to the* identity or whereabouts of the killer known locally as *The Beaconsfield Butcher*. A name given to him by the locals and not myself, you understand. You already knew of the five murders in this vicinity and I'm saddened to have to report a sixth. A small, nine-year-old girl by the name of Molly Wexham, (The fully documented report will follow this letter in a few days).

We were ever so close to catching him, sir. He was seen taking the life of the poor mite in a lane close to Macken Farm. Several field workers gave chase but he was fleet of foot and the workers weary after a long days toil harvesting. They did manage to keep sight of him in the distance and tracked him to West Wycombe, less than four miles away as the crow flies from the scene of the murder. I had been summoned by a worker sent to inform me. I saddled my horse and gave chase, catching the group of pursuers as they climbed the long hill to the caves. I quickly overtook them and saw the man enter the caves. He was very tall, very gaunt looking. Very pale. He was dressed all in black, blood covered his long fingers. I shouted at him to stop, that there was nowhere to run to, and he turned to me and I have never seen such an evil countenance before in my entire life. His eyes were so dark, almost black, and I don't mind admitting that I was scared by the look of him. I've been a parish constable for nigh on thirty years and this was the first time I'd ever been chilled to the bone by the look of a criminal.

I waited at the entrance until the rest of the chasing party arrived, they had asked an innkeeper in the high street for lanterns as the impending evening would have hindered their search. I intended to go in the caves by myself but thought it best if I had support there with me, especially as I'd seen the man and the look of him. Two of our group guarded the entrance, one with a pitchfork, while the rest of us would search the passages. It was thought there would be no escape for the man. We split into four groups of three men. Each group methodically searched each passage and the various offshoots of them. We intended to drive the man further into the cave system like the rat he was, trap him in there. My group could hear him shuffling away nearby, we knew we would soon have him and I contemplated giving him to the mob to deal with instead of making him stand trial. I know that is not how to administer the law of our country, sir, but feelings were rampant amongst the residents of Beaconsfield and there was always the chance that he wouldn't be convicted - even with the eyewitness testimony of the farmhands of his latest murder.

We were getting closer, our determination driving us ever onward. In the distance, about thirty feet away, there was a slight glow. We thought he may have a lantern of his own. As we neared we saw that it came from a small alcove along the tunnel. The passage had now reached a dead end and the only place he could be now was that small crevice to our right. There was a strange smell coming from the recess, like the charge in the air during a violent thunderstorm in summer. We approached slowly, very cautiously, ready for any attack from the cornered man, like a trapped fox would.

What followed was inexplicable, sir. The glow faded as we entered the alcove, the smell disappearing slowly too, changing to more of a damp odour. The place was empty. There was nowhere to hide but the man was gone. Not even a sign of a lantern. We all looked at each other in disbelief. The expected triumph at catching a mass murderer dropped from our faces like a pebble falling from a high cliff. We were confused and then the sense of fear spread amongst us and we realised that this was no man in the real sense. He was some spirit or supernatural

"It certainly does jibe with the suspicion that he is indeed a supernatural being. It's a shame I haven't found a reply from Kense, " sighed Jim. "Do you fancy a trip to the caves to check them out?"

"Sounds good, I'll leave Weatherby here to hold the fort, maybe go through the files again while we're gone.


Daly picked Jim up from his address in Paddenham around forty minutes later. They drove the twelve miles to West Wycombe and found the caves easily as they were signposted. Parking was difficult on the single track hill and the small car park was full so Daly drove to the top and parked not far away from the Dashwood Mausoleum, finding a level space amongst the deep potholes in the car park there. They walked slowly down the track again, Jim's bulk was not made for aerobic exercise, or even gravity. Eventually, they arrived at the gated entrance to the caves. The main facade and entrance were certainly impressive, maybe fifty feet tall with arches like a cathedral. It was flanked by two high stone walls, the left hand one housing a small shop where you could buy tickets, guide books, postcards and also various refreshments. There were around twenty white plastic chairs set around small round tables and large sun umbrellas to provide a little shade during the hot summer for those drinking tea, coffee and soft drinks or indulging in an ice cream. Half the chairs were already taken. A coach had arrived while they had been walking back from the Mausoleum and a group of foreign tourists, German by the sound of them, had occupied the seats while their tour guide was buying their tickets.

Daly and Jim queued behind the coach tour guide waiting to pay for their own entrance. Daly could have flashed his police I.D. and got them in for free but as this part of the investigation was off the books he decided not to and paid for them both. They exited the shop and saw the tour guide was still trying to organise her German charges so took the opportunity to dart into the entrance first so they wouldn't be stuck behind a bunch of babbling foreigners.

They squeezed through the turnstile, Jim was struggling due to his size and virtually climbed over while a huge trailing leg rotated the bar of the turnstile with a heavy clunk. After a few yards of a dimly lit, arched tunnel, their feet were crunching on the chalky gravel floor. There was a small caged alcove to their right with a sign saying 'Tool Store'. A mannequin of a man seated at a table was sat quietly in there. Daly thought it looked a little creepy. They took a sharp left and followed the path. Plenty of information on the caves, the legends and the people associated with the Hellfire Club were on plaques on the chalk walls every few yards. There was another small cave to their right before they approached 'The Circle'. Two paths branching off from each other and meeting again according to the cave map that was on the wall. Daly took the left branch and Jim the right. They emerged a minute later, nothing much to be seen there apart from some creepy looking faces carved into the short tunnels. They carried on down the slight descent towards 'Franklin's Cave'. They moved on to 'The Banqueting Hall', a well-lit cavern with a great domed ceiling. There were even more caged exhibits of scenes from the past, more creepy mannequins. At 'The Triangle' they each took a branch and met again on the other side. Two more large exhibits were situated at 'The River Styx' and 'The Inner Temple. There was nothing in the whole cave system that had any connection with the killer, Consus, as far as they could see.

On their reverse journey, they stumbled upon a narrow tunnel to their right, it must have been concealed by a shadow when they had approached from the opposite direction. The walkway was too constricted for Jim to get down so Daly investigated alone. It was pitch dark so he used the flashlight on his phone to illuminate the way along the narrow tunnel. After a few slight twists and turns, he came to a dead end with a small cave to his right. *This must be the one mentioned in the letter Mansbridge sent to Kense,* he thought. Daly nearly choked on the smell of damp earth and moss, mixed with something he couldn't quite put his finger on. He noticed a strange greying beige patch on the opposite wall. It looked very smooth and out of place compared to the rough chalk walls of the other parts of the cave system. He ran his fingers along the patch and was surprised that it was slightly warm which should have been impossible that far underground and deep into the chalk system. He touched the wall to his left. Stone cold as it should be. He took several pictures on his phone and, after checking they were captured properly, made his way out of the small alcove and through to passage back to Jim, glad to be out of that particular recess. He was not normally claustrophobic but that alcove gave him the shivers. It didn't feel right to him.

Outside again in the fresh air, Daly told Jim to wait there while he got the car. It would be a lot easier than have to witness Jim puffing and panting up the hill and possibly keeling over from a heart attack too. He almost reached the car when he saw a dark shape watching him from the woods next to the church. Daly decided to check it out. He moved quickly along the path to the graveyard, his eyes scanning over the tops of the stones there. It would be easy for someone to hide behind the old granite markers. He did walk along several rows of graves but saw nothing else. Daly laughed at himself for even thinking the dark shape was even Consus and he'd be able to apprehend the killer as easily as that. Life, and also policing, wasn't that simple.

Daly skirted around the outside of the mausoleum on his way back to the rutted car park. It certainly was an impressive structure. The church behind it was a bit strange though. Who the hell had the bright idea to put a big golden ball on top of it? He walked slowly back to the car and took one last look over his shoulder at the graves, hoping to see more movement. He thought that anything he saw now would be his own imagination playing tricks on him. Inside the car, he started the engine and sped away to pick Jim up. Loose gravel and dust flying in his wake. He took one last look at the churchyard in the rear view mirror and saw nothing. Jim was standing patiently opposite the gates to the cavern. *Just as well he didn't climb the hill,* Daly thought, the giant professor looked exhausted just standing up in the heat. Daly stopped the car next to him and Jim squeezed himself into the passenger seat of the Audi with a loud groan. *Don't you dare die in my bloody car, I need you,* Daly silently pleaded.

They quickly returned to Jim's house back in Paddenham and transferred the pictures from Daly's phone onto Jim's PC. Jim loaded the files into Photoshop and played with a few settings, trying to enhance the shadowy images.

"Any idea what that patch was, Gerry?" asked the professor. "It looks like it doesn't belong there."

"It was weird. It looked like a bad plastering job but it wasn't plaster. And it felt warm to the touch too, that shouldn't even be possible unless there was some sort of heat source behind it."

"Hell itself?" joked Jim.

"Christ, I hope not, we've got enough on our plate, Jim," said Daly. "Talking of which, have you got anything to eat in the place?"

"I can order pizza if you're sticking around for a while," smiled Jim, his mouth already watering at the thought of all that cheese, pepperoni, and spicy beef.

Jim opened his right hand desk drawer and pulled out a wad of takeaway menus and then went to the kitchen to make coffee while Daly chose his pizza. Daly wondered if Jim ever cooked more than a cuppa soup, pot noodle or garlic bread. He chose a fifteen-inch meat feast thinking he'd be stuffed halfway through and could take some back with him for Weatherby and then almost choked on his black coffee when Jim picked up the phone and ordered three of the same size for himself, an American Hot, a Pepperoni Passion and a seafood one with everything bar the Loch Ness Monster on it. Jim said there would be a forty-minute wait for the delivery so they got back to studying the images of the hidden cave.

"It looks like it *was* the small cave Mansbridge had found. He mentions in his letter a smell that I picked up on immediately," said Daly. "It was a sort of dank dampness but something underneath too, like ozone. I just don't get the connection."

"Let's break it down a bit," said Jim. "We have a small cave, part of the Hellfire Cave system, but apparently unknown to most people. There is no mention of it in any guide to the caves, no one who has ever made a documentary or put anything up on Youtube has ever found it or at least hasn't reported its existence. In that cave we have a smell, both yourself and this Mansbridge chap say it's a mixture of damp and ozone. Consus somehow disappeared in that cave when he was followed by Mansbridge's group. Frank says Consus told him he has to kill to return in some sort of cycle. He repeats his series of kills and then disappears for a set number of years which, looking back at all the cases is twenty-two. Why twenty-two? That is the big mystery to me. Why not twenty, or fifty or one hundred years? What is the significance of twenty-two? That really is the intriguing aspect to all this for me. If we can find out why it's that number then maybe we can work out a way to end this."

"Why that particular cave too?" added Daly. "Was that cave well known in his time as being unusual or did he find it by accident? What is so different about that cave? Was he dumped there after his execution? What is that smooth patch on the wall?"

"Sounds like science fiction to me but what if the cave is some sort of portal? No, hear me out, Gerry," said Jim as Daly raised his eyebrows at the statement. "Not to another world or dimension because he keeps returning to that spot, but a type of storage area where he regenerates after his kills. Maybe the acts of murder take so much from him that he has to hide away and recuperate before he returns?"

"Doesn't make sense, Jim," said Daly. "If taking these lives depletes his energy then why kill at all? He's apparently immortal, right? What is stopping him just leading a normal life without the killings and moving on every couple of decades when people start to notice he isn't ageing like everyone else? Turn it around and think what he gets from the kills?"

"You mean every time he murders someone he takes something from his victims? Their souls? Something else? Like a vampire but instead of blood he takes their life force? Then after the sixth, he hides away in this storage place and what? Processes that life force so he can return to begin again in another generation?"

"Sounds a bit X-Files to me, mate," sighed Daly. "It's all fantasy without any proof, just a theory. We're not Einstein you know. You've got a doctorate in history, mine's in catching scumbags… real ones, and not some bloody immortal, supernatural serial killer. How the hell do we stop something like him?"

The doorbell rang.

"Time for a break, it feels like I haven't eaten in days," Jim grinned. Daly rolled his eyes.


While Jim was polishing off all three of his pizzas, Daly gave Frank a call and filled him in on the pair's trip to the caves. Frank said he had an hour to spare and would come over to view the pictures of the hidden alcove. He arrived twenty minutes later and finished off Daly's leftover pizza for him while looking at the enhanced images. He'd lived near the caves most of his life and had visited half a dozen times but the passage to the strange opening came as a bit of a shock.

"I had no idea it was there," said Frank. "But this Constable Mansbridge did according to this letter, and so did his superiors, or at least Kense did. I'm amazed it is still such a secret. Why do you think this sort of information was suppressed, Gerry?"

"I think it was two things," answered Daly. "Firstly, the failure to capture the murderer. There was that initial embarrassment, especially as they were so close. Then you have the supernatural element of his disappearance, there was no way Scotland Yard would admit to such a thing. This is a private letter and not an official police report."

"No wonder Mansbridge was a lowly constable for thirty years. People like him would be blamed for the failure, they needed a scapegoat. I wonder how long he lasted in the job after this," said Frank.

"Who knows? They were a lot more dedicated to their communities back then. He probably stuck it out until he retired or died," said Daly.

"I've got a friend who is a Ripperologist," said Jim to Daly and Frank enthusiastically. "Maybe he can offer some help?"

"Those blokes are all nutters, Jim," laughed Daly, "Bloody obsessed, the lot of them. How could he possibly help?"

"He probably knows more about the Whitechapel killings than anyone in the country," replied Jim. "There could be something we've missed or not freely available on the internet."

"Okay, if you think it's worth a shot," admitted Daly. "You get on with that. I've got things to do back at the nick."

Frank stayed for a coffee and a chat, interested in hearing about the Ripperologist. Daly left them to it, wondering if Jim would order more food. He liked the professor a lot but he was a heart attack on legs if he didn't control his eating.


Daly chuckled to himself on the drive back to Watford. Ripperologist? He'd been on one of those Ripper tours in Whitechapel. A short, fat bloke dressed like Sherlock Holmes leading a group of gullible tourists around the various locations of the murders in the dead of night and charging fifty quid a pop. Not many facts and a lot of theorising about the identity of the killer. The chief suspect at the time was someone called Tumblety, he remembered. Before that, it was some Royal. The guide would shit himself if he knew what Daly knew. A Roman centurion. None of these so-called 'experts' would have worked that out in a million years.

It was fairly quiet for the next few days, the heat was stifling in the office Daly shared with Weatherby. They went over all the extensive reports and statements yet again, finding nothing new. He was reminded of the father of the first victim, George Linscott. Daly was convinced the man was a wrong 'un. Something definitely off about the man. He didn't know what and really didn't have the time to look into him further. He was pretty sure Linscott wasn't the killer. Couldn't really imagine him tackling the burglar in the woods and cracking his head open. He wasn't the type for violence in his opinion. But there *was* something dodgy about him.

*****

Jim Anderson picked up his phone. He was excited, ecstatic. This was just unbelievable. An amazing connection - or was it a coincidence? Can't be! He dialled Frank's number.

"Frank, it's Jim. Have you got a few minutes?"

"I'm on my break, waiting for a job," replied Frank. "What can I do for you, Jim?"

"How much do you know about your ancestry?" asked Jim.

"Well, my mum was born and bred in Kingsford. Her lot go back centuries around here, so she told me," he said. "My dad came from a fishing village called Moville in County Donegal, I've still got family over there in Ireland as far as I know, but we sort of lost touch a few years ago. That's all I know about his side of the family really."

"Fit's perfectly," said Jim.

"What do you mean?" asked Frank.

"I'm sure you've done your own research into Consus' victims, haven't you?"

"As much as I could find."

"Of course, but the most information is about the most famous case, isn't it?" prompted Jim.

"Well yes, the Ripper killings in 1888 obviously."

"I've got this Ripperologist friend, Alex McArthur, probably knows more than anyone in the country. He's virtually dedicated his life to the Ripper case. He does tours in Whitechapel dressed like Sherlock Holmes."

"He sounds mental," joked Frank.

"He's a nice chap actually, and very thorough in his research," said Jim. "So what do you know about the last victim in 1888, Frank?"

"She was the only one killed indoors, as far as the canonical victims go. The Ripper really took his time with her, disgusting mutilation by the look of the grainy pictures I've seen in books and on the internet. Mary Jane Kelly. His sixth victim before he disappeared again. Are you saying she was an ancestor, Jim?"

"Exactly, you are descended from her, Frank," enthused Jim.

"How? She lived alone, unmarried, according to records, just a common prostitute trying to survive in Victorian London. She came from Limerick apparently. She was only twenty-five when she was murdered."

"You are absolutely right, Frank," said Jim. "What you haven't uncovered about her, and my friend has, is that she had a child at the age of fourteen, a boy, who was taken in by her sister and Mary moved away in disgrace. The sister wasn't married but after she migrated away from Limerick she had pretended to be a widow with a young child, but still kept the name Kelly. She eventually settled in Moville further north, where your family on your dad's side come from. The boy grew up, got married, and had a family, and was working on the fishing boats until his death from drowning in 1903. He was your great-grandfather, Frank, and he was called George."

"Bloody hell!" said a shocked Frank. "Is it really true what your man says?"

"I believe him and it gets even stranger, Frank."

"How can it get stranger? Surely it's just coincidence?"

"There's more, Frank, a lot more."

"George produced two sons, Michael and Sean. Michael stayed in Moville, he was your grandfather. Sean moved to London, Kilburn in fact, had a son and a daughter. The daughter was married to a man called Wilson. Their young daughter, Jane, was a victim of Consus in 1932."

"Jesus!" said Frank," shock starting to overcome him. "Consus murdered two of my family line?"

"Three. Wilson's son, Arthur, eventually went to live in Hastings. He was a victim too, Frank."

"So, in 1888 he kills Mary Kelly, Jane Wilson in 1932 and Arthur in 1954, all related and connected to me. And I was an intended victim in 1976 until Gerry's dad saved me. This is unreal, Jim."

"He does seem drawn to your family is some strange way, Frank. I hate to say this, but where are your children?" asked Jim.

"Luckily they still live in Scotland near the ex-wife."

"That's a relief," said Jim. "Scotland seems out of reach to him. He hasn't really ventured much further north than Buckingham as far as I can tell, like he's somehow tied to a small area, maybe even the location of his death?"

"Doesn't mean that my kids or grandkids or even further down the line won't move nearer to here in the future! We've got to stop him, Jim. How the hell does he know some of his victims are descended from Mary? It doesn't make any sense!" said Frank, thinking of his estranged family for the first time in months.

"It's like he's drawn to them like a magnet somehow," said Jim. "I can't even guess how."

"So why only one from the family line in each of those years? Why didn't he kill Sean and his wife at the same time as Jane? Why does he wait another twenty-two years to kill Arthur?" asked Frank, confused.

"I can only imagine that several members of the same family at the same time would have been investigated a lot more closely by the police, especially with the Irish connection. Jane would just have been viewed as a victim of the serial killer in 1932. She wasn't the first victim then, easier to cover up the connection. Same with Arthur in 1954, the fourth one of that series in Hastings."

"But why my family?"

"Maybe something happened while he was mutilating Mary in her room in Miller's Court? Something we may never know."

"It's so bloody crazy, Jim," said Frank. "And you are right - we may never know. I doubt even Consus knows why."


*****


Arlyne Braughton was walking home alone from the pub after it shut early at ten. It was rare for her to be on her own as she was the sort of promiscuous teen who usually had a bloke in tow, sometimes more than one. She was sixteen and had left school a few weeks previously. She had hated school but she hated having no job and no money even more. Blokes would always buy her drinks in the pub but she needed money for other stuff, the things all her mates were buying for themselves when they would hang about in town, trailing from shop to shop and trying on clothes or browsing the makeup aisles at Boots or the cut-price CDs at the failing local music store. Going out clubbing too. She was starting to feel a bit left out. She had had no interest at school while she was there, she left with no qualifications because she didn't even turn up for her exams. She thought she could be a model or a singer but she wasn't that good looking and couldn't really carry a tune either. Her parents were always on at her to do better. Nag, nag, nag! That was when they weren't fighting with each other. Arlyne couldn't wait to leave home. She hoped that one of her friends would offer to put her up for a while but it never happened, despite the numerous hints she kept dropping. Some bloody friends they were. She'd be better off without them. Maybe she should just disappear for a while, see if anyone cared about her.

She needed to find a job soon or she may end up on the game. The fifty quid a week she got in income support from the government didn't last very long and she was forced to do a bloody boring training scheme as well. Typing and Word Processing. It was like being back at school and she hated it but if she didn't do it they would stop her money for a few months. The Job Centre made her apply for all sorts of crap jobs like shop work too. She would hate standing around all day in a newsagent selling fags and dirty mags to smelly old men for minimum wage. But she needed something! She was too young to drive and couldn't afford the lessons anyway, let alone get the money to buy a car or even rent a van to deliver parcels. Life wasn't looking too sweet for her at the moment, she thought. Arlyne walked slowly along the footpath between the new doctor's surgery and the playground. The cooling night air was beginning to nip at her bare arms and legs. She thought the heatwave was beginning to come to an end. There was a rustle in the bushes opposite the playground. Maybe a cat out for the last few minutes before being called in by its owners?

"Here puss," she whispered. "Are you looking for a mouse to take home for mummy?" She laughed at how evil cats could be to their owners. She'd had one herself before it died a couple of years ago. It was always bringing in headless birds. Disgusting! Where did they leave the heads?

The rustling continued, a little more insistent now. She moved closer to the tall browning foliage. The rustling came from higher up. The stupid cat was trying to climb up now, she thought. Was there a bird's nest in there it was trying to reach? She moved closer to the bushes and parted them with her hands and saw a pallid face staring back at her. She froze. A massive hand quickly shot out and took her by the throat and then pulled her into the growth, still thick despite the hot weather over the never-ending summer. She couldn't scream, could hardly breathe with the large, gloved hand squeezing her neck so forcefully. The man brought his face towards her, their noses almost touching. She could smell his foul breath. His eyes narrowed slightly as he grinned evilly at her. She stared into his cold, black eyes, finally realising what was happening to her and who the man was. It was *that* man, the killer. The red mist started to ooze from her, fairly bright even in the moonlight and then she knew. Knew that she would not survive the attack. Her last thoughts were if she would be missed by anyone, even her parents. She very much doubted it as her short, lonely life ebbed away in the dark.

Consus had greedily breathed in the red vapour and let the body drop to his feet, one of the girl's arms snagged on a lone thorn bush, tiny beads of blood appearing and then eventually gravity took hold and they ran down to her elbow and dripped onto the dirt floor. He exited the bushes from the other side and onto a football field, the areas around the goalmouths bare earth from the almost constant use during the long, hot summer. He crossed the pitch to the lane running uphill into the high street. At almost eleven-thirty he knew there would be very little traffic running through the village and could safely walk to the rented house and rest. There was no one on the streets as the police had deemed a curfew was necessary for the pubs in the area. Just one more victim to go. It would definitely be Frank Kelly this time. He would make sure of it. The unfinished business between them was almost over for good.

*****

Thirteen-year-old Colin Walker was playing football with his mates. The tall, blond-haired boy was in goal and had just made yet another world-class save… according to him. The ball had flown from his outstretched hand over the crossbar and had looped into the dense bushes behind the goal. His friends jeered as he celebrated keeping the ball out again with a beaming smile. One day he hoped to be playing for Arsenal, or maybe even a good team. Colin jogged over to the dense bushes to retrieve the ball, eager to get on with the game. He gingerly pushed his way in, trying to avoid any thorns or sharp twigs and saw the girl lying there, eyes open and mouth pulled into a silent scream. He shouted to his mates that he'd found a dead body, the panic in his voice told them he wasn't joking around, plus the fact a serial killer was roaming around and they were all being careful where they went and made sure they were never alone when they went out, even during daylight hours.

They all sprinted to where Colin had entered the bushes, trying to push their way in to get a look at the victim. Every one of them soon had their phone out and were taking pictures of the girl while Colin was staggering out from the scene. Shaky, but still thinking clearly, he used his own phone to call the police. He knew that normally the police got a lot of hoax calls, he'd even made a few himself when he was younger, but he was confident that a body found in Kingsford would get their immediate attention. 2020 had been a strange and terrifying year for the locals. Everyone was scared for their families and themselves. He'd recognised the girl from the brief sight he'd had of her. She was two or three years above him at his school, he thought she had possibly left that summer. The girl looked a lot different when not in uniform, more grown-up. She wouldn't be growing any older, he thought sadly.

Daly and Weatherby arrived at the scene and knew that time was running out. This was certainly the fifth victim and the chances of getting to Consus was now a lot slimmer. A couple of Plods were standing guard and they both pulled the bushes to the side so that Daly could get a better look at the crime scene. The girl was deathly white, the look of sheer panic on her face told him that she was understandably terrified at the moment of death. He could see the dark marks on her throat indicating another strangulation. *Why the hell don't these people learn?* He shook his head at the thought. Everyone had been warned not to go anywhere alone, especially at night. He supposed the folly of youth made them think they were all immune, safe from bad things ever happening to them. They were wrong - bad things could happen to anyone, at *any* age.

"SOCO should be here in about ten minutes, guv," said Weatherby, taking his phone away from his ear and putting it in his trouser pocket. The heat of the day was beginning to rise and both Daly and Weatherby had removed their jackets and discarded them in the car, left a hundred yards away in the car park outside the new doctor's surgery.

"I just wish they could give us something new. This guy is very good at what he does, he's well practised over the years. How the hell does a Roman soldier know what we'd be looking for now and how does he avoid leaving clues for us?" replied Daly. "I even considered he could read our minds the other night."

"It's all those factual TV shows on now, I reckon. True life crimes, re-enactments, detailed forensic examinations, it's all there for anyone to see. He must be a fan of them, he's learning more and more as he goes along. No fingerprints, no DNA, no secretions or hair samples. He's a bright boy, our killer."

"If he is as old as we think he is just imagine what he has learnt, what he's experienced. He's certainly good at adapting to his new surroundings. It would take a lot of intelligence to go unnoticed by everyone. Zero witnesses apart from Frank back in 1976, and he was lucky to survive," said Daly.

"We don't even know for sure that he looks the same as back then," sighed Weatherby.

"Frank said to my dad and a local Plod that the man was a dead ringer for Bela Lugosi but a lot taller. It's in the report from '76. I think if he were a normal man he'd develop a streak of arrogance after getting away with so many murders. Make mistakes. He'd almost have a wish to get caught to experience the fame and recognition of what he'd done. They want to go down in history like Bundy or Dahmer. Some even taunted the investigators like that Dennis Rader in the US, the BTK killer. They make mistakes, either by their own stupidity or their arrogance. I think our man is very different. He's very careful, very meticulous. He wants to continue this. He enjoys it so much now he never wants it to end."

Daly called Frank to inform him of the latest killing after they had identified the body of the teenage girl as sixteen year-old Arlyne Braughton, another local. They both knew that time was running out but left it unsaid. Frank suggested offering himself as bait to catch the killer but Daly obviously rejected the idea. Frank told him that now was the time for drastic action, one more murder and Consus disappears for another twenty-two years. Daly knew he was under pressure and needed to catch the man. He also knew that Frank had a valid point, despite the risk. So far the killings have been under the control of Consus. His choice of victim, *his* decision where and when. Daly could see the advantage of setting a trap for Consus, controlling the circumstances himself. It was just *too* risky though. If it went wrong there would be another death, Consus would get away again and he'd be finished as a copper. The only thing he was ever good at. Pretty much his life. He thought about using himself as the bait but the same thought gnawed at him. Consus had failed to kill Frank twice. Was he looking for his revenge and saving Frank for last anyway? It seemed very plausible, especially with the family connection that Jim had found. Daly told Frank he'd need to think about a plan of action to lure Consus out. He wished there was another way rather than using Frank as bait.

Frank took out his old, battered notebook from the drawer in his bedroom, his hand trembling slightly as he added to the list of victims.

**1. June 4th - Simon Linscott, 17, male, Great Elms estate, gutted with? Loc: Alley leading to the estate.**
**2. June 9th - Amanda Peabody, 42, female, Blackstone Avenue, strangled. Loc: Copse at top of Berrybush Farm Lane.**
**3. June 19th - Cassius Darwin, 23, male, Unknown address, choked/head trauma. Loc: Woods south end of Kingsford.**
**4. June 21st - Annabel Watts, 8, female, Ash Grove estate, multiple lacerations/ blood loss. Loc: murder scene unknown.**
**5. July 9th - Arlyne Braughton, 16, female, Ayreton Road, strangulation. Loc: Cypress Estate playing fields.**

He returned the green notebook to the drawer, lay on his bed and closed his eyes. He had to convince Daly to let him draw Consus out. If only there was a way to contact the killer and goad him into taking action. There must be some way. He was sure if they failed to catch Consus then Frank's name would be last on the list. But who would complete his list for him if he died?

*****

Weatherby called Daly early the next morning.

"We may have a witness, guv," said the sergeant.

"Who?" replied Daly, still trying to shake off the haze of a hangover sat at his kitchen table with a large, black coffee.

"A little old lady called Emily Raft, she was looking out of her bedroom window which overlooks the playing field. She saw a man walking a dog."

"That's not unusual," said Daly, trying to focus.

"She said he was acting a bit funny, in and out of the bushes, acting very suspiciously."

"Okay, send a Plod over for a description," said Daly.

"No need, she said she knows him." Daly could hear the smile in Weatherby's voice.

"Got a name?"

"George Linscott," replied Weatherby.

"The father of the first victim? Jesus, I knew there was something up with him. I'll pick you up in half an hour, Jimmy. We'll have a chat with our Mr. Linscott."

"Right, guv."

Daly questioned whether he was wrong to dismiss Linscott as a suspect too quickly. He'd heard of killers murdering a series of victims to cover up the killing of one of their own family before, but never the first victim. That just draws the initial suspicion to them. Third, fourth, or the last is more usual. No, he still didn't think their man was Linscott but he may have seen something. Linscott seemed too timid to be a killer. But then so was John Christie of Rillington Place infamy. He prayed this would lead to something, anything.

The black Audi arrived on the Great Elms estate just before ten. The media were no longer camped outside the Linscott house, they had already moved on to the family of the latest victim, Arlyne Braughton. Daly may not think Linscott was his killer but he was certainly up to something. He hoped dearly Linscott had seen something walking his dog but held back so as not to reveal what he was up to the evening of the girl's murder. Weatherby rang the doorbell and Mrs. Linscott opened the door, she was dressed in a baggy grey tracksuit favoured by frumpy middle-aged women. It was partially covered by a giant plastic apron with a large cow's face on.

"Inspector! I was just baking cakes. Can't seem to get enough of them since Simon died. Keeps me busy too. Otherwise, my mind wanders back to that awful day, come on in."

"Is your husband in?" asked Daly.

"George? Yes, he's still in bed, I'll give him a shout, shall I?" she said, slightly suspiciously.

"That would be great, Mrs. Linscott, thank you," smiled Daly, giving nothing away to the woman.

She trudged up the stairs and Daly could hear a groan and a muffled conversation. He wished he could make out the faint words. She reappeared a few moments later and told Daly that Linscott would be down as soon as he dressed and had a wash. She offered to make tea for the pair of detectives while they waited in the front room. While in the kitchen she opened the back door and a black Labrador bounded in and headed straight for the two policemen excitedly, tail wagging uncontrollably and slobbering all over them.

"If only you could talk, mate," Daly whispered to the dopey old dog, wiping his wet hand on a handkerchief.

They could hear Linscott shuffle down the stairs. He walked slowly into the front room and sat in his usual chair, a cup of tea was waiting for him in a mug that bore the legend: 'Busier than a cucumber in a women's prison'. Daly almost laughed aloud but needed his serious copper face on to question Linscott.

"Morning Mr. Linscott, , just a couple of questions for you, can you tell me where you were last night?"

"Err... nowhere really, walked the dog, I suppose," said Linscott nervously.

"What time was that?"

"Around ten, I think, inspector."

"Where did you walk the dog?" asked Daly.

"Normally all sorts of places, don't want to get bored you see. Last night was near the new doctor's surgery," said Linscott, now more visibly nervous."

"That's near the playing fields on the Cypress Estate, isn't it?" asked the detective.

"Yes, that's right. Look, what is all this about?" asked Linscott, even more worried.

"Another body was found this morning, a girl walking home was murdered and left in the bushes next to the playing fields," said Daly quietly, looking for any reaction from the man.

"Oh my God, that's terrible," said Linscott. "I hope you don't think I had anything to do with it?" Daly watched him very closely.

"You were seen in the area before she was murdered, so I'm just following up all leads at this point. Did you see anyone else when you were walking?"

"Just a couple of locals, more dog walkers, I suppose, maybe a few kids." Linscott raised his mug with trembling hands and took a sip and winced, the tea still too hot for him. He put it back down on a coaster on the table next to him.

"So no one out of place?" asked Daly.

"No, just the usual people really."

"What were you doing ducking in and out of the bushes several times?" asked Weatherby, right on cue, switching the attack.

Linscott began to look very uncomfortable. It was now clear to him that they knew something of his activities. The sergeant slipped that question in as he was beginning to relax. He had to confess.

"Jeannie, do me a favour and nip down to the shop for some fags, I'm out," Linscott asked his wife.

"Why can't you go yourself later, I'm baking!" she replied.

"Because I'm gagging for one and these detectives are still talking to me."

"Bloody hell! Alright, but you pay for them," she snapped at him.

Linscott took a crumpled ten-pound note from his wallet and handed it to her.

"Keep the change, buy yourself a cake or something," he scowled.

"Very funny!" She glowered at him as she took off her apron and hung it on a hook on the back of the kitchen door and then stormed out of the house.

"I take it you have something you want to tell me, Mr. Linscott? Something you don't want your wife hearing," said Daly with the sympathetic smile he gave to everyone when he knew they had something to get off their chest. Weatherby resumed taking notes for the time being, happy his direct prompt worked as planned.

"Err… well, yes. I didn't kill that girl, I want you to know that straight off! None of the others either. I didn't even see her last night." Linscott started to sweat, a drop running down the side of his face.

"The bushes?" cajoled Daly patiently.

"Oh, God. I'm not a bad person, I swear. Only… I watch people. Women. A lot of them go to bed around that time and some don't close their curtains. I suppose you think I'm a pervert, don't you?" Linscott was beginning to quietly sob.

"So you're a Peeping Tom? Is that it?" asked Daly.

"Yes! I wouldn't do anything to them, I wouldn't hurt them, honest. I just watch them!"

Daly rose from the armchair. Weatherby put his notebook back in his jacket pocket and quickly followed suit.

"I suggest you do your best to give up your little 'hobby', said Daly. "It's lucky for you I'm investigating a serious crime, a spate of killings which includes your own son, Mr. Linscott! Back in the day, some coppers in my position would drag you in and beat a confession out of you for the murders just on the evidence of you being in the area. Behave yourself in future because If I hear you've been spotted again I'll inform one of my colleagues. I doubt you want to be on the Sex Offenders Register, do you?"

"No, definitely not, thank you, Mr. Daly. I promise I won't do it again."

Daly and his sergeant left. Both frustrated that the interview with Linscott didn't lead to more than a confession from a pervert. They got into the Audi just as Mrs. Linscott was returning from the shops looking slightly worried.

*****

Gerry Daly was called to the Met. The Assistant Chief Constable, Winston Richards, wanted to see him urgently.

"Time is running out, Gerry," said the tall black man. "Five murders and not a lot of progress as far as I can see."

"I believe these killings are linked to the 1976 murders," said Daly, hoping the ACC would give him more time based on the link. He hoped Richards would at least listen to the possibility and not replace him just yet. There was plenty going on that Daly couldn't reveal. How could he confess he believed an immortal Roman was responsible for the killings?

"Did you know I eventually took over the 1976 cases?" Daly nodded. He'd been through every inch of the files from that year several times. "Paddy Mallen was a good man and a bloody fine detective, the best I've known, but it was all too much for him in the end. Maybe he got stale or maybe it was just his drinking? I don't want you to end up in that state, Gerry. Tell me what you know."

Daly decided to tell the ACC half the truth. If he told him everything they'd found he'd be off the case immediately. No enquiry from the brass - just gone.

"Well, we believe the cases are linked with a group of murders in Tring in 1998 and possibly other years before 1976. Possibly a cult," he lied.

"I remember the Tring case. I was involved in that too but Superintendent Evans personally took charge. Probably thought a result for him would mean the top job and a bloody knighthood. He was always was a bloody glory hunter. I could see the possibility of a connection but there was no evidence, and that's what we have to work by, no mad theories, Gerry. There was a tip from some nutter come down from Scotland screaming that the two killing sprees were linked but no one really took him seriously."

"Maybe they should have listened? That 'nutter' was Frank Kelly, the boy my dad saved in '76."

"Christ, I never knew his name, said Daly's superior. "If I did he would at least have been interviewed. You know how many nutters try to associate themselves with big cases, attention seekers, needy losers mostly."

"I know, but in this case, he's been a big help. He's been a sort of unofficial consultant working with me on this. His knowledge of what happened in '76 is invaluable to us and he feels he owes me for my dad sacrificing himself to save him."

"Okay, you've bought yourself a bit more time Gerry, and in light of this information you've presented I have something that may help, something that wasn't and will never be part of the official police reports, understand?"

Daly nodded and was certainly intrigued as Richards rose stiffly and went to the filing cabinet in the corner of his office. He pulled a ring of keys from his pocket and inserted the smallest one into the lock. He opened the top drawer and flipped through some files then returned with a two-page letter, the pages stapled together at the corner, it was wrinkled as if it had been screwed up and thrown away and then later retrieved.

"This is from my personal files, Gerry. Maybe one day I'll write a book like your mate Mason. This was from Mallen. I got this a few years before he died." He handed Daly the rumpled pages. He read slowly and silently until the end of the second page.




*I don't like how you replaced me on the Kingsford murders but do accept why the brass made the change. In my heart of hearts, I knew we would never catch the killer but I'll get to why in a moment. These are my own thoughts and never said a word to Carter about them. Carter is a good lad and him buying into my theory would hinder him in his career. He's destined for the top, hopefully even higher than me, but doesn't have your advantage of being a box ticker when it comes to advancement. Look after him and he'll be as invaluable to you as he was to me.*

*After Danny Daly was butchered and there was still no evidence, I knew that this killer wasn't flesh and blood in the normal sense. Maybe he was a demon or a ghost or something, but I felt he wasn't a man! I know that to the bottom of the soul I would have gladly sold to catch him. I don't know if you are religious or anything or even believe in the supernatural. It's all part and parcel of being a good Catholic to believe. Absolute faith in what can't be proven by us mere mortals. If you are any sort of a copper you'll have come across things you can't explain too. Maybe you've shrugged them off as coincidence or a fluke or maybe they've gnawed at you for years as they did me? Maybe that hasn't happened to you yet, but it will.*

*Look back at my record in Ireland, both north and south. Plenty of cases where a lot of things were never explained, especially out in the countryside and even in towns. Look at the cases in and around Derry in particular. But how the hell can you put those things in an official report? The truth is you can't or you'd be booted off the force very quickly.*

*Many things in that spate of killings didn't make sense to any of us. We found absolutely no evidence whatsoever. How many cases have you seen like that? No witnesses apart from the Kelly boy. The one Danny sacrificed himself for. I'm sure that kid was deliberately targeted by the killer. There's no other explanation for it. He'd seen the killer previously and had to be silenced even though the killer would have assumed he'd already given a description, but I was sure there was another reason. That's why I had Daly follow him. Danny died because of my decisions but we just didn't have the manpower to send anyone else. Danny was part of my team and I feel guilty as hell. Christ, he has a son who is just a toddler! He'll never really know his father and I hope to God he never finds out exactly how he died. That was the worst day of my career, no, my life, and I never got the chance to catch that bastard. I've confessed my crime. How I let Danny down, and have been absolved by a priest and by God but I just can't forgive myself for his death.*

*I should have written to you long before now and maybe you'd have caught him. There's no chance now as he's gone to wherever he hides. I know he WILL kill again. I don't know where or when but trust this advice for when he does: Don't look on him as a man. He is not. Get him, Richards. For ALL his victims dead or alive, especially Danny's wife and boy.*

"Jesus," said Daly, a tear forming in his eye. "Mallen knew something was really off. He just couldn't make something like that official. Maybe, as he wrote, it would have helped if he'd sent you that letter days after he was taken off the case and not years afterwards. After the killer had disappeared."

"I showed you this because I thought if you got inside Mallen's head it would help you. I know you think this cult stuff you told me is bullshit and you only told me that because *you* believe there is a supernatural element to this too. I can see it in your eyes, Gerry. You've got the same haunted look Mallen had when I replaced him. It destroyed him. Don't let it do the same to you, for Christ's sake. Don't let one of your lads end up the same way as your father.

I can put you on another case if you want, there are plenty of other detectives who are struggling and maybe fresh eyes will help with those cases? I'm giving you the chance to walk away from this, with your head held high and your mind intact. If you want to, Gerry. But I already know your answer, don't I? You want this man, this thing or whatever. But you have to understand you are on your own. I can't help or back you up any more than I have. It's my nuts on the chopping block if I don't pull you off this case in the next week or so, another ten days tops. Use that time to find the killer, Gerry."

"Understood," Daly said as he rose and left the office, knowing he needed to think and act fast. Maybe using Frank as bait really was the only option he had left?

*****

Daly got an urgent call from Jim to come round.

"I think I found something significant," enthused the big professor.

"What have you got?" asked the detective.

"It will be easier to show you, can you spare thirty minutes, Gerry?"

"There was another killing last night but I can leave Weatherby here to supervise. I'll be there in about twenty minutes," Daly said as he ended the call. He gave Weatherby his instructions, told him he'd fill him in on Jim's news when he returned, and then quickly drove to Jim's house in Paddenham, his mind racing. What the hell has he found? It had better be good.

Jim was waiting with a large grin on his face at the open door of the red-bricked Victorian house as Daly got out of the black Audi.

"Come in, dear chap," Jim beamed as Daly wearily climbed the steps to the front door.

"You look happy, mate," said Daly.

"I am. I think I've possibly found the answer to stopping Consus… for good."

"Jesus, I bloody well hope so, there isn't much time left, Jim," sighed the dark haired copper.

Daly followed Jim down the narrow corridor to the study. He was thinking if Jim got any bigger he'd get stuck in that corridor one day. Three massive pizzas in one go didn't help. Daly was suddenly grateful his diet was mainly kebabs and scotch. At least the kebabs had plenty of salad and he counted the scotch of one of his five a day. They got to the small study at the rear of the house, the afternoon sun shining brightly through the pair of old windows, and Jim flopped into the generously padded seat behind the huge desk that had seen better days. Daly stood by Jim's shoulder as the big man wobbled the mouse to stop the screen saver, a witch burning at the stake. The large twenty-eight-inch monitor burst into life revealing a page of emails and several other tabs at the top of the browser.

"So, we already know that Consus was executed in 62 A.D.," said Jim. "What we didn't know was how."

"Go on," said Daly, his anticipation growing, hoping Jim had the answer to all his prayers.

"The Roman Governor General of Londinium at that time was Festus Augustus, a well-travelled man, but I'll get to that part in a moment. A dear friend, the lovely Maria Bettega at the Sapienza in Rome, it's one of the oldest universities in the world, founded in 1303, you know. I'd probably marry her if her tastes didn't involve bronzed, skinny guys of around twenty," he smiled ruefully.

"So what did she find?" said Daly, desperately trying to get Jim back on track.

"Yes, well, she probably has the most complete records of the Roman Empire at her disposal, most not available to even recognised academia like me. Apparently, Festus Augustus himself struck the fatal blow to Consus."

"So how does that help us, Jim?" asked Daly.

"It was what he executed Consus *with* that is the interesting part. I assume you've heard of Lazarus from the Bible?" The professor was virtually bubbling, eager to impart the news.

"My religious studies are a little rusty but wasn't he supposedly the man brought back from the dead by Jesus?" said Daly.

"Very good, Gerry," smiled Jim. "I doubt you know what happened to him afterwards, not many people do. He wasn't heard from again, at least, according to biblical text, never mentioned in the later books of the New Testament.”

“So what *did* happen to him?” asked Daly, now intrigued and hopeful Jim had possibly found a solution to destroying Consus.

“Allegedly, after Jesus resurrected him after four days in his tomb, Lazarus was a marked man. The Jewish lawmakers were not happy bunnies and wanted both Jesus and Lazarus dead for that ‘crime’ of resurrection. As we know, they succeeded in contriving to get Jesus arrested and crucified by the Romans, but the Romans had very little choice if they wanted peace and co-operation in Jerusalem and the surrounding states. Pilate didn’t want an uprising that would make him look bad, he probably had ambitions to be Emperor one day. He went along with the plot to get rid of Jesus, probably got well paid for it too although no one knows for sure, I wouldn’t be at all surprised,” said the big professor.

“With you so far,” said Daly.

“Anyway, Lazarus knew if he stayed in the region he was a dead man, no pun intended. He escaped to Cyprus and lived another twenty-two years.”

“Twenty-two!! Really?”

“I thought you’d pick up on that,” laughed Jim. “Yes, apparently he lived another twenty-two years in Cyprus, in Kition, in fact, which is now known as Larnaca in modern times. He wasn’t exactly in hiding but thought he was far enough away from Jerusalem to be safe from those lawmakers who wanted him dead. The apostles Paul and Barnabas found him on their travels and made him Bishop of Kition, where he guided the flock for several more years. Word of his ministry finally got back to the Jewish conspirators, who then sent assassins after him. They finally tracked him down to his new home and there they plunged a spear into his heart. Apparently a strange light then emitted from the lance and when it was removed Lazarus lay dead for the second, and final time. The assassins were captured by Roman guards and the spear came into the possession of Titius Marcellus, the Roman governor on Cyprus. Festus Augustus claimed it from Titius as payment for a gambling debt on a visit to Cyprus before he was dispatched to his own governorship in Britain.”

“So you’re saying that the spear used to kill Lazarus for the second time was used by Festus to execute Consus?” said Daly, wide-eyed.

“Spot on,” said Jim, pleased with himself.

“Bloody hell! What do you make of it all?” exclaimed Daly.

“The theory I’ve formulated is that when Jesus resurrected Lazarus he gave him something. Some ‘force’ that resided in the body of Lazarus until his second death at the hands of the assassins. When Lazarus was murdered in Cyprus that force somehow transferred itself to the spear and by killing Consus with that same spear the force entered Consus to make him immortal. I think Lazarus was immortal himself until then. Does that sound plausible to you,

Gerry?”

“So that force entered Consus, but he needs to kill to ensure he remains immortal? Why? It’s not as if Lazarus was a serial killer, was he?”

“Maybe it’s a force that could be used for good *and* evil?” said Jim. “Good when it entered Lazarus, but switched to evil when the good man was killed, sort of like switching polarity, the force transferred to Consus made him evil and with it the need to kill and if used again could reverse that polarity.”

“So, what you are saying is that the spear gave Consus eternal life and it can be used to kill him again, like Lazarus?” asked Daly.

“I believe so, it’s the best theory we have at the moment, Gerry. Does it make sense?”

“There’s only one problem, Jim,” said Daly. “We don’t have the bloody spear!”

“I know where it is,” smiled the professor, slyly.

“You’re shitting me, Jim!” Daly exclaimed. “Where is it?”

“I traced the spearhead to a museum near here, in Stevenage,” said the professor. “Festus was buried with the spear and his tomb was excavated in the late sixties, ironically by my old friend, Stuart Pearson, God rest his soul. It’s been exhibited on and off at the museum ever since the early seventies, usually when there is a display on the Roman occupation of Britain. They obviously don’t know the spear’s significance, just a possession of a Roman governor. The spear was nearby when the 1976 killings took place. If only your DCI Mallen had known and had the knowledge of what it was and what it could possibly do.”

“So how do we get hold of it?” asked Daly. What sort of paperwork do we need to fill out? Do we need a court order?”

“What court is going to grant us access to a two-thousand-year-old artifact to kill an immortal Roman, Gerry?”

“Shit! So what do you suggest, Jim?”

“As a professor, I can get access to it at the museum,” Jim smiled.

“What use is that if you can’t take it out of the building, do we drag Consus there and stab him with it?”

“I’m going to steal it and hopefully return it before anyone at the museum notices,” grinned Jim.

“Oh Jesus… I didn’t hear that, mate” sighed Daly.

Daly left Jim to work on his mad plot to steal the Lazarus spear. Now he had two stupid and risky plans to deal with, both Jim's and Frank's. Both risky as hell and neither guaranteed to work. He hoped he could come up with a better solution than either of them. He called Weatherby to find out where he was and the sergeant told him he was at the post-mortem of the girl, Arlene Braughton. Time was running out and Weatherby somehow got the girl bumped up the queue of autopsies. Weatherby reported what Daly expected. Death by strangulation. SOCO had found no evidence at the scene either, as usual. Why couldn't Consus make just one mistake? Something that would lead to wherever he was holed up. He decided to go and try and talk Frank out of his plan to be bait.

He got to Frank's flat within minutes, Frank buzzed him through the security door and was already at the open door of his ground-floor flat. Frank looked like he hadn't slept for a week and it seemed like he'd lost weight in the short time Daly had known him. Frank ushered the detective into the small kitchen and made coffee.

"Look Frank, this proposal of yours to offer yourself as a sacrificial lamb to draw him out is mad. It's too risky," pleaded Daly.

"I doubt you have a better idea," said Frank wearily. The skin below his red-rimmed eyes was darker than before.

"Not yet, but sacrificing yourself won't help. What if it goes wrong and he gets away again? He comes back in another couple of decades and starts again and then it will be some other poor sod's job to catch him, only they will be as clueless as I was at the start," said the detective, starting to get angry.

"At least I wouldn't have to carry around all this guilt inside," sighed Frank, visibly depressed.

"What guilt? You've done nothing wrong! You're just as much a victim as those dead kids. You've lost your best childhood friend to him, even some ancestors. And if you think I blame you for my dad being killed in your place you can forget that too, you muppet!"

"What other choice do we have then? What if we fail?"

"I don't know for sure. Jim may have something, but I don't want your death on my conscience if it goes tits up, mate, is that clear?" said Daly.

"I really can't see any alternative, Gerry. What is Jim up to?"

Daly told Frank about the Lazarus Spear and Jim's absurd plan to steal it from the museum at Stevenage. Frank hoped Jim could actually get away with it and they would have a weapon that could possibly kill Consus. If he couldn't pull it off there would be another victim.

Consus was outside in the shadows, staring at Frank's flat. He'd seen the other man enter. He knew it was the policeman in charge of the investigation. He'd seen his picture in the papers and interviewed on the television news. He wondered why the detective was there. He chuckled at the thought that Frank could be a suspect for the killings. Soon Frank would be a victim too. He'd make sure of it. Another spectacular one, he thought, another to go down in history like the last victim of 'Jack the Ripper'. Consus smiled and returned to his rented house to wait for his opportunity.

*****

Jim reached the museum at just after noon carrying his scruffy black briefcase. His Doctorate gave him almost unlimited access to such places all over the country but he was very nervous about being detected, terrified, in fact. It would ruin him. His reputation would be in tatters and he'd never work again. He moved apprehensively towards the small reception desk and showed his credentials to a pretty auburn-haired girl of about twenty who put his sweaty face down to the heat outside and his alarming size. She smiled at him and waved to a skinny, ginger male assistant with a short goatee who was standing near the glass main entrance, looking bored. The man scampered over and ushered Jim to the doors of the inner sanctum, the warehouse where they stored the exhibits which were not currently on show in the main part of the museum. The young assistant used his keycard to open the twin doors and Jim thanked him for his help. Now alone, he felt a little more confident although the sweat still ran in rivulets down his face. He walked to the exact location of the spear, knowing precisely where it was because he had already checked the manifest of the museum's warehouse in the restricted access area of their website. He just hoped he could return it without it being discovered missing by the museum staff or security.

Jim found the spear on a thin, grey steel shelf and wrapped in thick cloudy plastic. He carefully unwrapped it, opened his tatty briefcase and put the spear inside. He then took out the heavy iron poker he'd taken from his own fireplace and wrapped it in the almost opaque plastic bag which had stored the lance, hoping that no one would notice the difference. An empty shelf would look too suspicious for his liking and would be investigated very quickly. The air in the warehouse was cool at a constant twelve degrees Celcius, but Jim was still sweating profusely, his light blue shirt was now stained darkly and stuck to his broad back. His severe anxiety not helping his normal state of bulk induced perspiration.

Jim took a couple of very deep breaths, trying to calm himself before attempting to exit the impressive glass and steel building. He walked slowly to the main doors of the warehouse. He reached the doors and pressed the pressure pad that opened the doors from the inside, no keycard needed. Both doors swung open towards him with a swishing sound and he was immediately blinded by the harsh sunlight streaming in from the clear front of the building. It took a few seconds for his eyes to adjust, giving him a little more time to breathe deeply and still himself for the seemingly endless walk to the main doors and out into the car park where the Lincoln was waiting for him. He started to walk slowly towards the exit, trying not to attract any attention.

"Professor Anderson? Wait!"

Jim froze in terror. He turned pale. *Oh God, I'm finished!*

The pretty girl from reception was running up to him. Jim was on the verge of panic, his heart banging fiercely in his huge chest. If he was discovered there would be no chance of stopping Consus from returning in another generation. He bravely turned to face her, hoping to bluff his way out.

"This card dropped out of your wallet when you showed me your I.D. I didn't want you to leave without it," she smiled sweetly.

The pretty girl held up one of Jim's credit cards. The big man almost fainted in relief. He thanked her in a hoarse whisper and tried to walk calmly from the building on his wobbly legs. He exited out into the hot sun, the sweat pouring off him now, partly the change in temperature but mostly the stress of the last fifteen minutes. He reached the black Lincoln and rested his arms on the roof and lay his head on top of the fleshy limbs, the hot roof of the car was burning his skin but he didn't even notice the scorching heat of the metal. Jim finally felt composed enough to unlock the driver's door and flop into the seat. He started the car and reached for the air-con and set it to full blast straight at himself. He sat there for another ten minutes with his eyes closed while his heart rate slowly lowered. He hoped returning the spear would be a lot easier than that. If he had the chance to.

Later, Daly was back at Jim's house. Jim showed him the Lazarus Spear. Technically it was just a spearhead - unattached to any sort of wooden shaft. It was about a foot long and made from a dull, dark bronze. It looked exactly like a thousand other Roman spears excavated by archaeologists in the past couple of centuries. Daly lifted it, it was a lot heavier than he'd imagined. The point was honed to a sharpness he hadn't expected after two thousand years, most of that time buried in the tomb of Festus. This was the spear that had killed Lazarus and Consus. Had it killed others too after Consus? Were there others like him roaming the earth or was he a one-off? He shuddered at the thought there could be more like him.

Daly called Frank and reached his mobile. Frank was about to finish his shift at work, the policeman told him to meet them there at Jim's house. Frank replied that he'd go home to get out of his work clothes first. Daly said he'd send Weatherby round at 8.30 to pick him up. Frank said that was fine as he didn't fancy driving anywhere else as he'd been on the road for twelve long hours that day without much of a break. He asked if Jim would be ordering any food in or did he need to pick something up for them all on the way. Using all his detecting skills Daly told Frank that he expected Jim to order food whether Frank brought anything or not and laughed. Daly hung up and turned back to Jim and hefted the spear in his hands again. If only they could be certain Jim's theory was correct and this would kill Consus… again. If not, Consus could kill all of them.

Daly left in the Audi, intending to go back to the station to write up the day's events and then stop off at home to change before returning for the meeting with Jim, Weatherby and Frank. He really wanted to stop off for a couple of large scotches but really needed a clear head for the rest of the evening, coffee will have to do, strong and black and a lot of it.

Consus had been waiting patiently in the alley opposite Frank's flat. Frank arrived back in his van at just after 8 pm and let himself into the communal area and then his ground floor accommodation. Consus waited around ten minutes and quickly crossed the road. He tried to open the door to the foyer but it was locked. He needed to enter a code on the number keypad on the wall. He was frustrated. Through the large glass panel in the door, he saw a large bald man descending the stairs from one of the upper flats. The fat man opened the door to leave and Consus pulled the heavy wood and steel door even wider for him.

"I'm here to see Frank," said Consus and pointed to the door of Frank's flat. "I work with him."

"No problem, mate," said the large man and went through the door sideways, not suspicious of Consus in the slightest, thinking more of the Indian takeaway he'd ordered and was about to collect.

Consus waited for the man to walk slowly away from the building and then another thirty seconds to make sure. He crossed the area to Frank's door and knocked. After a minute or so Consus was about to knock once again when he heard Frank shout, "Coming, Sergeant Weatherby!"

Frank opened the door and Consus barged his way in, pushing Frank heavily in the chest, the door slammed shut. Frank shuffled backwards, unable to believe what was happening. No need to draw Consus out now, but he wasn't ready for him, he was totally unprepared to confront him yet.

"Nice to see you again, Frank, you must have guessed I was saving you for last," said Consus with an evil looking smile. "You escaped me twice, not for a third time though! No policeman to save you now." The immortal's red-tinged eyes bored into Frank, maybe as deep as his very soul.

"Shit!" cried Frank, his eyes darting around the room, looking for something to defend himself with. *Think!*

"I've been watching you, Frank. Observing your activities. Planning for the best time for us to meet again. Alone... and uninterrupted."

Frank backed up to the wall of his living room, almost tripping over the corner of his armchair. Consus advanced grinning like a cat stalking a bird.

"I think I told you I've never truly enjoyed all the killing, Frank, but you are special. No one has ever avoided dying at my hand before, but you did it twice all those years ago. I wasn't quick enough the first time at the farm and that policeman sacrificing himself to let you get away was unexpected. Truly heroic of him. He did suffer greatly for that intrusion."

"Did you know the policeman heading the hunt for you is his son?" said Frank.

"Really? That's an interesting development," mused Consus. "I didn't know. Maybe I should have killed him too?"

Frank was truly corned, nowhere left to turn in the small living room. He picked up a framed photo of his two children when they were young, happy and smiling, and threw it at Consus. The frame struck the man just above the left eye causing a deep gash. There was no blood. Consus smiled and moved forward again.

"There is nothing you can do to hurt me, as you can see, Frank," he smiled smugly, pointing to the wound. "You will not prevent me from killing you this time. Third time lucky as the the old English saying goes."

Consus pulled a long knife from his coat pocket.

"I've had this knife many years, it's honed to perfection. I used it to kill the daughter of the man who executed me, he wasn't very significant. I took it from her. When I returned the first time I discovered Festus was then governor of the area I was in. I met his young daughter in the woods. I needed to kill and when she told me who she was, who her father was, it seemed so fitting that she had to die. She wasn't afraid of me at first and she stabbed me with this knife. Then I sliced her open with it, all over her scrawny body, before I cut her throat and ended her. I revelled in the torturous mental pain Festus would endure when he discovered she'd been mutilated but was disappointed he would never know it was me who had inflicted the many cuts. It was still so exquisite though. I will enjoy your death just as much, Frank, possibly even more," he smiled at the prospect.

Consus inched forward again, Frank flattened himself against the wall, fear threatening to ooze from every pore of his body. Consus lifted the knife above his head, ready to plunge into Frank's limbs first. He wanted to disable Frank to take all the red mist he knew was coming to him. He wanted to make this kill last, extract every ounce of fear from Frank. This would be so special, he'd waited so many years for it. Consus could see Frank was not as fit or thin as he used to be and would be easy to subdue, unable to bolt like a frightened rabbit this time.

The door suddenly burst open violently, slamming against the wall and splitting the frame. A wooden coat rack on the wall was crushed. Sergeant Weatherby charged in. Consus turned and screamed in frustration, pausing his attack on Frank. Weatherby flung his arms around the legs of Consus bringing him to the ground. Frank snapped out of his frozen state and kicked Consus viciously in the head, opening the bloodless gash even more. Consus swept the knife behind him, catching Weatherby on the right ear, slicing off the lobe. Weatherby howled in pain but did not let go of the killer. Consus struck again, opening up Weatherby's scalp. Blood gushed and ran into the detective's eyes, blinding him. He released Consus to wipe his eyes, knowing he was dead if he couldn't see, hoping he could clear the blood before Consus struck at him again, wishing Frank could do something to distract the killer. Frank did, he continued to kick out at

Consus before grabbing a reading lamp resting on a cabinet near him. He ripped the lead from the wall socket and wrapped the cord, still attached to the lamp, around the neck of Consus, pulling it tight. Consus stabbed at Frank, catching his left bicep a glancing blow. Frank shrieked, dropping the electrical lead, giving some respite to the serial killer.

Consus shrugged Weatherby off from on top of him. Frank scuttled back to the wall. Consus got to his feet again, the knife still in his hand. Confident that the other man, the interloper, was disabled enough for him to finish what he came for. He had wanted to kill Frank slowly but the presence of the other man lying on the floor frantically trying to clear the blood from his vision gave him little time. He would take what he could from Frank and then finish off the other man. He lunged at Frank with the blade again. Frank dodged to one side, the knife struck the wall, chipping plaster away and skidding off to the left of him, leaving a long scar in the paint.

Consus had underestimated the resilience of the big policeman. Weatherby had regained his footing after wiping the blood from his eyes and dived at the killer, smashing Consus' head against the living room wall. Consus turned, dazed, and without thinking stabbed the man in the chest. The red vapour flowed from Weatherby. The copper knew he would die. Consus screamed in frustration that it was not Frank's essence pouring out and into his lungs. Consus could still kill Frank after he was finished. He'd killed a seventh a few times in the past and knew there was no mist to be gained from them. He would have to settle for only satisfaction and closure. He saw Frank inching towards the damaged door.

"Nooooo!" Consus screamed, "You will not escape again."

He breathed deeply again, taking as much of Weatherby's fear as he could before he tried to shrug the policeman off him and get to Frank. Weatherby clung tightly around the neck of Consus. The killer could not cast him aside easily. This allowed Frank the opportunity to run. He was grateful to Weatherby but knew there was nothing he could do to help him. He ran from the flat, across the foyer and out through the heavy security door, wincing as pain radiated down his arm from the knife wound. He got to his yellow van seconds before Consus emerged from the door to the flats about thirty yards away. Despite the pain in his arm from the knife, he found his keys in his pocket. Frank got the door open and quickly pushed the key in the ignition and turned it. The engine roared into life. He painfully put the van into gear and Frank sped away with the driver's door swinging before Consus had covered half the distance to the vehicle. Consus bellowed in frustration and disappeared into the shadows. Windows all along the street were lighting up and beginning to be populated by people hearing the commotion. No one dared venture outside, it wasn't safe in Kingsford anymore.

Frank drove slowly to Jim's, trying not to pass out from the pain. He was safe now but every time he tried to change gear pain shot from his left arm so he decided to leave the van in third and avoid the gear stick, resting the arm on his lap and steering with only his right hand. He started to worry about weakening from the blood loss and his vision blurred a couple of times. He felt sorry for Weatherby, he died a hero saving him just as Danny Daly had done all those years ago. He had to get to Paddenham to find help.

The van struggled on the hill to the small town,. He plodded on up it with a boy racer in a

Corsa flashing his lights at him and revving his engine from the rear, unable to overtake because of the constant stream of cars coming from the other direction. Even that late in the evening the road was busy. He reached the row of Victorian houses in Jim's street and coasted to a stop beside the Lincoln parked in the drive. Frank eased himself out and winced as he climbed the half dozen steps to the front door and slammed the heavy door knocker. Jim eventually opened the door and immediately started to panic.

"Frank! What's happened?" he shrieked.

"Consus… Weatherby dead," was all he could manage before he was close to collapse. Jim supported Frank's weight and almost dragged him to the bathroom. Frank sat on the edge of the bath clutching the rim with his right hand. Jim removed Frank's sweatshirt carefully and rolled up the sleeve of his t-shirt to reveal the bloody gash in Frank's bicep.

"Christ, that's deep Frank, all I can do is disinfect it and wrap it up and drive you to hospital. I'll call Daly to meet us there. Tell me what happened to you and to Weatherby."

"Weatherby saved me just as Danny did. I was a goner for sure, Jim. No escape," he said through gritted teeth, swaying on the edge of the bath. "Consus came to my flat to kill me. Saving me for last. Daly told me Weatherby would be picking me up to drive me here for a meeting so I opened the door thinking it was him. It was Consus though. Fortunately for me, Weatherby was early, not for him though. I never really liked him, never comfortable around him, but he gave his life for me, deserves a lot of respect at the very least." Frank hissed as Jim applied the antiseptic to the wound.

"I'm sorry Frank. If I'd set the meeting for earlier, Weatherby's death could have been avoided."

"Not… your… fault," groaned Frank, eyes shut tight from the pain. "Consus would have come sooner or later."

"Right, we're off to the hospital," said Jim as he finished wrapping Frank's arm. "Can you hang on a moment while I ring Gerry first?"

"Sure, go ahead, I'll be fine," slurred Frank, even though he was starting to feel drowsy.

Jim rushed to his study as quickly as his bulk allowed and found his phone under a batch of papers strewn across his desk. He dialled Daly's mobile number with a slightly shaking hand and gave the detective a quick version of events. Daly said he's meet them in A&E. Jim got back to the bathroom and put Frank's good arm over his shoulder and then tried to negotiate the narrow hallway leading to the front of the house side on. Jim got Frank out of the door, down the steps and into the passenger seat of the Lincoln, then returned up the steps to lock his front door and joined Frank in the massive, black American car, more like a canal barge than a vehicle designed for roads.

On the twenty-minute drive to the hospital, Jim filled Frank in on recent events. He gave a more detailed version of the story of the Lazarus Spear, how he and Daly had believed the spear had given Consus the immortality and the theory that using the lancehead on him again could possibly kill the Roman. Jim also told Frank of his daring raid on the museum to steal the artifact, leaving out the absolute terror he felt with his entire career on the line. Frank listened absently and said nothing, fighting the drowsiness of his blood loss and hoping Jim would drive the giant car a little faster.

They reached the hospital Accident and Emergency department. Jim parked the car where he shouldn't, intending to move it to the car park once he'd got Frank booked in and settled on a chair in the waiting area. Jim was at the desk trying to explain that there was significant blood loss and Frank needed to be seen quickly when Daly burst in through the double doors.

"Right, *you*!" he said forcefully to the receptionist, "I want this man seen to NOW! He's a witness to a murder and I need him coherent!"

The receptionist seemed totally un-flustered, probably used to such bellowing instructions from the police in the past. She pressed a button on her desk and an orderly with a wheelchair and a nurse immediately appeared out of nowhere to take Frank to a cubicle. Jim and Daly sat in the waiting area which was crowded, as usual, with drunks, even though it was still before nine in the evening. Also there were a couple of beaten wives by the look of it and a pre-teen who had a marble stuck up his nose, sat with his mother. Daly remembered he'd done the same at about that age. Jim told Daly exactly what had happened when Frank knocked at his door and how he'd done his best to clean and staunch the wound.

"Jesus, what a bloody mess," said Daly, trying to keep his voice down, trying hard to mask the anger he felt. "Weatherby was a good copper. I had Plod and paramedics sent to Frank's flat but there was nothing they could do. Plod did a quick search in the flat and outside too but came up with nothing and are now knocking on doors to try and find a witness. Some hope. The whole town is hiding away and pretending it's not happening. SOCO are on the way too."

"Frank told me he'd thrown a framed picture at Consus," said Jim. "It hit him above the eye and gashed him but there was no blood, maybe they can finally get some DNA from it?"

Daly slapped Jim on the shoulder and quickly jumped up and ran outside to make a call on his mobile, it could be the break they needed. He walked back inside and sat next to Jim again, feeling a little more hopeful. The child sitting behind them tried to snort the marble from his nose and sat crying when he failed yet again. Eventually, a nurse came over to escort Daly and Jim to the cubicle where Frank was lying on a trolley where a tube full of blood was flowing from a plastic bag on a stand and into his arm at the elbow. Frank was very sedate, Daly assumed he's been given a shot of morphine or whatever they used. A white, middle-aged doctor gave them an update on Frank.

"I'm Roger Fisher, nice to meet you. This is Nurse Jude," he nodded at the East Asian on the other side of the trolley, engaged in hooking Frank up to a monitor to track his vital signs. "Well, we've washed and sutured the wound, the weapon used managed to avoid any arteries or major blood vessels luckily, but there is a long road of physio needed to get the bicep back to good working order again, it will take time but there shouldn't be any lasting damage to the patient.

"Thanks, doc," said Daly, "When can we take him out of here?"

"A couple of hours, I should think, until the sedation wears off a bit. You are quite welcome to wait and try and get a statement in the meantime. I understand he's a witness to murder so I appreciate time is of the essence for you."

"He's also a friend," said Daly. "And another friend was the victim."

"Oh, I'm really sorry to hear that," said the doctor. "Mr. Kelly should be a bit more with it in less than an hour, I really hope he can help you."

The doctor smiled thinly and he and Nurse Jude left them in the cubicle with Frank and, after a few minutes of silence apart from the beeping monitor, Jim volunteered to get them coffee.

After Jim had left Daly turned to Frank and said quietly, "You're the luckiest bugger I've ever met, mate." He patted Franks good forearm gently and thought about how his sergeant wasn't so fortunate.

Jim returned with the coffees and they sat and quietly sipped until Frank broke them out of their thoughts with a groan, he was coherent enough to tell Daly exactly what had happened in his flat and how Weatherby had saved his life. Daly swore that he was going to get Consus, for his dad and his friend Weatherby. Frank asked if what Jim had told him in the car was true and not an hallucination, forgetting Daly had already told him they had the spear. Daly confirmed that it was and they indeed did have the Lazarus Spear… and they were going to use it.

*****

Three days later Consus knew he had to get to his cave, his work was done for another generation, and the initial manhunt had been scaled down. Frank Kelly had escaped for the third time. How? How he wished he'd ended Frank's life the first time they'd encountered each other at the farmhouse at the far end of Kingsford. He wouldn't be feeling the utter frustration he was at that very moment. He hoped Frank Kelly would still be alive when he returned in another generation. Frank would be around eighty if he survived that long but there would still be plenty of fear in him as he remembered back to the previous confrontations with the Roman. He'd thought about making Frank a seventh victim. No refreshing red mist, but at least the satisfaction of knowing he'd finished with the man for good, he could concentrate his efforts on his offspring if they were close enough. But he knew that taking him now wasn't possible. Frank would be protected by the police and he didn't know where they were hiding him. He couldn't risk trying to find out. He had to leave the area and he knew they would be hunting him for killing that policeman. That meddler! He'd make sure Frank was the *first* victim next time, no mistakes.

The killer wished he could drive one of those cars. They'd been around for over a century and he should have learnt the basics of driving one. It would be easier to steal one and make his way to the caves rather than have to rely on someone else to drive him. A potential witness. He picked up the phone provided by the landlord of his furnished house, called a taxi service he'd found in the online phone directory and waited impatiently. He was ready to rest again. He'd got the vital essence he needed to hibernate and recharge himself for the next twenty-two years. He would be back. For Frank Kelly *and* his family.

The taxi arrived, a fairly new silver Volkswagon Passat. The Asian driver was told the destination and proceeded to drive the twenty miles to West Wycombe town centre where Consus would walk up the hill to his usual resting place. The journey was uneventful, the driver thankfully uncommunicative. Consus had no wish for conversation. Not for a long time.

Frank and Daly had been parked opposite the gated entrance to the caves. They were in Weatherby's Toyota Avensis in case Consus recognised Daly's Audi. Daly nudged Frank from a light doze as he saw the immortal make his way up the steep hill. They saw Consus walk in the small alcove to buy his ticket and then make his way to the turnstile. Once through they exited the car and jogged towards the ticket office. Frank winced from the slight pain in his arm even though he was dosed up on strong codeine painkillers. This time Daly flashed his I.D. to the rotund dark-haired woman about to issue two tickets to him and they made their way to the turnstile themselves, anxious not to lose Consus in the tunnels. At least they knew exactly where his destination would be.

They silently followed the creature into the cave, careful not to scrape their feet on the rough floor, or even breathe too heavily after their jog to the caves from the car. Frank was determined. This was his only chance of stopping this monster. He'd be almost eighty if the beast was allowed to come back again and murder even more innocents. Consus seemed unaware they were there, or at least unconcerned. The figure moved slowly towards the passage that held the chalk wall, ready to be absorbed into it for another generation. Frank's bicep ached but pure adrenalin and the medication was blocking any real crippling pain. He was driven on and Daly followed a couple of feet behind, equally determined to reach the killer.

"Consus!" shouted Frank, his voice echoing off the walls. "This ends now!"

"You are too late, Frank. Oh, it seems you have brought your friend with you," Consus mocked. "I brutally slaughtered his father, I believe. You seem to have recovered quickly from the wound from my knife. I expected you to still be hiding from me. Terrified of my wrath."

"Yes, I'm Detective Inspector Gerry Daly," the policeman interrupted. "We're here to make sure you'll never return and murder again, you bastard."

"Frank told me about your father. I remember him well, died like a true hero saving that boy. I assume you've been told my story, you know I can't be killed?" he said triumphantly as he walked confidently towards the mortal pair.

"That's not strictly true is it, Consus?" said Daly with a slight smile.

The creature paused and looked slightly confused, suddenly unsure of himself. What did the policeman know that he didn't?

"You made the mistake of telling me your name all those years ago before you killed the policeman," said Frank. "Consus the centurion. We soon found out you were Consus the traitor, betrayed his people, and his friends, for gold. Executed by his own general. Information is available to anyone now, and it's all easily accessed, especially if you know the right people."

Consus looked at them both warily and weighed up which one was more dangerous. The policeman with cold revenge in his heart and slightly younger and fitter, or Frank, who seemed to have knowledge about him, his history, his shame.

"I found out why you were executed and what with, Consus. Your greed killed you and you still have that greed, although you take fear now instead of gold," said Frank.

"You can't possibly know what happened!" screamed the Roman.

"I do! You were a traitor, you exchanged troop strengths and movements for gold from the Britons. You hoped a second uprising after Boudica died would drive the Romans back and you could return to your family, with plenty of money for a new life with them. You were discovered, tortured and executed. There are records, just one of the things the Romans were very good at, Consus."

"You know about the spear?" asked Consus.

"The Lazarus Spear? This one you mean?" Frank pulled open his dark coat and produced the spearhead which Jim had stolen for him. The one that had given Consus eternal life when it had supposedly killed him at the hands of General Festus.

A look of panic was etched on the face of Consus now. It *was* the spear, he'd never forgotten it, he knew the dull bronze of the blade. It was etched into his memory. Was it possible that the spear which gave him eternal life could also kill him? Doubts of his own immortality crept into his now confused mind. He tried to back away towards the hidden passage, he had to get away to his haven. Take no chances. Daly moved to cut him off as Frank walked towards him. The spear in his right hand.

"Stay away!" screamed Consus. "You too," he hissed at Daly, who had blocked off the route to the passage which led to his resting place. The only way to escape was to kill the old man and turn the spear on the policeman. He lunged at Frank, knocking the spear from his hand and gave him a backhand swipe that sent Frank flying against the wall, hitting his head on the chalky surface, momentarily stunning him. Consus tried to pick up the spear but Daly swung his arm around the neck of the immortal from behind and squeezed tight. Consus struggled and tried to reach behind him to shake the detective loose. Daly was hanging on for dear life. Consus used his weight to slam Daly against the chalk wall, once, twice, a third time and he was free of the policeman's grip, his hand going towards his coat pocket for his knife. He turned towards Frank and suddenly felt a sharp pain in his chest. Frank had thrust the spear deep into it. Consus gazed down at the lance protruding from his thin torso and then looked into Frank's eyes, behind the shock that he would finally die, there there something else, Frank saw. Gratefulness? Acceptance? Maybe even peace.

The spear that ended the life of Lazarus and gave Consus eternal life, or maybe damnation, two thousand years ago had now ended it forever. His body sagged and fell to the floor of the dimly illuminated cave, the stench of decay wafting from the body already filling the place. Frank and Daly covered their faces with their hands and watched as first the body of Consus began to liquefy, and then rapidly dried and turned into a fine grey dust. It was finally over. Consus the disgraced centurion who was once known as Jack the Ripper, the terror of Whitechapel, was finally dead. Well over five-hundred victims, including friends and family of both men, conclusively avenged. Daly walked to the pile of dust, unzipped and urinated on the powdery remains. The liquid taking the dust down the slight slope towards the concealed tunnel which had hidden Consus in its secret alcove for nearly two millennia.

"That's for my dad, you bastard! Jimmy too," hissed Daly.

The sense of relief was evident as Frank and Daly turned and walked up the minor incline towards the mouth of the cave and the outside world, safe now from the multiple killer from down the ages. The new sun was close to rising and the lives of those in the shadow of Consus rid of another evil. They were ready for a large drink despite the early hour. They trudged across the road to where the Avensis was parked and slumped into the front seats. It was several minutes before Daly collected himself enough to start the car and drive back to Paddenham. Jim needed to return the spear to the museum as soon as he could. That was still hanging over the big man. Why he had taken it could never be fully explained to the authorities if he was caught putting in back in place. Where the hell would they start? 62 A.D.?

Later that day, Jim, accompanied by Daly for moral and maybe physical support, managed to replace the iron poker left in the warehouse with the Lazarus Spear. Daly had to wait outside in the reception area while Jim was left alone to complete the mission. As Jim exited the warehouse door he breathed a sigh of relief, comforted that he'd managed to save his career and his reputation.

Frank had been dropped off on their way and he entered his flat for the first time since Weatherby's murder. Daly had arranged for the place to be thoroughly cleaned. No evidence that an attack ever took place except for the broken picture frame, replaced on the table, and the coat rack behind the door, which had been disposed of. Frank dropped his keys on the floor and slowly shuffled into the bedroom. He was utterly exhausted. He fell untidily onto the bed and immediately lost consciousness, woken sixteen hours later by his landline phone ringing beside the bed. Daly was checking up on him whilst in a drunken stupor.

"We did it mate!" Frank could hear the grin on the detective's face as he slurred the words before the phone went dead. Frank smiled to himself, all those people avenged, more than five hundred, he thought. So many, including his old mate Martin and Danny Daly. He felt happy for the first time since he was fourteen when he worshipped Bridget from afar. He was particularly happy for Daly, retribution for the father he had barely known. For Mallen and Carter too. He wondered what Bridget was doing now and if he could track her down somehow, maybe Daly could help? Frank took more painkillers and began to doze again, thinking back to his youth before Consus had arrived in Kingsford. Football, great music and Bridget occupied his thoughts until he nodded off into a deep sleep.

*****

A week later Daly, Frank and Jim were gathered around the oblong hole in the ground where Weatherby's mahogany coffin had been lowered into. Daly had lost a friend and partner. Jim shed a tear for the policeman. Frank's arm was in a sling and it rested strapped in the light blue support across his chest, in contrast to his black suit. He'd burst his stitches thrusting the spear into Consus. He hadn't even noticed until he'd stripped for a shower after almost two days of deep sleep. Frank was grateful his children and their bloodline were now safe from Consus as well as hundreds of other potential victims in the future. The man known as Jack the Ripper, the Beaconsfield Butcher, the Kingsford Killer and maybe other names over the centuries was finally gone for good.

Daly and Jim were already friends, involved in an encounter with a witch that Mark Mason had destroyed a year earlier at the Marsham stones. Frank was now part of their club. The Survivors Club headed for the nearest pub to toast Weatherby, a man not much liked, but very much respected. They also toasted Danny Daly, the legendary DCI Paddy Mallen and all the other victims of Consus.

*****

Thanks for sticking around to the end. Hopefully you've enjoyed the second book. I do think I've improved a little from the first one, maybe a lot? For those who are interested, Lazarus died thirty years after being resurrected and not twenty-two, no evidence he was murdered by Jewish assassins either and the year of his second death is allegedly 63 A.D. which was the year after Festus used the spear to execute Consus. I changed all those things to fit in with the timeline. Twenty-two fit perfectly in 2020 to include that legendary hot summer of 1976 and Jack's reign of terror in 1888 and so going back to 62.A.D for the execution was necessary.

Frank Kelly is pretty much based on me. His interests and thoughts back in 1976 and mine were almost the same, we both played a lot of football and loved the same music and there was indeed a Bridget and I do hope she is happy and well today. I recommend visiting the Hellfire Caves in West Wycombe, they are very cool… but don't go investigating any strange passages. The mausoleum at the top of the hill is well worth a visit too, as well as the church with the big golden ball on top.

No apologies for some of the thoughts and language used by some characters in 1976 - they were different times and I wanted to be as authentic as possible.


Thanks to my usual proof readers, Erika (who survived in the first book), Julie (who appears briefly in this one) and Phyllis for their help and encouragement.

Massive thanks again to Sue Massey for permission to use her amazing art for the cover. Check her out at:

https://www.deviantart.com/suemart  https://www.artistsandillustrators.co.uk/suemassey


Mark Mason, Nat, Ellie, Kendra Watkin, Anrok the demon and Daly from my first book Cast The First Stone will return in the sequel called Second Chance. We get to sample Mark and Nat's travels, I won't say where or even when, and more of Ellie's lovely cooking. And maybe one or two real life friends will pop up so be nice to me or Anrok may get you.

2020 has been a strange old year for pretty much everyone. On the one hand I've completed my first book and was close to finishing this and I hope I entertained a few people. But on the other hand it seems to be the year all Hell broke loose - my wish for 2021 is for people to rediscover that, after all the differences we all have, we are basically just PEOPLE. Let's all get back to that or the human race will suffer. Keep on reading, whoever the author may be, don't let literature die.

Peace and love X.